Man's World

RUPERT SMITH is the author of ten novels, in his own name and as James Lear and Rupert James, and of several biographies and books about television. He was born in Washington DC, grew up in Surrey and has lived in London since 1978. As well as writing fiction, Rupert has a long career as a journalist, contributing to dailies, weeklies and monthlies in Britain, America and Europe. www.rupertsmith.org.uk

Man's World

RUPERT SMITH

ARCADIA BOOKS

Arcadia Books Ltd
15–16 Nassau Street
London w1w 7AB

www.arcadiabooks.co.uk

First published by Arcadia Books 2010
Copyright Rupert Smith © 2010

ISBN 978-1-906413-40-8

Typeset in Garamond by MacGuru Ltd
Printed and bound in Finland by WS Bookwell

Arcadia Books gratefully acknowledges the financial support of Arts Council England.

Arcadia Books supports English PEN, the fellowship of writers who work together to promote literature and its understanding. English PEN upholds writers' freedoms in Britain and around the world, challenging political and cultural limits on free expression. To find out more, visit www.englishpen.org or contact
English PEN, 6–8 Amwell Street, London EC1R 1UQ

Arcadia Books distributors are as follows:

in the UK and elsewhere in Europe:
Turnaround Publishers Services
Unit 3, Olympia Trading Estate
Coburg Road
London N22 6TZ

in the US and Canada:
Independent Publishers Group
814 N. Franklin Street
Chicago, IL 60610

in Australia:
Tower Books
PO Box 213
Brookvale, NSW 2100

in New Zealand:
Addenda
PO Box 78224
Grey Lynn
Auckland

in South Africa:
Jacana Media (Pty) Ltd
PO Box 291784,
Melville 2109
Johannesburg

Arcadia Books is the *Sunday Times* Small Publisher of the Year 2002/03

For Marcus

and

In memory of Tim Clark

01

Jonathan was supposed to meet me at nine o'clock this morning, but he turns up at eleven with some story about how he went out with his yoga teacher last night and they ended up getting drunk in Soho and going back to the yoga teacher's house, where Jonathan spent the night, and now of course he is being quite coy about what if anything actually happened. I've said all along that the only reason he got into yoga is so he can keep his legs in the air for extended periods of time.

By the time Jonathan actually turns up I've started loading the van myself. I'm going up and down in the lift completely knackering myself, although on the third or fourth trip I realise that it's actually like an extra session at the gym and is working my quads, glutes, calves and hip flexors quite hard, not to mention burning a lot of calories, which is no bad thing because I had pizza last night. And even though I only really ate the cheese and pepperoni and mushrooms off the top, and threw the base into the bin, I'm sure that I accidentally had some bread, which means I broke the most important rule of all: no carbs after five p.m. So I start using the stairs instead of the lift, and it's taking ages longer than it's meant to, not least because I'm doing it on my own, but when I've done about ten trips I take a photo of my abs on my phone and they are looking really defined, so in fact when Jonathan arrives I'm not cross with him at all but in quite a good mood.

Jonathan isn't much help anyway, not being as he puts it 'the lifting type', but we manage to get everything into the van; it's mostly clothes in black bin bags, a few books, the television, boxes of kitchen stuff including food, my weights, a couple of rugs and cushions and some bedding. The only furniture is the Eames chair, the Philippe Starck coffee table, the computer desk and the ergonomic chair thing that is giving me back problems. Everything else belongs to the landlord. Jonathan says that the Eames chair and the Philippe Starck coffee table might as well go in the recycling, because they are really old-fashioned, and I should get new ones like the ones he saw in *Elle Decoration*. I tell him he doesn't realise how much it costs to buy a flat, and that I can't afford to start throwing away perfectly good furniture. Not throwing away, says Jonathan, recycling, he would never throw anything away, it's unethical, but he still thinks I need new furniture and that I should start with an empty shell. I say this is just because he wants to come shopping with me and buy stuff that he can't afford, and he says that's not true, he can buy anything he wants, and I say yes but it's all on credit which you never pay off, and so by the time we finally set off in the van we aren't speaking to each other. This is not unusual. In all the years that we've been best friends, Jonathan and I have fallen out so many times that we've got the routine down to a tee.

When we get to the new flat Jonathan has to start speaking to me again so that he can tell me everything that's wrong with it. The building is facing the wrong way, so the Feng Shui is all out of alignment, apparently, although I thought he gave all that up when he stopped going out with that Feng Shui astrologer last year, and he started referring to it as 'Feng Shit'. When we park the van and take the first load of stuff up the stairs, he complains that there isn't a lift, so I tell him that this is a post-war block and that they didn't put in lifts in those days, people didn't mind walking up a few flights of stairs and it's only on the third floor. He doesn't like the red brick, and he doesn't like the external landings that run along the front of the building, and when he catches sight of some plant pots and window boxes on the second floor with primroses and crocuses and geraniums in,

I think he's going to faint with disgust. When I get the key in the door, he walks in first and starts looking around as if he owns the place, while I'm still struggling with boxes and bags, and he makes helpful remarks like 'not much storage space' and 'very little light in this room'. I console myself with the knowledge that Jonathan will never own his own home, that he is living in a Housing Association flat that could be taken away at any moment when they find out that he got it under false pretences, claiming that he was a victim of homophobic harassment in his last place. In fact, this never amounted to much more than the old lady downstairs 'looking at him funny' but he made such a song and dance that they re-housed him just to shut him up, which I can totally understand.

We get the rest of the stuff into the flat in about ten more trips, and I can't work out exactly what Jonathan was doing because I seem to recognise all the things that are now stacked up in the middle of the living room as being things that I carried. Jonathan says he sees himself in more of an advisory capacity and that he is going to be my home stylist, which if it's anything like his personal shopping service when we go out looking for clothes means that the flat will very soon resemble a knocking shop.

By the time I've taken the van back and we've managed to make a cup of tea and sit down it's nearly six o'clock, and Jonathan is getting fidgety about *Star Search* which starts at seven. Jonathan will not go out on a Saturday night any more; he says it's because town is full of naffs at the weekends, but I know that it's really because he wants to stay in and watch *Star Search*. If I phone him when it's on he doesn't answer, and there are only two reasons why Jonathan doesn't answer his phone, and the other one is sex.

He's ready to leave at half past six which would just about get him home in time, when I tell him that I've got a bottle of champagne in a cold bag and I was planning to share it with him as a kind of house-warming. So he looks at me for a while as if he's doing a few calculations, and then he says okay, he'll stay for a drink if I can get the TV hooked up as well. So I put the TV on top of a packing case and I pop the cork just as *Star Search* starts, and Jonathan glares at me and tells me to shush, because he can't concentrate on two things at once. So we drink the champagne in silence watching *Star Search*, and Jonathan is completely obsessed by this boy, Lukas, who he thinks is gorgeous and talented and the sort of boyfriend he'd like to live with, basically because he would match Jonathan's current colour scheme which is chocolate brown and olive green. Lukas has dark brown curly hair and olive skin and he is cute in a retarded-child sort of way. Lukas does a really bad rendition of 'Wind Beneath My Wings' and something horrible by Stephen Sondheim, and Jonathan keeps telling me to shut up when I make remarks. I actually catch him crying when Lukas gets a bad score off the judges, and then he asks me if he can use my phone and he votes for Lukas about ten times which considering it costs £1 per call is quite a lot of money.

I tell Jonathan that he is wasting his time obsessing over people on television when he should be going out and meeting a real boyfriend, and then he comes over all enigmatic and says he has plenty of irons in the fire, and besides what would I know about real boyfriends, I haven't had one since before Christmas. Which is true, but seeing as it's only March I don't think that's so bad, and I tell Jonathan that I'm quite enjoying being single for a while, at which point he looks at me like he's about to phone for an ambulance.

When *Star Search* is over we are allowed to have another drink, and Jonathan says that I've got a bottle of vodka in a box somewhere, although how he worked that out I really don't know, seeing as he never went near any boxes when they needed moving. I haven't got any mixers so he says he'll put some music on if I'll go down to the corner shop and get tonic and lemons, and we can have a party. I leave him fiddling around with his iPod which has about 20,000 club tracks on it which all sound exactly the same, although Jonathan spends hours making different playlists and insisting that he would actually be a really good DJ.

I'm glad to get out of the flat for a while, even though I've only just moved in, and there is a shop literally across the road OPEN 24 HOURS which is good news. I might as well make myself known, as I will be going in there every day for the rest of my life. Planning meals has never been my strong point, and as long as they sell microwaveable rice, a bit of salad and some herbal tea I can make up the rest of my diet with protein shakes.

When I get to the bottom of the stairs an ambulance really is pulling up with its blue light flashing, which seems like a bad omen on my first night, and I wonder for a moment if Jonathan's made another bogus emergency call like he did that time he fancied a fireman, and thought that if he dialled 999 he might come round and 'rescue' him. But there are two paramedics going to a flat on the second floor.

Jonathan is looking very pleased with himself when I get back, and he says he's bought me a flat-warming present, and can I guess what it is? He wasn't carrying anything when he turned up, and I really, seriously hope that it's not another of his joke presents like the subscription to *The Watchtower* which I was never able to cancel and will probably keep turning up at my old address for the rest of time. I say thank you, because I believe in good manners even with people like Jonathan, and I ask him what is it? He says I have to guess, and so after I've mentioned a few things that I would actually like, like a juicer, and an Xbox, he says, 'Close your eyes and hold out your hands.' Jonathan is the sort of person who is quite capable of placing something disgusting in your hands under these circumstances, like for instance parts of his own anatomy, but on this occasion it is something small and cold and square. 'Now open them!' he says, and it turns out be a hand mirror with four enormous lines of cocaine chopped out on it. 'I used your credit card, I hope you don't mind,' he says, and then I remember that he cut up all his cards last week when he decided that consumerism was blocking his path to enlightenment, and anyway they were all maxed out.

The cocaine mixes very nicely with the champagne, and I'm feeling quite cheerful when we hear a siren whooping from downstairs. We run to the window and lean out and we can see the paramedics loading a stretcher into the back of the ambulance. One of the paramedics is really good looking, with a shaved head and an earring, and when I mention this to Jonathan he wolf-whistles and shouts out, 'Oi, mate, my friend fancies you!' The paramedic looks up and scowls which is quite sexy and I smile and wave, thinking that this might defuse the situation, but he just shakes his head. This is when I notice that the person on the stretcher actually has the blanket pulled up over the face and is therefore almost certainly dead. I pull my head in quickly and pull Jonathan in after me, just as he is drawing breath and opening his mouth to say something 'funny'. Jonathan's funny remarks, which he tends to say very loud when he's had a drink and a line, quite often cause fights, and I have no desire to get into this kind of trouble on my first night in my new home.

'What the bloody hell are you doing?' says Jonathan, and I say that I don't want him saying anything stupid. And he says, 'Like what? You think I'm going to shout out, "You've got a big stiff one there, mate!"' then he looks a bit sheepish, because obviously that's exactly what he was planning to say.

Then Jonathan gets upset because he says he's never seen a dead body before, which isn't strictly true because there was that time we saw someone being loaded into an ambulance at the back of Fire, and everyone said he was dead as well, but Jonathan was so out of it that night that he couldn't remember his own name, let alone details like this. He starts crying and saying that if he died nobody would find him for weeks, and so to cheer him up I say we can share the last line. He cuts it into two, one rather bigger than the other, and no prizes for guessing which one goes up his nose, but at least he stops talking about death and starts talking about Madonna instead. He spends the next twenty minutes telling me a long and involved story about how he managed to get six tickets for her shows in Holland which he is now selling for a vast profit on eBay. I know that the coke has really kicked in when he tells me that the lyrics to 'Confessions on a Dance Floor' are very spiritual and that he's thinking of going over to Kabbalah and changing his name to Habakkuk.

Jonathan says he needs to go online to check the status of his auction, and that he will make us some more drinks if I get my laptop up and running, which fortunately doesn't take very long because I have mobile wireless broadband, which I only ever seem to use when Jonathan comes around, because most of the rest of the time I use the internet at work. But he persuaded me that I had to have it at home, which is convenient as he no longer has internet access at home, what with the chopping up of the credit cards and other 'cashflow problems', all of which will be remedied if he manages to make the expected profit on the Madonna tickets. As soon as I have the computer unpacked and plugged in and connected to the outside world, Jonathan starts happily surfing away, checking his emails, his Gaydar profile and various other profiles that I have never even heard of, chuckling away to himself as he writes replies. When I try to see what he's writing he shields the screen with his hand, which is a bit much seeing as it's my computer he's using, but I say nothing and have my drink quietly on the landing. I presume that these are the 'irons in the fire' he was talking about.

It's very quiet now that the ambulance has gone. I can hear someone's TV, a dog barking and a child crying, other, more distant sirens, a train rumbling along the railway lines, the usual medley of sounds that make up 'silence' in London. I can smell Indian food coming from one of the flats. I can see for miles up here – right across the railways lines, over towards Hammersmith and the west. There should be some great sunsets.

Jonathan calls me in because he's found the tattoo that he wants to have on his back; it's a very colourful picture of the Virgin Mary, standing full length, surrounded by an orange and yellow sort of halo thing. I say that he's not a Christian, but he says it's about the design and the colours, not about the 'meaning' of the image, and that I wouldn't understand because I am not a graphic designer like him. I mention that he hasn't actually worked as a graphic designer since leaving college, which is more years ago than either of us cares to remember, and he says that he's been doing some freelance work, which is news to me, but he doesn't elaborate. He quickly changes the subject by saying that it's high time I got a tattoo, that there are some really beautiful Maori tribal symbols I should have on my arms and shoulders, but I say that I'm not Maori, I come from Surrey.

Jonathan thinks I don't take body adornment seriously enough, that I might get more sex if I had some decent tattoos, but I have no desire to be one of those saggy old men you see in the clubs who got covered in ink when they were our age and now look like smudged photocopies. Jonathan has already got quite a tattoo collection, reflecting various phases of his life, the most recent being his yoga name Steady Stream in Hindi script at the base of his spine. I once happened to mention that I didn't like the idea of 'steady stream' so close to his arse, but he said I was just jealous and that I was too scared to have a proper tattoo done, and that means I'm frightened of commitment.

Eventually Jonathan decides it's time to go, which could be something to do with the fact that the vodka bottle is empty and I'm not opening anything else. I do mention that the shop across the road is open twenty-four hours a day and has a small selection of wines, beers and spirits, but he chooses not to take the hint and instead announces that he's got a date. When I ask who with, he gets quite mysterious and will only show me a text message on his phone which says 'u r fuckin hawtt'. Then he starts scrolling through his texts and screams when a big picture

of a knob comes up and says, 'You weren't supposed to see that –
now you know what I'm going to be doing tonight.' I don't think
it's the yoga teacher.

Jonathan leaves at midnight and I do a bit of unpacking, but
it's late and I'm tired and drunk, so I leave most of it in a heap
in the middle of the floor. It can wait until the morning. The
cocaine is wearing off but I don't feel like going to bed, not least
because I won't actually have a bed until Monday, and so I decide
to stay up and write this blog instead.

One

The first thing we had to do today was a Freedom from Infection parade, which meant we all lined up in nothing but our 'drawers, cellular, green' so that the Chief Medical Officer and the nursing orderly could lecture and examine us. It was much like being back at school, lining up to take a shower after games, and there was the same amount of fooling around and jostling and name-calling, the big difference being that we're all young men now, all over eighteen, and no longer children. There were as many different types of body as there were accents. Some looked as if they had stepped straight off the pages of *Health and Strength*. Others must have bribed their way through the medical, because if they're fit for service I'd hate to see the ones that got rejected. Some were short, some were tall. Some were broad at the shoulder and slim at the hips, others were as wide as they were high. There were hairy ones and smooth ones, pale ones and dark ones, even a couple of black ones, who attracted a certain amount of curiosity. There was blond hair, brown hair, black hair, red hair, curly and straight, thick and thinning – all of it shorn within half an inch of its life at the barbershop yesterday. Someone had written on the wall in pencil 'This is just a fucking farce, they shave you like a duck's arse.'

I wished I had my sketch book or my camera with me, because waiting in line for sick parade was like a life class with a hundred different models, every physical type, every imaginable pose – leaning against pillars, standing tall and straight, arms folded, arms hanging, sometimes sitting or squatting, running on the spot to keep warm, clutching hands under armpits to thaw cold fingers. There was much banter about the cold, and how it would make things shrink – 'the old feller', 'the todger', 'the willy' (this was from some of the posher lads) and 'the cock/prick/dick' (from the cockneys, Scousers, Geordies and so on). 'That nurse is going to be disappointed,' said one, looking down his pants and scowling. There was a great deal of laughter because the nurse, of course, was a man, and the general idea seems to be that all male nurses are queer. I joined in the laughter, but of course one of the reasons why I'm glad to be here, at RAF Reville, a medical base, is precisely because the medical corps has 'that' reputation. And that's why this diary will remain hidden in the lining of my suitcase, along with the copies of *Health and Strength* and *Man's World* that I brought with me. If anyone asks, they're to help with my art studies. If anyone reads the diary, God help me. I'll end up in the loony bin.

We shuffled across the dirty wooden floor of the lecture hall, getting splinters and black feet and God knows what else, it didn't seem very sanitary, then when our time came we climbed the five steps up to the stage to be inspected. It was quite theatrical. People whistled. Some of the lads turned round and waved or took a bow. Others were shy, blushing furiously, the flush going right down their necks and over their chests. This was particularly the case with the blonds and redheads.

My turn came, and I walked up trying to look confident. Nobody whistled. I stood before the nurse, who wasn't bad looking, in a Jack Lemmon kind of way, at least from what I could see, because he never looked above belly button level.

'Name?'

'Medway.'

'First name?'

'Michael.'

'Number?'

I gave it.

'Any trouble passing water?'

'No, sir.'

'Any rash discharge swelling or smell?'

'No, sir.'

He took notes and ticked boxes.

'Drop your drawers.'

I did so, just at the front. Some of the lads pulled them right down to their knees and showed their arses.

'Pull your foreskin back.'

I did so.

'Right. Good.' Tick, scribble. 'Now I'm just going to … Mmm-hmm. Ah-hah. Okay.' He broke a little wooden spatula out of its paper wrapping – it looked like a lolly stick – and lifted my cock up, pushed it to the left, to the right, raised my balls. I stared up at the ceiling, and thought about Mum. Anything to avoid getting a stiffy. He threw the spatula in the bin.

'Now I'm going to inspect you. This won't hurt.'

His left hand – the one with which he was not writing – was sheathed in a rubber glove. He felt around my balls, around the tops of my thighs, his fingers gently poking and prodding. I thought of Granny. Finally, he picked up my cock between thumb and forefinger and squeezed the tip.

'Good. All clear. No discharge.' Finally he looked up at me, with the hint of a smile. 'You can put it away now. Get dressed and report to the CO.'

'Thank you, sir.'

'Next …'

I returned to the pile of clothes that I'd left on a bench near the door. I was buttoning up the itchy shirt when there was an outbreak of wolf whistles and catcalls from those still waiting in line. A pale, skinny figure, looking like something out of an Egon Schiele painting, had mounted the stage, thin arms crossed over his sunken chest, knees clamped together, toes delicately pointed out like a ballerina's. His hair was cut short, of course, like everyone's, but somehow he'd contrived to keep a lock or two at the front, and they fell over his forehead. His face was white, apart from two bright red spots on the cheeks. His shoulders were bony, and his ribs stuck out. There was not a single hair on his body. Oh, he's going to have a rough ride, I thought, and felt relieved that there was an obvious one to draw any unwelcome attention away from me.

The nurse went through the usual routine, businesslike as ever, but I thought I detected a blush on his face and a certain unease in his manner. A hush fell over the room. When it came to 'drop your drawers', you could have heard a pin drop.

The boy said and did nothing, but hung his head and kept his knees together.

The nurse looked up. 'I said drop your drawers, Airman Poynter.'

'Do ... do I have to?'

This got a big laugh.

'I'm afraid so,' said the nurse. 'Orders is orders.'

This too got a good reaction. It was turning into a farce.

'I don't ... like to ...'

'Why not? Is something wrong?'

'No,' said Poynter, glancing over each angular shoulder. 'But really ... in front of all these ... men.'

This got the biggest laugh of all. I couldn't work out if he was playing to the gallery or not. But his head was still hanging, and I thought I could detect moisture on his eyelashes.

'Come on, Poynter,' said the nurse, in a gruff voice, 'we've seen it all before.'

Eventually the poor boy did as he was told, and of course by now he had made things much worse for himself. Everyone was crowding the front of the stage, trying to get a good look. Out it popped, and the commentary began.

'Cor, what a beauty!'

'Pass the magnifying glass, I can't see it!'

'Don't get many of them to the pound.'

'Ooh, Daddy, what's that?'

And so on. The nurse, who had turned several shades darker in the face, dispatched it as quickly as possible, and said 'Next' with a great deal of relief in his voice. Poynter strutted across the stage with his nose in the air, trying to regain some shred of dignity, which is not easy in a pair of RAF-issue drawers, cellular, green. He got dressed, but nobody went to talk to him. He stood in the centre of an invisible cordon, as if the men were afraid of catching 'it'. Queerness. Just by talking to one. Or perhaps, like me, they didn't want to give themselves away. For whatever reason, Poynter was alone.

When everyone had been poked and prodded and squeezed, we were sat in rows as the CO took to the stage. He was an old chap, looked like he'd been in the RAF since the First World War, big moustache and everything, row of medals on his chest, red face, white hair.

He gave a speech that he had obviously given a thousand times before, to each new intake. The script had not changed since the twenties.

'On the seafront at Blackpool you are likely to be approached by a number of undesirable characters, some of whom will offer you the services of prostitutes, or women of the night.' This got a big cheer, and the old fellow beamed, cleared his throat and carried on. 'Others will be persons of a class to which I hope none of you will ever have the misfortune to belong, the unfortunates who can be identified by their collar-length hair and bright shirts and … erm … neckerchiefs.' This prompted a lot of whispering, and sideways glances at Poynter, who had developed an absorbing interest in his boot caps.

'Moving on to Lytham St Anne's, an equally dangerous location but less awash with what I might call the refuse of society …'

He chuntered on in the same vein before coming to the main business. The nurse rolled down a white screen.

'Could some of you men close the curtains, please? Jolly good. Lights, please, Austen.'

The lights went out, and there was the usual outbreak of wolf whistles, quickly silenced as the first slide came up – a technicolour close-up of a syphilitic chancre. 'Venereal disease can kill,' intoned the CO, sounding like the voice-over to a Cecil B. DeMille biblical epic. 'It only takes one false step to give you this' – the slide changed to a messy study of a face destroyed by soft tumours – 'or this.'

Deadly silence, and then a crash. Someone had fainted.

Now that he had our attention, the old man rattled through the rest of the repertoire: the shame of gonorrhoea, the horror of herpes, the discomfort of crabs. The cures, it seemed, were even worse than the infection.

'And now,' he concluded, sounding quite pleased with himself, 'fall out for tea and buns.'

We dawdled over to the NAAFI in silence, many of us a little green around the gills. I was more cheerful than most – but then, I have no intention whatsoever of screwing the whores of Blackpool or even Lytham St Anne's. I shall, as my mother advised me, 'keep myself nice'.

I think Mum was rather relieved to see me off when I went to basic training – at least as relieved as I was to get away. Our letters (I received one this morning and will reply tomorrow) are friendly but already distant. She tells me that the daffodils are up and there is frogspawn in the pond, that Nicola has been riding and that they're hoping for a week in Sheringham at Easter. I tell her how busy I am, that I won't have a long enough leave to make it worth the journey home, that I'm meeting some good chaps and that I'm hoping RAF Reville will give me an opportunity to put my knowledge of anatomy to good use (this was a sop to my father, who still grumbles about me going to art school).

Neither of us shed a tear when I left. For me, it was an escape, and for her, an end to the embarrassment of having me at home, from the duty of dangling 'suitable girls' under my nose at parties, from dropping hints about her ravenous appetite for grandchildren. An end to my brother's 'off-colour' jokes about my 'artistic tendencies', an end to parrying questions from aunts and uncles about whether I'm courting. An escape from sub-urban Buckinghamshire and half-timbered houses and Hillman Minxes in the drives. Basic was hell for some, but not for me. It got me fit, and it got me out. It was a gateway to a new world – RAF Reville, a few flat acres on the Lancashire coast, low build-ings huddling on strips of grey-black tarmac, surrounded by square green fields, and beyond them the estuary reflecting the dead grey of the sky. The limitless sky, all over us, huge, blank, criss-crossed by planes and geese. Here to serve our country for two years from 1957 to 1959, to learn something useful, to clean bedpans and change dressings and make beds and maybe even save lives. To make friends. To start life.

I write this diary at night, either in the toilet, where the rest of the men assume that, like them, I'm wanking, or in bed, with a torch, where they assume that I am 'some kind of religious nut'. I'm in no hurry to correct them on either count because the less interest they show in it, the better. Often, I sleep with it at the foot of my bed, under the blankets. In the morning, during the ritual of washing and shaving and tidying the barracks, I squirrel it away in the little suitcase that lives under the locker. We all have our secret places. Most of them are respected. The only way anyone would find this diary is if I gave them a reason to look for it – and that I will not do.

Today we had basic anatomy, the first part of our medical train-ing. Thirty of us in a classroom, windows closed, stuffy, the chalk squeaking on the blackboard as the corporal outlined a skeleton, in white. I did it much better in my notebook.

'And this one?' He tapped the board with the chalk.

'The thigh bone,' we chorused.

'Connected to?'

'The shin bone.'

'And what's this?' Tap tap tap.

'The knee bone.'

'Thank you, Airman Wright. We can do without the accompaniment on paper and comb.'

'Yes, sir!'

Wright is the class clown, a loudmouthed Welshman, always at the centre of a gang. He has a big, square skull, a full mouth, and a good build – I noticed him yesterday, of course, the loudest of the lot, showing off, showing his arse, whistling and shouting and doing handstands while he was waiting in line.

The corporal picked up his red chalk, and made a blob somewhere in the middle of the chest. We began again.

'What's this?'

'The heart.'

'And what does the heart do?'

'Belong to Daddy?'

'Thank you, Wright. Anyone else?'

'Beats?'

'Good. And why does it beat? Anyone? No?' He drew a thick red line from the heart to the head. 'It pumps blood around the body.'

There was a general 'aaah', as if this was news to most.

'Taking oxygen to the brain, to the limbs' – more thick red lines – 'and to all the vital organs.' He picked up his blue chalk. 'And bringing deoxygenated blood back to the lungs, where it will be ... I see I'm going too fast.'

The mysteries of circulation explained, the corporal selected his pink chalk.

'Now, the muscular system.'

Whistles from the audience, and a bodybuilding pose from Wright, who sprang to his feet and started modelling in the aisle.

'Here we have the arm muscles,' said the corporal, at work on the blackboard.

'Biceps, sir.'

'Correct …'

'Then the triceps, deltoids, pectorals, latissimus dorsi, trapezius …'

'Thank you, Wright. As you seem to know so much about it, perhaps you'd like to come up here and do my job for me.'

'I'll do better than that, sir.' He started unbuttoning his tunic. All heads were turned towards him, apart from Poynter, who sat in the front row, staring fixedly at the blackboard. I could feel sweat breaking out on my forehead – but it was very warm in the classroom.

'What are you doing, Wright?'

'A demonstration. Better than a diagram.' He pulled his shirt over his head, vaulted over a desk and took up a position in front of the blackboard. 'There you go. And you won't see a finer specimen in Her Majesty's forces.'

There was much clapping and cheering, and the corporal, fortunately for Wright, seemed to be a good-humoured fellow, glad of the distraction. 'Very well, gentlemen, as we seem to have a stripper in our midst' – more cheers – 'I may as well save on chalk.' He picked up a ruler, and prodded Wright in the chest. 'So, here we have the pectoralis major.'

Wright flexed his chest.

'Bloody hell, it's Diana Dors!'

Wright winked and blew kisses.

'The biceps …'

He flexed again, and someone sang 'Popeye the Sailor Man'.

'The triceps …'

He bent his arm back and the muscle popped up – a pose I'd seen hundreds of times in physique magazines.

'The deltoids … trapezius … rhomboids.' He had a pose for every muscle. 'Moving downwards, the abdominal obliques, transverse and rectus abdominis.' His stomach muscles looked like cricket balls under the skin. 'You didn't go short of protein during basic, then, Wright?'

'No, sir.' Wright grinned. 'I always make a point of having a woman in the cookhouse.'

More laughter. The corporal signalled for silence. 'Now, Air-craftman Wright, we won't trouble you for anything below the waist, much as I'm sure you're dying to give us the benefit of your gluteus maximus.'

Wright made as if to unbuckle his belt, looked around the room – caught my eye – daring us to egg him on. Then he took a quick bow, picked up his clothes and returned to his seat, with much back-slapping along the way.

'Bad luck, Poynter,' yelled a voice from the back. Poynter bent his head over his notes.

'That'll do for this morning,' said the corporal. 'Fall out for a smoke.'

I walked to the perimeter and looked out towards the estuary. They already think of me as a loner. There are plenty of us, and we're not disturbed. But today someone came running up behind me. It was Poynter. I looked to left and right; thank God there was no one near enough to see.

'I saw your drawing,' he said, in his rather nasal voice. 'It was very good.'

'Oh. Thank you.'

'You're very artistic.'

'Well … I went to art school before call-up.'

'I knew it!' His face brightened, and he looked quite animated. 'As soon as I saw you, I thought you were.'

'Right.' I smoked and looked out to sea, unwilling to pick up on whatever he was driving at.

'I'm artistic too,' he said, getting something out of his tunic pocket. 'Would you like to see?'

He unfolded a sheet of paper torn from a notebook. His ana-tomical drawing resembled an exaggerated Michelangelo sketch, complete with long eyelashes, curly hair and a cupid's bow mouth etched in blue ink. The chest, the buttocks and the groin were all greatly enhanced.

'What do you think?'

'It's a little … out of proportion.'

'I draw what I see in here.' He tapped his smooth, ivory forehead.

'I don't think even our very own Steve Reeves is quite that well developed.'

Now his face really lit up, and he clasped his hands in front of his chest. 'Oh I do like Steve Reeves. They're showing his film in Blackpool this weekend. Shall we go?'

This sounded too much like a date, and I threw my cigarette end through the chainlink fence and walked on.

'Sorry,' he called after me. 'I didn't mean …'

I kept walking.

'My name's Stephen!' he shouted after me. 'What's yours?'

I didn't reply.

02

There is a NEW BOY at work this week who has already caused quite a stir of excitement in the advertorials department. At least Anna and I are excited, and that counts as the entire department. The rest of them get in at eight o'clock in the morning, keep their heads bent over their computers all day, don't take lunch breaks, don't take coffee breaks, don't get social calls even on their mobiles, in fact don't have mobiles, so Anna and I barely regard them as human and certainly don't socialise with them. When we leave in the evening, they are still at their desks – in fact I am beginning to wonder if they exist at all outside the office, or have just been put there to test us. If that is the case, I suspect we have failed.

The New Boy arrived yesterday. Anna and I have not yet decided if we officially fancy him or not. He is quite good looking in a rather nerdy way, that is to say he wears glasses, but quite stylish glasses, although I haven't got close enough yet to find out who they are by, if they are 'by' anyone at all. He wears a suit, which probably means that he is an accountant, and although we have always said that accountants are against the rules we are both prepared to change the rules if necessary. Again, I am not sure who the suit is by, which is one of the reasons I have not yet mentioned New Boy to Jonathan, because the first thing he will want to know before he pronounces judgement is about the labels.

NB walked through the office yesterday wearing his suit (charcoal with a very faint stripe, not sure if it's stylish or just conservative) and a sky-blue shirt with a pink tie, which I think is very gay but Anna says that if wearing a pink tie is gay then her father is gay. His hair is short and neat and looks freshly barbered, which again is a good sign because I could never really love someone who did not get their hair cut at least once a fortnight, preferably weekly. Anna likes him too, which could mean the end of a beautiful friendship but we both agree that would be a small price to pay if it means one of us gets a husband out of it.

He arrived in the building today at the same time as me, carrying a cup of takeaway coffee, which means he has some standards and is unwilling to drink the horse piss that comes out of the coffee machines we have here. Although I don't drink coffee since reading that it disrupts absorption of proteins and vitamins, I smile at him in the lobby in a way that says 'I see and approve of your choice of hot beverage, please feel free to ask me for a date and I can tell you at great length about my diet and exercise regime, you don't think I was born looking this gorgeous, do you?' He looks back at me in a rather watery way, which is not good. By the time I get to my desk I have decided that it's all over between us, that he is a weak personality with addictive tendencies and that it could never work.

I don't see him for the rest of the day which is probably just as well because Anna and I are supposed to be working on a fairly important new pitch which if it comes off could be good for both of us, what with appraisals around the corner, so we opt out of the human race and join the drones with our heads bent over our desks, although obviously taking time to email each other every five minutes and discreetly checking our Facebooks on a need-to-know basis. It's perfectly possible to create first-rate online marketing strategies and do social networking at the same time. It's called multitasking, which is one of the skills for which they employed me.

I have not mentioned to anyone in the office apart from Anna that it is my birthday today and so I am not too upset that there are no cards or flowers. However at three o'clock Anna pushes a very small, very elaborate box from her desk to mine, and at that precise moment an email pings into my inbox saying 'Happy Birthday Fatso'. I open the box and there is a perfect miniature chocolate ganache cake, exactly the sort of thing that she has heard me fantasising about a thousand times a day for the last two years. On top there is a letter R in pink icing. 'Go on,' says Anna, 'indulge yourself for once in your life.' I am tempted to stuff the whole thing in my mouth in front of the entire office, making pig noises while I do so, but I would never hear the last of it. She is watching, so I take a bite, chew and even swallow, which satisfies her, and she gets back to work. I still have the taste of chocolate in my mouth, however, which is activating all sorts of addiction centres in my brain, and so I go to the kitchen and make myself a cup of nettle tea, which is enough to spoil anyone's appetite.

At five o'clock I get a text from Jonathan saying 'Happy Bday 2 U, squashed tomatoes & stew, U look like a hamster & ur hung like 1 2', and then it says 'Barcode 7.30.' which is where we are meeting for tonight's magical mystery tour in honour of my special day. So at six I switch off my computer and pick up my kit bag and am just heading off to the gym when I see New Boy coming through the office again, this time he's looking around as if he wants something, and when he sees me he smiles and sort of half waves, which is a bit pathetic. He looks a bit scruffy this evening, and I'm fairly certain that the suit is not Agnès B or Paul Smith but Marks and Spencer or even Next. I look straight through him, throw my bag over my shoulder in a way that shows my arms to good effect and walk out.

At the gym I'm doing arms and chest and talking to Andy, the guy I see every time I go to the gym or to a club, he's always there, he's always super-friendly, I don't know if he fancies me but we've known each other for so long now and he's never made a move that it doesn't really seem likely. I know absolutely nothing about him other than his name, his training regime and his drug preferences. I don't know where he lives, where he works, if he's got a boyfriend – he could be a serial killer for all I know, and then when they interview me on the news I'll be the one saying, 'He always seemed like such a nice, normal guy.' Andy is friends with all the serious gym people and tonight I find out why, because for the first time, after hinting about it for weeks, he asks me outright if I need any steroids, because if I do he can get them for me. I say no thanks, but I'll bear it in mind for the future, and we carry on chatting about creatine and protein shakes and carbloading as if nothing has happened, which I suppose it hasn't although I think it's probably illegal to sell steroids. For all I know it's illegal to buy them as well, in which case a hell of a lot of the people I know are going to end up in jail.

For the record, I don't do steroids because a) I don't want to get huge, and b) I don't want high blood pressure, acne, baldness, heart attacks, loss of libido, low sperm count, testicular atrophy, liver damage, depression or mood swings. I've mentioned this to one or two people and they look at me as if I've just started speaking in Uzbekistani, or whatever they speak in Uzbekistan.

Anyway the penny finally drops about why Andy has such big muscles when he seems to spend his whole time in the gym chatting to people. I look at him a little more carefully this evening and I notice that his back is quite spotty. I'm surprised I never noticed it before.

After an hour I have a shower, and avoid the glance of the guy I call Sauna Slut, who comes into the changing room, gets undressed and goes straight into the shower, doesn't even bother to go into the gym to make a pretence of working out. Then he spends the rest of the evening going to and from the shower and the sauna, occasionally coming out into the changing area to cool down a bit and stare at people like me, as if he could hypnotise us into following him. He's actually not bad looking, and he does have a very big one, but he looks so mad that I try not to catch his eye. Who knows, if I ever get desperate enough I'll smile at him and see what happens. He'd probably run a mile.

I make up my protein drink, and have it while I'm getting dressed. I brought a change of clothes today because I don't want to go out in my office stuff, even though Anna says that I wear to work what most people would wear to a nightclub. For tonight I've got a pink Abercrombie and Fitch polo shirt with sky-blue lettering, and my DSquared jeans which Jonathan made me buy on the grounds that they were the ones Madonna wore in the 'Don't Tell Me' video, with the cowboys. I check myself in the mirror and accidentally catch Sauna Slut's reflection so I have to beat a hasty retreat because he starts waving his thing at me again.

It's a nice evening although not really warm enough to be out in just a polo shirt but if I put my sweater on (John Smedley, white with an argyle pattern in light blue and brown) then no one will see my arms and chest, which I've just spent the last hour working on. So I knot the sweater loosely around my shoulders, but then I see myself in a shop window and decide that I look like a girl, so I tie it round my waist but then you can't see my arse, so in the end I fold it up and put it in my gym bag. As a result of this, by the time I've walked into Soho I'm actually quite cold, and my nipples are sticking up through my shirt, which turns out to be a very good way of making an entrance into Soho. Heads turn. I shall underdress more often.

Jonathan is always late for every date, and tonight is no exception, even though it is my birthday. I have time for a Coke Zero and a chat with the barman and a read of the mags and he's still not there. It's eight o'clock and I'm starting to look at my watch just to let everyone know that I am expecting someone, that I haven't come to Barcode on my own/on the pull, but even I am finding it hard to remain aloof and self-contained and am starting to attract a certain amount of interest. I now wish that I'd kept the sweater on because I might look less obviously like an escort. I keep texting Jonathan WHERE R U? but he's either got his phone switched off or is not bothering to reply.

Eventually at eight-fifteen he breezes in, carrying Selfridges bags, only forty-five minutes late which is not bad for him. 'Don't be cross with me,' he says, holding up one hand in a traffic-stopping gesture, 'I've been shopping for your present and I have found you something absolutely perfect.' He puts all the bags down – there are four in total – around the base of a stool. 'And I'm absolutely bloody parched.' This is understood by all Jonathan's friends to mean 'Please buy me a drink', so while I'm getting the barman's attention and ordering two large vodka and Coke Zeros, Jonathan is bending down and fishing around in the bags. I try not to look as it would be bad manners, but I can't help noticing in the mirror above the barman's head that he has pulled out the smallest imaginable Selfridges bag and is clutching it between his hands with a very pleased look on his face. The other bags are obviously full of stuff that he's bought for himself. I say bought, but 'borrowed' would be closer to the truth, because ever since Jonathan discovered that Selfridges has a no-quibble returns policy, he stocks up on new season clothes which he wears once or twice then takes back for a refund. He regards Selfridges' menswear department as a kind of fashion lending library, and has trained himself to ignore the poisonous looks that the staff give him every time he goes in there.

The barman is quite a cute Brazilian who always gives me large measures and tries to get my phone number so I busy myself with him for a moment, while Jonathan squirms in his seat and clears his throat to get my attention, but he's kept me waiting for three quarters of an hour so it won't hurt him. I keep a close grip on both glasses because he's quite capable of downing one and wanting a refill while you're still getting change.

Eventually I relent and hand him the drink, and he doesn't wait to say cheers but gets the straw between his lips and sucks so hard that it looks like his head is going to implode. I often wonder what it would be like to receive oral sex from Jonathan, but fortunately I have never had to find out. Even when we met at college, and everyone assumed we were lovers, we weren't, which suited both of us just fine. The liquid in Jonathan's glass zooms downwards, until there's only ice, and he's still sucking. I expect to see the ice cubes going up the straw.

'Aaaaaah!' He's panting, like a little boy who's just drunk a glass of squash in one go. 'That's better!' Jonathan takes his pleasures at a gallop. I've barely sipped mine. He's got an expectant look in his eye, but I can see that he's torn between wanting another drink and giving me my present, so I say nothing.

'Dis is for yoooo,' he says, adopting a baby voice, holding the bag out with both hands, dangling it from its rope handles. 'I hope you love it.'

It weighs next to nothing.

'Thank you, Jonathan.'

'Open it open it open it!'

When Jonathan gives a present — which isn't very often — he does so because it gives him an opportunity to display his good taste.

It's a wallet. I have a wallet, of course, but I'm too polite to mention this — although Jonathan is familiar enough with its contents. Perhaps he feels that he's worn it out, and that I need a new one.

'It's lovely. Thank you very much.' It's made of brown leather, and it's got about enough room for a credit card inside. You certainly couldn't keep cash in there, but as Jonathan never carries cash that probably wouldn't have occurred to him.

'Look,' he says, grabbing it off me and turning it over, 'it's Ungaro.'

If I hold it at the right angle, I can just about read the words EMANUEL UNGARO embossed into the leather.

'Wow … It's great.' It occurs to me that it might make a handy holder for my Oyster card, which is probably not what Jonathan had in mind.

'Go on, then. Transfer everything.'

'Not now, Jonathan.'

'You don't like it.'

'I do. I love it. I just don't want to …'

He snatches it out of my hand. 'I've got the receipt, you know. I can take it back and exchange it for something else.'

'No, really, I do like it, please give it back.'

The wallet has been returned to its bag, and will go back to Selfridges along with the rest of this week's wardrobe.

Jonathan sticks out his lower lip and swirls the ice around in his glass, making sure it clinks audibly. I am not going to be made to feel guilty just because he's stolen my present back. It's my birthday and he can buy a round. Jonathan finds it hard to pay for things. I sometimes think that 'share', to him, means only the singer of 'Believe'.

Suddenly it's time to leave, probably because I'm not putting my hand in my pocket, but also because Jonathan has seen someone he knows walking down the street, so he leaps to his feet and shoots out of the bar, screaming 'Hadley!' I should mention that tonight Jonathan is wearing what I call his yoga drag, a sort of loose raw linen trouser suit that's five sizes too big for him, and some horrible Prada leather flip-flops that, apparently, are going to be everywhere this summer, and he's determined to wear them first even though it's far too cold. His hair is still quite long, gelled up into a complicated birds' nest, which doesn't really go with the outfit, I think he ought to shave the lot off but he says he doesn't want to be mistaken for a bloody monk.

I finish my drink, leave a couple of quid for the barman who sniffs and doesn't seem to find me quite so irresistible any more, and follow Jonathan out into the street, where he's deep in conversation with the person I assume is Hadley. Hadley is five-feet-ten tall, and about the same across; I have never seen anyone so built up, he looks like a saveloy that's about to burst its skin. Speaking of skin, he resembles a saveloy in that department too, it's a rich deep terracotta colour, particularly in the folds around his neck. He looks old, but not in the normal way of having wrinkles or grey hair, but in the new way of having a completely immobile forehead and a permanently wide-awake expression. His face is stretched and shiny, but if you look at the backs of his hands, oh dear, they tell a very different story. In order to stop you from doing this, Hadley moves his hands around a lot. I would guess that he's in his mid-forties, but he could be anywhere from thirty to sixty, depending on how good, or bad, his plastic surgeon is.

I'm left hovering on the margins for a few minutes, while Hadley shoots appraising glances at my tits and arms. He's obviously not that impressed, because after a while he looks straight through me. There's another much younger guy also hovering in the background – he is dark and handsome in a rough kind of way, he looks like a Romanian gypsy dressed by Vivienne Westwood, ill at ease in his designer gear, shifting from foot to foot, waiting for Hadley to move on, but Hadley and Jonathan are deep in conversation about Madonna tickets and circuit parties, so neither of us is going to get a look-in. Eventually I step around Hadley – which is quite a detour, as he's so large – and offer my hand to the young guy and say, 'Hi. I'm Rob.' He's confused, and quite possibly doesn't understand English, and looks up to Hadley for guidance. Hadley is suddenly very attentive, and interposes himself between us.

He takes the hand that I'm still holding out. 'Hi Rob.' I can't work out whether he has an American accent or not. 'Hadley.'

'Hello Hadley.'

He doesn't introduce the Romanian gypsy, who is now busy texting someone.

'Anyway, I don't know yet if I'm definitely going, it depends if I can get some you know what,' says Jonathan, who hasn't stopped talking.

'Oh, sure,' says Hadley. 'Charlie will be there. And Tina.'

'Fabulous,' says Jonathan. 'I've never met Tina, and I'm dying to make her acquaintance.'

'You'll love her, Nathan,' says Hadley. I raise my eyebrows at Jonathan, who gives me one of his 'don't you dare' looks. We'll discuss this later.

'And are you going to be there?' says Hadley, turning to face me full on. This has an effect rather like a total eclipse of the sun; I swear Soho suddenly gets a little bit darker.

'I don't know,' I say, because I haven't got a clue what they're talking about.

'Bring him,' says Hadley to Jonathan, as if it's an order for a takeaway. And then he's off, with the Romanian gypsy trotting along after him, still texting. As he recedes down the street I notice that he's actually got a normal person's legs, which look far too thin to support the massive superstructure. Perhaps the mirrors in his gym only go down to waist level.

'So, *Nathan*,' I start, and Jonathan turns on me and is about to launch into a number, but he twizzles himself off his flip-flop and lands with one bare foot in a patch of chewing gum. This takes the wind out of his sails, and for the next few minutes I'm squatting down scraping sticky peppermint-scented crap off his heel, which is pretty dirty already as it would be if you insist on wearing flip-flops in London. Disgusting as this job is, it does show my thighs to quite good advantage, and it completely puts me off the idea of eating, so I don't have to worry about fat and carbs.

Jonathan is obviously hoping that I've forgotten the whole 'Nathan' thing but I haven't, I'm waiting for him to say where we're going next, as this is supposed to be my birthday treat and he's been hinting about 'something really special' for weeks now. I'm actually quite excited although I should know better, having known Jonathan for as long as I have.

'So,' I say, as we walk along Old Compton Street, 'where now?'

'You'll see,' says Jonathan, in a way that makes me nervous, because if he's excited about something I'm almost bound to hate it. And I'm not disappointed.

We turn into Charing Cross Road and my heart starts to sink.

'Oh God, Jonathan, we're not going to GAY, are we?'

He looks offended, like an angry duck.

'Don't you know who's on?'

'Don't tell me, some has-been from the nineties who's got a best of to flog.' I'm quoting Jonathan almost verbatim here, because he's said as much, in a very loud voice, when sailing past the queues on our way into Soho.

'No. As a matter of fact, it's Lukas.'

For a moment the name doesn't register.

'Don't stand there looking like a fucking mong. Lukas.' He shouts. 'Lukas!'

Of course – the olive-and-brown twink who came second in *Star Search*. Jonathan is still obsessed, because he can't resist an underdog, and he's been muttering darkly about how he was prevented from winning by some homophobic conspiracy. Obviously we have no proof of this, we don't even know that Lukas is gay, but we know he's aggressively courting the gay audience, which is always a sign of a career in trouble.

'Lukas,' I say. 'So that's my birthday treat, is it?'

'Well I'm going.'

'Enjoy yourself.' I'm angry, not because Jonathan is being selfish – he's never anything else – but because I could have done something else to celebrate my birthday, like going to my parents' for dinner, for instance, and seeing my sister, whom I've not seen for a year, but I told them I was being 'taken out'. Now I see what a mistake that was.

Jonathan's already forgotten it's my birthday, and is talking to someone he seems to know on the door, presumably so he can get in without paying.

'See you, Nathan,' I shout, trying to sound as sarcastic as possible, but he either doesn't hear me or does a very good job of pretending not to. I get the bus home. I'm not particularly upset. In the six years I've known Jonathan (or Nathan as he's obviously about to become, Jonny and Jon-Jon as he has been in the past) this is not the first time an evening has ended this way.

Why do I bother with Jonathan? How many times have I asked myself that question? How often have I decided that enough is enough, he's just a user, our friendship has run its course, it's time for me to move on? And then I remind myself that a) he was the first gay person I met when I went to college, b) he helped me to come out (in fact he told me I was gay before I told him) and c) my social life isn't so full of exciting alternatives that I can afford to cut him out. Jonathan is my best friend, my 'sister', more like family than family, and although he's a constant source of irritation I could never really chuck him. I like to think that we'd do anything for each other, that we'd be 'there for you' as they say on *Friends*, although if this was actually put to the test I wouldn't put money on the outcome. Jonathan. A fact of life, like housework, or taxes. Neither of which he 'does'.

It's only ten-thirty when I get home, and there's a lot of old men coming down the stairs from the second-floor flat, the one where someone died. They seem to be quite drunk, which means they've been having a better time than I have, which is a bit galling as they're at least three times my age. I can't help noticing that a few of them give me the once-over, even though my tits and arms are now covered by the argyle sweater.

'Oh,' says one, deliberately blocking my way as I climb the stairs, 'you're the boy next door, aren't you?'

'I beg your pardon?'

He's an obvious queen – a tight-fitting grey suit, cinched in at the waist, a bright red shirt with a huge collar, large specs on a chain and woofy grey hair that is probably a wig.

'Upstairs.'

'That's right.'

'Thought so.' I try to sidestep, but he mirrors the move. 'You might want to pop in and pay your condolences.'

'Sorry?'

'To the grieving widow.'

'Oh,' I say. 'I ... I don't really know her.'

'No, you don't, and that's the trouble with you young ones, you don't make the slightest effort.' He's had a few drinks, and he's gesturing with long, skinny hands, covered in signet rings. 'How long have you been here? Weeks. And not once have you popped down to offer a bit of tea and sympathy. And him with his husband barely cold in the ground.'

I'm losing track of this, and mumble something about being tired and wanting to go to bed, but he won't let me past.

'You're coming with me.' He grabs my wrist, and I'm about to shake him off when I realise that it would be very stupid to grapple with a drunk old man on a concrete stairwell, and I can really do without broken hips on my conscience. So I follow meekly along the second-floor landing.

'Michael! You have a late arrival!' he shouts, walking straight through the open door.

Another old man appears in the doorway, wearing a sludge-green cardigan and a check shirt with a brown tie, and a pair of very worn carpet slippers.

'Who is it?' He looks exhausted.

'Look what I found hanging around on the stairs, dear.' He ushers me in. 'Go on. Introduce yourself.'

I put out a hand and say, 'Hello, I'm Robert. I live upstairs.'

'Oh,' says the old man, 'I know, I mean I've seen you coming and going. How are you getting on?'

'Fine, thanks.' I can't think of anything else to say, and I'm about to leave when the other one says, 'This young gentleman wanted to say how sorry he was for your loss. Didn't you.' It's not a question.

'Oh, er, yes,' I mumble, although I'm not quite sure who's died.

'That's very kind of you,' says the old man. 'Will you come in for a drink? There's still some sherry left.'

'Sherry?' screeches the Other One, pushing me in. 'Don't be ridiculous. Young people don't drink sherry. Give him some gin.'

I don't drink gin either, but I don't like to be awkward, and so I accept the gin (warm) and tonic (flat) that is pressed into my hand.

'I'm so sorry,' says the old man, and I think he's apologising for the lack of ice. 'I'm forgetting my manners. I'm Michael, and this one,' he says, nodding towards his friend, who is leaning in the doorway with his arms folded, looking down his long nose at me, 'is Stephen. Don't worry. His bark is much worse than his bite.'

'What would you know, dear? It's many years since I've bitten you.'

We all shake hands and I am shown into the living room. Michael's flat is the same basic layout as mine, but looks tiny in comparison, it's so full of furniture and books and pictures and what Jonathan would call 'knick-knackery'.

I sit down on a sofa that's covered in that sort of tapestry material, with big flowers on a grey background that might once have been white or cream. There are crocheted covers on the arms, probably to cover holes. Every surface has something on it – framed photographs, model aeroplanes, tacky souvenirs of foreign holidays including – I can hardly believe my eyes – a Spanish lady flamenco dancer doll, complete with tiny castanets. The walls are painted a muted pinky brown colour, like liver, and the light fittings are made of brass.

'I'm sorry I've not asked you down for a drink before, to welcome you to the block,' says Michael, 'but I've been unusually busy. You see, we buried my partner today.'

'Ah,' I say.

'He died a couple of weeks ago.'

'Yes, I ...' I suddenly remember Jonathan wolf-whistling the ambulance man, so I stop in mid-sentence.

'It takes so long to get things sorted out these days. I'd much rather have got him planted the next day, to be honest, but there seems to be so much paperwork involved.'

'It was a lovely service,' says Stephen, who's perched on an arm of the sofa and is leaning rather too much towards me. 'Nice music. Lovely readings.' He brushes away a tear. 'Sorry, here I go again.'

'She's been like Vicki Carr all day with the crying,' says Michael, and then stops short. 'Sorry. I mean he.'

'It's all right, Mickey,' says Stephen. 'I think he understands.'

There's a silence, during which I think I'm meant to make a declaration, but I don't know what to say.

'You are, aren't you, dear?' says Stephen, touching me lightly on the shoulder. 'I mean, you're not one of them that just looks the part.'

'No,' I say, 'I'm ... one.'

'There,' says Stephen, pointing at Michael, 'I told you. God takes away with one hand, but gives with the other.'

I finish my drink. 'It's been lovely meeting you,' I say, getting to my feet, 'but I really must go to bed. I've got an early start in the morning.'

'Of course, of course!' says Michael. 'It's very kind of you to pop in. I do appreciate it, and it's nice to know that there's someone friendly in the block.'

I'm about to leave, but I can see Stephen looking daggers at me.

'I'm very sorry about your partner,' I say. 'Had you ... er ... been together long?'

Michael and Stephen look at each other, and burst out laughing.

'Yes, I suppose you could say that, Robert. If you think forty-eight years is a long time.'

I can still hear them laughing when I turn the key in my front door.

Two

Life here would be fine it wasn't for Sergeant Kelsey. We all hate him, from the tip of his dazzlingly polished cap badge to the mirror-like toes of his boots. There is a huge roll of fat at the back of his neck bulging over the tight collar of his shirt, which has earned him the nickname Sausage. It is covered in stubble – rumour has it that he goes to the barber every day – and often nicked and bleeding. Kelsey likes to think that he 'runs the show' at Reville although it's quite clear that the officers can't stand him any more than the men, and if he is so bloody great then why hasn't he been promoted above the rank of sergeant?

His main purpose in life seems to be picking on the weak, especially among the conscripted men, but the regulars will do just as well. I could see him, on our very first parade, picking out his victims. He has a sixth sense for strangeness, deviation or queerness. He can't stand brown faces but he's under orders from above to curb his treatment of these 'black bastards' as he calls them under his breath. So he takes it out on everyone else. He picks on the university men, the Taffies, Jocks and Micks, men who are shorter than him, men who are taller than him, men who stutter, men who cannot march properly, men who wear glasses and, particularly, men who display the faintest trace of effeminacy. He gave me a good going-over that first day, found out that I had been to art school and called me Botticelli, called me a poof – but then, he called nearly everyone a poof. It's the word that you hear from his lips more than any other. He puffs himself up like a toad, and it all comes out in that single syllable: Poof! He's not allowed to say wog, nigger, coon or spade, but poof he can say with impunity. It also enables him to spit in a man's face, which he obviously enjoys.

A little down the line, of course, he found Stephen Poynter.

'Hello hello hello, what have we here?'

A bit of tittering from other airmen who were probably just as relieved as I was that Kelsey had found his supervictim. He didn't stop until he'd made Stephen cry – real, big, fat tears dropping off his face and splashing on to his boots.

Then, 'What is this on your boots, Poynter?'

'Water, sir.'

'Water, Poynter? Have you pissed yourself, boy?'

'No, sir.'

'Then what's it doing there?'

'I …'

'What's that, Poynter? Speak up. I can't hear you.'

'I'm crying, sir.'

'Crying!' He sounded like a crow. 'Crying! What sort of fucking poof are you, Poynter? I said what kind of poof are you?'

And so it went on until Stephen looked as if he was going to faint. Kelsey knows exactly when to stop – and not a moment before.

Poynter came into the barracks while I was writing my diary one afternoon, and everyone else was out on the football field or on furlough in Blackpool. As usual, I hid the diary under the bedclothes – but he wasn't paying attention to that. His eyes were red and swollen, and he was paler and thinner than ever. He stood by the window, looking out, his fists bunched.

'What's the matter?'

'What do you think.'

'Kelsey?'

'Of course.'

'I'm sorry.'

He started to speak, gulped back some tears and was silent for a minute, breathing hard.

'I think he wants me to kill myself. People do, you know. It's quite common.'

'Don't be ridiculous.'

'Well, after all, why not?' He turned to face me. He looked awful, as if he hadn't slept in weeks. I've been avoiding him since we arrived, since he tried to make friends that day, because it's better if we're not linked. 'Might as well give him what he wants. I'm of no use to anyone here. I've got no friends. My family can't bloody stand me. I might as well be dead.'

'Why give him the satisfaction?'

'Isn't that what we're here for? To be good little airmen, to do what our superiors tell us? To follow orders? Like you?' His voice was getting shrill.

'All right. There's no need to take it out on me. I didn't do anything.'

'No, you didn't.'

'What's that supposed to mean?'

'I thought you might stick up for me. Be a pal.'

'Well, I …'

'Don't worry, Medway. I don't want you to hold my hand as we skip merrily around the base.'

'Good.'

'I just need a friend.' Nobody has ever spoken this directly to me before. 'And I think you're the only friend I've got here. With the possible exception of Nurse Austen, or Jane as I call her. But she's so prim and proper, a right little lady with the lamp. Won't even catch my eye. Is something the matter, Medway? You look as if you're about to vomit.'

'I can't stand that sort of talk.'

'What sort of talk, dear?'

'You know. All that … all that "dear" stuff.'

'You mean camp talk.'

'If that's what you call it.'

'I do. What do you call it?'

'I don't know.'

'Tell it to the marines, duckie.'

I lowered my voice to a whisper. 'What do you mean?'

'You know perfectly well what I mean. You may fool them, dear, but you ain't fooling me. Takes one to know one. Isn't that what they say? Hmm? Botticelli?'

It was my turn to stare out of the window. 'Shut up, Poynter. I don't know what you're talking about.'

He came closer. 'Do you want me to show you?' His hair has grown out a little now, and is suspiciously yellow. He smelt sweet, perfumed.

I heard a noise outside the barracks, and bolted.

'Oh Medway!' he called. 'You've left your diary lying around.'

I ran back in, my heart pounding.

'Silly boy,' he said. 'Careless talk costs lives. See you on a pink cloud, duckie.' He walked out, waggling his fingers over his shoulder, chuckling to himself.

Since we completed our six-week basic medical training, we have been split up into different groups with different duties. I'm a filing clerk, sorting out rotas and filling in order forms in the Station Sick Quarters. I think I was given this job because I have A levels. Stephen Poynter is a hospital porter, or 'bedpan Johnny'. The SSQ is a busy place – it's not just military personnel, but locals as well – and so he has his hands full. Wright of course is one of the very few who was picked as a trainee pilot, and spends most of his time out on the airfield. The flyers are like royalty. Even Kelsey treats them with a certain amount of respect. And Wright, from what I observe around the camp and in the NAAFI, is the king. Not only is he popular and good looking, he is also a champion boxer – and they take their boxing very seriously at Reville. He spends a lot of time in the gym, training for fights. I've watched him sometimes; people take an interest in his training, so there's nothing particularly unusual about this. They know I'm an art student – Kelsey made very sure of that – and so sketching doesn't draw a great deal of attention either. I don't know what they'd make of some of the sketches I've done at the back of this diary, partly from memory, partly what I'd like to see, Wright in the showers, Wright without his shorts …

Today Wright came to see me in the SSQ office. My head was bent over the rotas, as usual, and I only noticed he was there because something was blocking the light. He was standing in the doorway, one arm crooked above his head, leaning on the frame, one leg crossed, resting on the toe of his boot.

'Airman Medway,' he said when I looked up, blowing a long thin stream of smoke out of the side of his mouth.

'Yes, Airman Wright?'

'The lads say you've been doing drawings of me.'

'Oh.'

'Have you?'

It was hard to read his face. The eyes were half closed, the lips slightly open around his cigarette. What did he want? Trouble?

'Well?'

'Yes, I've made a few sketches. I'm an …'

'Artist. Yeah. So they tell me.'

He shifted his weight to the other leg, rummaged in his tunic and pulled out a packet of fags. 'Want one?'

'Not in here. Not allowed.'

'And who's going to know?' He lit it from the butt of his, and handed it to me.

'If the MO comes in …'

'Tell him I led you astray.' He perched on the edge of my desk. His thigh muscles fill his trousers. Clothes hang off most of us in the oddest ways. There's a saying about uniforms here: 'If it fits, you're deformed'. Wright's uniform fits like a bespoke suit, and he certainly is not deformed.

'So. Medway. These … sketches.'

'What about them? They're nothing.'

'I want to see 'em.'

'Why?'

'Why? Why do you bloody think, mate? Because I'm bloody gorgeous and I want to see what you've made of me.'

'Oh. Right. Well … I think I might … Somewhere …' I keep a sketch book in a buff envelope at the back of one of the filing cabinets, where no one would ever look. There are Reville landscapes, drawings I've done in the NAAFI, caricatures of 'Sausage' Kelsey … and pictures of Wright.

He liked the caricatures. 'Look at the fat cunt! Christ, Medway, that's brilliant. You ought to get that printed up, sell it to the lads.'

'Yeah, and get discharged for my troubles.'

'But what a great way to go, eh? Ah. Now this is more like it.' He'd found a sketch I did in the gym – a series of rapid figure drawings of boxing positions. 'This me, is it?'

'Well, sort of.'

He turned the page to a much more recognisable head and shoulders. 'Ah! That's my boy! Wow! I like that!' He ran his fingers down the lines of the neck. 'What a beauty, eh?'

'It's not bad.'

'Not bad? It's bloody lovely, Medway! You're a fucking genius.'

'Oh well …'

'Mind you, with material like this, how could you go wrong?' He jumped up into a boxing pose. 'You should paint my portrait.'

'Well, I suppose it could get …'

'You got a camera, Medway?'

'Yes.' I've barely used it since call-up. 'Why?'

'Know how to use it? You know, properly?'

'Yes. I used to do a lot of …'

'Good. You're my man, then. I thought you would be.'

'For what?'

He lit another fag. 'Publicity manager. I need some glossy ten by eights. For the big fight.'

'I don't know about that.' But I was thinking: there's a Reville

Photography Club, a darkroom, and the chance of getting Wright to pose for me …

'Yes, you do.'

'Okay. It's a deal.'

He took my hand in his big square paw and squeezed it. Then, on the way out, he turned his head and said, 'You going to the pictures tonight?'

They were showing *Jailhouse Rock* at the Astra. I wasn't intending to go, but I said, 'Yes, of course.'

'Right. Pick you up at eight, and don't be late.'

He whistled 'Love Me Tender' as he walked across the parade ground.

When I finished work I shovelled down some chips in the refectory then went back to the barracks to change my shirt. I was excited, like I was going on a date.

I could hear sobbing from the washhouse. This is not unusual, and we all turn a blind eye to it. Everyone, at some point, has a bad day, and it's bad form to intrude. Stephen has more than most.

I was cleaning my teeth at the sink, and he came out of a cubicle. 'Oh. I thought it was you.' His voice was dead and flat, and he mechanically washed his hands, wringing them over and over again under the tap until they were red and raw.

'God, you look terrible.'

'Thanks a lot.'

'You should be in bed.'

'I'm all right.'

'You're not.' I glanced at the door – the coast was clear – and put a hand to his forehead, like my mother did when I was poorly. It was hot and clammy. Stephen sighed and closed his eyes. 'I'm not a well woman.'

'You're as skinny as a rail.'

'I've been off my food.'

'You're making yourself ill.'

'Yes,' he said. 'That's the general idea.'

'What?'

'Have you seen what's written on the wall in there?' He jerked a thumb towards the toilets. 'Roll on death, demob's too far away.'

'What's the idea? Starve yourself to death? You'll get shoved on the ward and force fed and then they'll put you back to the beginning of the course, with the new intake. Or worse, they'll bump you back into basic. What'll you do then?'

'Kill myself.'

'You'll do no such thing.'

'Ooh!' he wailed, 'I didn't know you cared!'

'Don't be stupid, Poynter.'

He leaned against the basin, staring at his thumbnails. One was bitten to the quick, the sides ragged and bloody; the other was long and carefully shaped by surreptitious filing against brickwork.

I looked at my watch. Two minutes to eight. Wright would be here soon.

'I've got to go.'

'Okay.' He watched as I splashed my face, dried it on a towel, straightened my collar, combed my hair. 'Oh, by the way, I've got something for you.' He unbuttoned his breast pocket and pulled out a newspaper clipping. 'My friend in London sent it to me. I thought it might be of interest.'

'What is it?'

'Take it. It won't burn you.' He laughed and a spot of colour returned to his cheek – then he started coughing, a deep, rattling cough from the lungs. 'Fucking hell, dear,' he gasped, 'it's like Greta Garbo in *Camille*.' He tottered towards me, holding a handkerchief to his mouth. 'It's not a dream ... I'm here with you in my arms, at last ...'

'Cut it out!'

'Armand!'

There was whistling from the dormitory. 'Medway! Are you in there?'

'Coming!'

I checked my reflection one more time, stashed the newspaper clipping in my pocket and left Stephen spitting into the sink.

Some of the men whistled when Wright and I walked over to the Astra together. I blushed, but he blew kisses. The crowd parted, so we were at the front as soon as the doors opened. Wright jumped over the seats and plonked himself in the middle of the back row, spreading his legs wide enough to reserve the seat on his left. I went round the more conventional route, and joined him.

The cinema was full, standing room only, hundreds of cigarettes glowing in the dark when the lights went down. Wright was wriggling around in his seat.

'Hey, Medway,' he whispered in my ear, 'I've got something to keep us warm.' I could smell the tobacco on his breath. He pressed a bottle into my hand. It was warm – body temperature.

'Cinzano,' he said. ''Fraid it's not cold. I've been sitting on it since I nicked it.'

'You know it's against standing orders to bring alcohol into the cinema.'

'They say forbidden fruit tastes sweeter. Have a slurp. Personally I can't stand the bloody stuff ...' He unscrewed the top, took a swig. 'But you know what they say. Any port in a storm.' He wiped his lips on his sleeve, passed the bottle to me. It was disgusting, but I wouldn't have exchanged it for the finest champagne.

The newsreel began.

'Go on, Wright,' said the airman in front of us, 'give us some.'

'Bugger off. This is a private party.'

'Bloody queers,' said the airman, and immediately found his head locked in Wright's legs. Everyone cheered. The airman, released and gasping, got thumped by his mates.

'Thirsty work,' said Wright, extending his left arm along the back of my seat. 'Ah. Here comes Elvis.'

Wright enjoyed the film, and I enjoyed Wright enjoying it. Every time there was a laugh, he dug me in the ribs. When there were love scenes with Elvis and Judy Tyler, he squirmed around and pressed his legs against mine. In the musical numbers, he drummed his hands on his thighs, using mine when required. Sometimes his hand rested there for a while, before grabbing the bottle. I had knots in my stomach and felt sweaty and sick – not just from the Cinzano. My groin felt like a block of stone. I've dreamed of this sort of thing often enough – drawn it, even – but now, I sat there like a prim schoolteacher.

'I wish I had that bird with me right now,' Wright whispered after Elvis had serenaded his leading lady. 'I'd bloody treat her nice …' He lit two cigarettes and handed one to me, the tip still wet. His hand was picking at his crotch, as if it was uncomfortable.

As soon as the house lights went up, he jumped up on his seat. 'Watch this, lads!'

He whipped out a comb, and with a few flourishes he converted his regulation RAF haircut into the nearest thing Reville has seen to an Elvis Presley quiff. Arms at right angles to his hips, one knee swivelling inwards, he began: 'Warden threw a party at the county jail …'

We were bombarded with caps and sweets and cigarette ends. Wright vaulted over the chair-back and ran, still singing, out of the cinema. I shuffled out with the crowds.

He was surrounded by a gang, still doing 'Jailhouse Rock'.

'Number forty-seven said to number three, you're the cutest jailbird I ever did see …' He bucked his hips wildly.

'Elvis the Pelvis!' yelled one.

'Merv the Perv!' yelled another. Wright's name is Mervyn.

I walked back to barracks, but he ran after, fell into step with me. 'Where you going? The night is young!'

'I'm tired, and I feel sick.'

'You need a breath of fresh air, mate.'

'I need my bed, Wright.'

'Come on. It's Merv the Perv now. Didn't you hear them?'

'All right, Merv.'

'I've got a bottle of Scotch in my billet. We could go and drink that somewhere, if you like.'

'Where?'

'What's your office like at this time of night?'

'Very quiet, and very boring.'

'Won't be boring when I get there.'

'I thought you said I needed fresh air.'

'Once round the ablutions block, by the right, quick march, while I get that bottle of moonshine.'

He raced away before I could stop him. I could trace his progress by the whoops and shouts that greeted him at every turn. I strolled on, not thinking where I was going, towards the perimeter fence.

'Hey! Medway!' Footsteps thumping across the grass, and Wright was at my side again. 'Where are you going? I thought I'd lost you. Look. I've got it.' He opened his tunic; a plain corked bottle full of brown liquid was inside. 'Can't guarantee it's the finest single malt. Could be Dettol for all I know. Keeps the cold out, though. Come on. Your office, wasn't it?'

'I don't think so.'

'You frightened of something?'

'Do you know what would happen if we got caught drinking in the SSQ?'

'Well there's a simple solution to that.'

'What?'

'Don't get caught.'

He put an arm round my shoulder, and led me back.

'What's your name, Medway? I mean your first name.'

'Michael.'

'Michael.' He tried it out, didn't like it. 'Can't call you that. What do your mates call you? What does your bird call you? Mickey? Mike?'

'I haven't got a bird.'

'Christ! Haven't got a bird? Fucking hell, we'll have to do something about that. I know the WRAFs aren't much to write home about, but some of the nurses are all right. And there's plenty of birds in Blackpool.'

'We've been warned about them, haven't we?'

'They're not all slags. Plenty of them are nice. Not exactly Kim Novak, but …' He delineated curves in the dark with his hands. 'Good enough.'

'I'm all right, thanks.'

'Your fucking wrists must ache, Mick, that's all I can say.'

We were at the door of the SSQ. Wright pulled the cork out of the bottle with his teeth, handed it to me. 'Come on. You only live once.'

'I won't, thanks.'

'Sure?' He was looking at me through those half closed eyes, his brow furrowed.

'Yes. Thanks.'

'Okay.' He put the bottle back inside his tunic. 'I'm off to see Gladys in the cookhouse. She's always got something tasty on the go.'

He walked back across the grass, combing his hair.

The camp was quiet now. The men were back in the barracks, preparing for bed. They greeted me with more warmth than usual, now that I was Wright's friend.

Under the covers, with my torch, I drew Wright, again and again … And now I was no longer like a block of stone, a prim maiden schoolteacher. Now I was on fire.

Afterwards, I couldn't sleep. I fumbled in the dark and found the press clipping that Stephen had given me. Curiosity made me read it.

Report on Homosexuality ran the headline. *Recommendations Aimed at the Protection of the Citizen.*

I could hardly breathe. I read on.

> The report of the Departmental Committee on Homosexual Offences and Prostitution, published yesterday, considers the function of the criminal law in this field to be to preserve public order and decency, to protect the citizen from what is offensive and injurious, and to provide sufficient safeguards against exploitation and corruption of others ...

My fingers were sweating into the paper, making damp patches.

> Certain forms of sexual behaviour are regarded by many as sinful, morally wrong, or objectionable for reasons of conscience, or of religion or cultural tradition; and such actions may be reprobated on these grounds ...

My breathing sounded too loud, as if I might wake up the entire billet. I broke off, came up for air ... Nothing, just the sound of snoring, the odd creaking mattress spring. I went back for more.

> The committee's first recommendation in the matter of homosexual offences is that homosexual behaviour between consenting adults in private be no longer a criminal offence.

My hands were shaking so much I could barely make out the words. I switched off my torch and closed my eyes, screwing the paper up into a tiny pill. I will dispose of that tomorrow, somewhere out on the parade ground.

03

Hadley lives in a huge flat in Shoreditch which apparently he has owned 'forever' i.e. long before property prices in the area were so high that you have to be a millionaire to buy something the size of my bedroom. It's basically one big space on the first floor of what used to be a sewing machine factory, and he's got one of the old machines displayed on top of a plinth right in the middle of the room, under a spotlight, like a museum piece. The rest of the space is divided up by cast-iron pillars and screens that create, according to Jonathan, a 'flexible live-work space'. There is a futon in one corner, with a white folding screen in front of it, and a lot of nightlights in glass holders on a shelf that runs the entire length of one of the walls, and apart from that very little. It's barer than my flat before any of the furniture was delivered. There's a huge trestle table at the far end, covered in bottles and glasses and white linen. The bathroom is concealed behind an invisible white door in a white wall. I can't see any sign of a kitchen and there is no food.

The place is already packed when we arrive even though it's only three o'clock in the afternoon, but Jonathan says that they will have been going since they got back from the clubs at eleven o'clock this morning, and that wasn't really 'this morning' or even 'very late last night' but in fact 'even later the previous evening'. Hadley and the rest of the club crowd operate in their own unique time zone, in which what the rest of us think of as 'Sunday afternoon' is actually still 'Friday night' as far as they're concerned. Everyone is smoking. There are signs on the wall saying YOU CAN SMOKE HERE.

There are waiters going round with trays of drinks, they're all wearing tight black T-shirts and black jeans, and I'm pretty sure that one of them is the Romanian gypsy that I saw with Hadley in Soho a few weeks ago, but I could be wrong because they all look the same. Perhaps Hadley has imported an entire Romanian village, or encampment, or whatever they live in. They are working the room very efficiently and there is so much drink that I am already wondering if I might have to have flu tomorrow morning, and spend a few extra hours in bed.

Hadley fights his way through the crowd to welcome us, and he's grown quite a lot since the last time I saw him. The material of his grey Abercrombie and Fitch T-shirt actually appears to be thinner than his brick-red skin, which has got thicker, probably as a result of too many sunbeds. His biceps are so pumped up they look like bags of rocks, with thick white veins crawling over the surface.

'Nate, Robbie,' he says. Nate? 'Great you could come.' His eyelashes are wet, his eyes twinkling brightly blue, like doll's eyes stuck in the wrong face. Jonathan offers to kiss him on the cheek, but Hadley pulls back, and instead grabs my right nipple and tweaks it hard. 'Help yourself to anything you like,' he says, 'but not Nico.' He nods towards one of the interchangeable bits of foreign trade. 'He's mine. Say hello, Nico.'

Nico manages to say hello in a way that sounds flirtatious and contemptuous at the same time; I must perfect that. All his clothes are expensively frayed, and don't actually cover much of his body. I can see a thick bush of pubic hair filling the gap between his shirt and the waistband of his trousers. It looks very warm, and I'm tempted to stick my hand in and find out, but he's already turned his back on us to take a phone call.

'I have to go, Hadley,' he says. 'I need money.'

Hadley peels off three twenty-pound notes. 'There you go.'

'I need more,' he says, and gets another forty.

'He's got to pay his college fees,' says Hadley, who might be blushing but it's impossible to tell. 'And I owe him for a job. He's working for me.'

I'm dying to ask in what capacity, but I don't feel I know Hadley well enough yet. I have my suspicions and ask Jonathan as soon as Hadley is out of earshot.

'So is Nico a rent boy?'

'Of course he's not. He's a very talented photographer.'

'And is he working for Hadley?'

'Yes, that's what he said.'

'And what does Hadley do, exactly?'

'I've told you before, he runs his own PR company,' says Jonathan, burying his nose in his glass, but I think that Hadley is a drug dealer. Hadley has started to loom very large in Jonathan's life recently, and we've already had one row about him, in which I said, 'It's all "Hadley this, Hadley that" with you these days,' and Jonathan said, 'Hadley has a lot of connections,' and I said, 'So does a box of Lego,' and we left it at that. Jonathan thinks that Hadley can do something for him; Jonathan is always looking for people who can do something for him, because he's too lazy to go out and look for a job and is just waiting to be discovered. As *what* I'm not exactly sure; he has a degree in graphic design and nothing on his CV so if he does have hidden talents, he's hidden them very well. As such he's probably ideal for PR.

We've come to this party largely because Jonathan thinks 'we should', because 'it's time we started moving in some more interesting circles', but also because I think that there will be men there and Jonathan thinks there will be drugs there. We get ready at my house, mainly because I have hot water (Jonathan is having 'a spot of bother' with the gas board over a small matter of unpaid bills), and so of course Jonathan ends up not wearing the clothes he arrived in, but borrowing and 'customising' a lot of mine, which means I will never see them again. He's ditched the yoga drag, and is now going for what he calls 'banjee realness' but looks more like the sort of thing you see in the B&Q

car park on a Sunday afternoon. He's got a pair of my gym sweatpants rolled up to the knee, white tennis socks up to the shin, a pair of pink Converse Allstars and a zip-up cardigan with black-and-white check trim, that looks like something a rather effeminate policeman might wear. He's teamed this with an outsize pair of aviator shades with white frames. I suppose this is the look that goes with his new name of Nathan or 'Nate', and I really hope it doesn't last because on the bus we get quite a lot of abuse from some real-life young black men and have to sit downstairs.

I'm wearing my usual polo shirt and jeans, which Jonathan calls my children's television presenter look. I say if I'm a children's television presenter, then we'd better have a line of coke before we go out, but this time I make sure that I'm in charge because I only have a gram and I need it to last all evening. Jonathan hoovers it up and then starts pouting but I've already put it in my pocket. 'If only I had a handy little leather wallet to keep it in,' I say, but he just shrugs. Needless to say I never got a replacement present, nor has Jonathan apologised for chucking me in favour of Lukas on my birthday, but then you don't expect apologies from Jonathan.

Lukas is another reason we've come to this party, because Hadley has told Jonathan that he is pitching for the Lukas account, which could mean that Hadley genuinely has a PR company and is hoping to represent him, or, which I think is much more likely, is hoping to become his dealer. Jonathan is convinced that Lukas is going to be at the party, that he'll see 'Nate' in all his banjee realness and soon they will be photographed in *Heat* magazine together, 'Lukas and mystery brunette'. So while I'm trying to talk to Jonathan, he is looking over my shoulder in case Lukas turns up.

This is so distracting that I have to look around as well, because I have this weird feeling that something or someo⌐ behind my back, and that's when I see HIM for the a bit like seeing myself in a distorting mirror: he's also wearing a polo shirt, but he's taller than me, bigger than me, better looking than me, possibly a year or two older than me. He's big – not freakishly big like Hadley, but he wouldn't look out of place on the cover of *Men's Health* or any of the other closet gay mags, shot in high contrast black-and-white with the words GET A SIX-PACK NOW! in bright orange letters.

He's looking at me, as if he was just waiting for me to turn round, and he raises his glass to me. I feel butterflies in my stomach but fortunately I have the kind of face that can express absolutely no emotion whatsoever, and so I just raise my glass in return and turn slowly back to Jonathan. I've drawn breath to say, 'Who is that gorgeous man behind me?' but then I stop because, in the time it's taken me to turn away and turn back, Jonathan has disappeared. I do a double take, and look around in every direction, but he is nowhere to be seen.

I must look completely flummoxed because the gorgeous man comes up to me, laughing, and says, 'Your little bird has flown,' as if I've somehow been stood up. 'Oh, that's not my little bird,' I say, 'that's just my friend.'

'Friend as in friend,' he says, 'or friend as in *friend*?'

'Friend as in friend,' I say, sounding like a complete cretin, but he smiles again and says, 'Pleased to hear it,' and we clink glasses. He is extremely good looking, with a strong jawline, narrow eyes, deep creases down his cheeks when he smiles and straw-coloured hair that looks as if it might even be natural. It's cut short on the sides, with a long, thick bit at the back, which I want to grab. His shirt is even tighter than mine, and I can see that he spends a great deal of time in the gym, so we have that in common. I'm already planning a future together when he says, 'What's your name, mate?'

'Robert.'

He puts out a big, square hand and says, 'Stuart.' We shake, and I'm relieved to find that he shakes hands like a normal person, not one of those complicated handshakes that I always get wrong. The shake goes on for quite a long time.

'Good to meet you, Stuart,' I say, taking back my hand. 'How do you know Hadley?'

He laughs, and his eyes are so narrow that you can't see any white at all, just two black slits, like in a mask. 'How does anyone know Hadley?'

This makes me even more convinced that he's a drug dealer.

'What are you doing later?' he asks, openly running his eyes up and down my torso. I was planning to be in bed by about ten o'clock, in order to get into work early and prepare for this big pitch meeting, but I say, 'Nothing in particular.'

'Good,' he says. 'Don't go away.'

And then he, too, disappears, and while I'm tracking his broad shoulders and powerful arse through the crowd until he's swallowed up by Romanian gypsies, Jonathan rematerialises. I almost expect there to be a puff of smoke. He is sniffing, so I know where he's been.

'Who were you talking to?' he says, as if I'd been neglecting him.

'Just a guy. His name's Stuart.'

'Stuart indeed.' Jonathan hates all my boyfriends on principle, because they disrupt his social life. 'He looks like a rent boy.'

Coming from Jonathan, who looks like something from a 1980s public information film about the peril of prostitution, this is quite funny.

'You may laugh,' he says, so I say, 'Thank you,' and do. 'But a lot of the guys here are, you know.'

'Are what?'

'Escorts.'

Jonathan is obsessed by escorts, and is only prevented from using them by economic factors, but looking around I realise that he might have a point. Suddenly I understand what kind of 'job' the lovely Nico might have been doing for Hadley. Is

Hadley a pimp, as well as a drug dealer? Or simply a punter? What kind of party is this?

'Have you met Miss Tina yet?' asks Jonathan, rapidly changing the subject. I wonder if she's a drag queen, and say, 'No.'

'Well you should. I just met her, and she's faaaaabulous.' He's wiping his nose, and clenching his jaw, and looking around even more than normal, and I suddenly remember which 'Tina' he's talking about.

'Crystal meth? Are you insane?'

'Oh, don't look at me as if I've just turned into a filthy junkie or something,' he says. 'I know what I'm doing.'

'They all know what they're doing,' I start, and Jonathan joins in the refrain 'until they're carried away in the back of an ambulance.' I've said this to him a hundred times before but he never listens.

'You're a fine one to talk, with what you've got in your pocket.'

He's right, and I can feel the little wrap pressing against my thigh.

'Cocaine is different. It's like having a pint of beer.'

'That's crap and you know it.' Jonathan then launches into a spirited defence of 'intelligent drug use' which lasts until his mouth goes so dry that his tongue actually stops moving, and he's obliged to swipe a glass of champagne from a convenient tray.

'I just think you should be careful, that's all,' I say, taking advantage of the brief respite while he drinks. 'You don't know what that stuff does to you.'

'And you don't know what all those supplements you take are doing to you.'

We've been over this ground before, and we both know our lines.

'I'm investing in my health,' I say, 'and my future.'

'No, you just want big titties so that you can pick up men.' Jonathan's failure to pick up men is a constant bone of contention, and he blames me for 'distracting' them.

'I'm only trying to help you …'

This is the wrong thing to say.

'My God, you've become so boring recently,' he begins, his mouth now well lubricated and the crystal meth kicking in. 'You've been spending so much time with that old queen downstairs that you're becoming middle-aged already. You're only twenty-four for Christ's sake! You should be out there!'

Jonathan can't abide my new neighbour and shudders every time I mention him. And he hasn't even seen inside the flat, with the swirly carpet and the ornaments.

'I don't want to be dead at thirty!' I say, quite loud, to make myself heard.

'Well I bloody do if living means becoming booooooooring.'

'You think anything that doesn't involve Class A drugs is boring …'

'You got that right.'

'But in fact Michael has led quite an interesting life.' It's not that interesting, in fact, from what I've heard, but I'm not willing to concede the point. As far as I can make out, he met his boyfriend forty-eight years ago, and did absolutely nothing ever since, didn't even get Civil Partnered because 'it takes so much organising', and is regretting it now he's dead. I haven't told Jonathan any of this because the words 'Civil Partnership' are like a red rag to a bull, and he'll start on his speech about 'apeing heterosexual norms'. Jonathan would be more than willing to ape if anyone asked him, but until that happy day he's quite political about it.

Fortunately for me, the discussion is cut short by a lot of jostling around the door. Jonathan stops in mid-sentence and says, 'OMFG! It's him!' and runs off with his mobile phone held above his head, snapping pictures as he goes. Through the scrum I can just about see a mop of dark brown curls so I guess that Lukas has arrived after all, and that's the end of any conversation with Jonathan.

'He's even shorter than he looks on TV,' says a voice behind me. It's Stuart again, standing so close that I can feel the heat from his torso on mine. 'He looks a bit chipmunky.'

'He's got weedy arms,' I say.

'Yeah, and no arse.'

That seems to have exhausted the conversation for now, but fortunately Stuart takes the initiative, puts a hand at the back of my neck and kisses me on the mouth. I'm so taken aback that I open up and his tongue goes straight in. He has a stubbly chin but very soft lips, which is a particularly effective combination as far as I'm concerned. He pulls me towards him, and our bodies touch from chest to knee. He's quite obviously got a hard-on.

'I've been wanting to do that ever since I saw you walk in,' he says. 'Hope you don't mind.'

I don't mind, and so I grab the hair at the back of his head and pull him in for another go. This time my tongue is in his mouth.

'Woah, woah!' he says, as if it's me that's taking things too fast. 'Easy, tiger!' He takes a step back. 'Shall we have a drink?'

I don't want a drink, I want to leave the party right now and go back to his place, my place or any place that's near, but he grabs two glasses of champagne and hands one to me.

'So, Robert,' he says, 'tell me about yourself.'

I'm not used to this, because most people only want to talk about themselves, but I shouldn't have worried, because I've got no further than 'I work for a media company ...' than he's interrupting.

'I can't stand parties like this, can you?' he says, knocking back Hadley's liquor, which is very good. 'All these fake people. What do you think?'

'Well, I don't really know Hadley ...'

'What clubs do you go to?'

'Oh, I don't go out that much, but if I do ...'

'I really like Base at the moment, I always used to go to Redemption but the music there is so shit now and they closed down the VIP bar.'

There doesn't seem to be much answer to this.

'Come on, let's go.' He grabs me by the arm and starts walking towards the door.

'I can't, I came with …'

'You can.'

And so I do.

He lives way out in north London somewhere, he's vague as to the exact location, and so we get a taxi back to my place, which I would never consider because of the expense but with him it seems the natural thing to do. In the back of the cab he is all over me, and when the driver makes a tutting noise Stuart says, 'What's your fucking problem, pal?' and carries on exactly where he left off. He's got one leg thrown over my lap and he's basically humping me, so I can see the driver's point to some extent, but at least this means that we get home in double-quick time, presumably so the driver can get rid of us as soon as possible.

I hand over thirty quid and tell the driver to keep the change (four quid) and when Stuart hears that he starts laughing again.

We take the stairs three at a time, and he catches me on the second landing and grabs me and starts kissing me again, this time he's got his hands up the back of my shirt, and we collide with one of the recycling boxes on the landing which makes a loud clanking sound. I catch sight of Michael's hand moving the net curtain at his kitchen window, and dimly see his face looking out, before Stuart pulls the shirt right over my head and I can't see any more. Somehow I manage to get him up to my floor, and just about push him into the flat before my trousers are round my knees. We have sex right inside the door, on the floor in the hall, knocking over a pile of books that I still haven't found a home for, rolling around and thumping and grunting like a couple of animals.

We don't do much apart from rubbing and wanking, we're too excited to get into anything more complicated like fucking or sucking, besides which Stuart seems to want to spend the whole time kissing. When we finally come, we're breathing the air out of each other's lungs. I open my eyes and he's got his screwed up so tight that the lines around them are white, he's driven all the blood away.

We lie there for a while, and I half expect him to get up and leave, but he doesn't. He ruffles my hair, bites the lobe of my left ear and then finds his way to the toilet to clean up. There's cum everywhere, and I wipe it up with my shirt, which has to be washed anyway.

My phone is beeping in my trouser pocket, and there's a message from Jonathan that says WHERE THE FUCK R U?, to which I don't reply. Stuart comes out of the bathroom, naked apart from his socks, and stands over me as I lie there on the floor, my trousers still bunched up around my shoes.

'Time for bed,' he says, and he's getting a hard-on again. I can't help noticing that he is also sniffing, but perhaps he has a cold.

Three

As Wright's friend, girlfriend, bum-chum or, as the padre rather wistfully calls me, 'Jonathan to his David', I am basically bulletproof at Reville. In fact, I'm popular. I'm one of the lads. My drawings are admired, my 'scribbling' tolerated and even respected (it's been put around, by whom I don't know, that I'm writing a novel of National Service life), I'm included in pub runs and barrack-room bonhomie. I would not say I have friends, other than Wright himself, but suddenly I have plenty of mates. People know me, and through me, Wright. We've become inseparable in people's minds, a team, a duo, like Laurel and Hardy, Flanders and Swann, or, as Kelsey calls us, Wright and Wrong. It's the nearest he can get to picking on me. Even Kelsey beams when Wright deigns to talk to him.

So of course all his venom is saved for Stephen. The nearer I come to the light, the further he's banished to the outer darkness, and there's little I can do to help him. He doesn't bother me. He hasn't tried to corner me since that evening in the bogs when he passed me the newspaper clipping. I can see he's getting sicker, sadder, more desperate, but what can I do? I'm not going to risk my new-found status by consorting with someone who, by his own admission, is trying to work his ticket out of here. The way he's looking, he'll manage it sooner rather than later.

He won't be the first one to get chucked out for being queer. The place is full of rumours. There was the Squadron Leader who, many years before any of us got here, was caught with an Aircraftman Second Class and had his stripes torn off in front of the whole camp. He was marched off the parade ground by two Warrant Officers, stripped of his uniform and pushed through the gates in civvies. He has since been sighted, they say, in London, 'hanging round the West End' in brown shoes. There were the two ACIs who were caught in the back of one of the old ambulances one night, bouncing away on top of each other with their trousers round their ankles; it was the creaking of the suspension that alerted the guard, who opened the doors and shone his torch inside. They disappeared the next day, carted off to RAF Halton, 'the loony bin', where they send all the queers and the would-be suicides and the more obvious nutters, 'for tests', and were never heard of again.

Wright has not referred to that night at the cinema, and I suppose I got the wrong idea, although I'm haunted by the certainty that I had not. He has, however, been pushing me to take his photograph, there being a regional tournament next month. He wants to plaster the camp with posters and sell glossy ten by eights to his 'fans', as he calls them. Wright has big ideas about stardom. When we get out of here, he's convinced he's going to be famous, although he's not quite sure as what – athlete, actor, singer, he's not bothered, as long as he gets the adulation and the birds. He talks a lot about birds.

I wrote to Mum and Dad asking them to send me some film, on the pretext that I was taking a few snaps of the chaps, and it duly arrived, along with a note complaining about how they had to go all the way into High Wycombe to get it, which was an inconvenience as the parking there is so poor, but Dad managed to find a space near the Odeon which is not too far from the shops. But there they were: four rolls of Kodak 200 ASA, 36 exposure, undamaged and ready for use. I've been practising with my camera – without film – refreshing my memory of aperture and exposure and all that jazz. When I get Wright into my viewfinder, I don't want to get flustered. I want to be cool, calm, professional. I've gone over the scene so many times in my head, at night, after lights out when mine is not the only mattress creaking and squeaking like the suspension of that old ambulance, which I think about a lot too, what they were doing in there, trousers round their ankles, faces glued together, eyes closed, unaware of the torch shining on their bare bums … I've drawn the scene many times, but scribbled it out, torn it into pieces, and dropped the scraps in the pig bin behind the cookhouse.

We set the date for 'the session' for a Wednesday afternoon, when the camp would be quiet, the rest of the men playing football or getting clap in Blackpool. I was nervous all day, couldn't concentrate at work, buggered up the rotas, got a ticking off from the MO, felt sick and had the shits. Even Wright looked nervous when he arrived at the classroom that we'd got permission to turn into a studio. I'd never seen him like this, smoking furiously, dancing on the balls of his toes, punching his hands, pushing his hair back. One of us would have to be calm, and it was going to have to be me. I'd been fiddling around with the 'set' since lunchtime, arranging the folds of the old blackout curtain that hung over the blackboard, trying to conceal the worst of the holes and patches. I borrowed arc lights from the operating theatre, grouped on retort stands, angled towards the curtain like they tell you to in *Amateur Photographer*. I'd even made a classical column – just like the ones in *Health and Strength* and *Man's World* – out of a roll of corrugated cardboard that was kicking around the quartermaster's stores, getting damp. White-washed and shaded with pencil to suggest fluting, it would look all right in photos – as long as Wright didn't lean on it. It was a bit wobbly.

'Quite a set-up you've got here.' He came in, leaving the door open, throwing his kit bag into a corner.

'It's not Hollywood, but it'll do.' I busied myself with my camera, which was set up on a tripod.

'Hope you've got some film in that,' said Wright. 'I've heard about dirty old men like you.'

'Oh yeah. I've lured you here on the pretext of taking photos, but I just want to get your knickers off.'

We both laughed, and stopped abruptly at the same time.

'Shut the door, Wright. You don't want to be covered in goosepimples.'

'Christ, no.' He kicked the door shut. 'I've got to look bloody gorgeous. I brought some chip oil from the cookhouse. Thought it might do.'

'What on earth for?'

'You know. They all do it in the mags. Grease themselves up.'

I opened the bottle and sniffed. There was a layer of brown crumbs at the bottom. 'It stinks.'

'Well nobody's going to know that, are they? Give it here.' He took off his tunic and hung it carefully over the back of a chair. 'Right then. I suppose I'd better strip off then, hadn't I?'

'Yes,' I said, very busy with the camera. 'You get yourself ready.' I couldn't watch. This was the point at which, in my night-time fantasies, things started to get interesting. My heart was beating too fast, my hands were shaking. I took deep breaths and tried to calm myself.

'No time like the present, is there?' I glanced sideways; he was unbuttoning his shirt. His chest was pumped up, his biceps bulging. 'I did fifty press-ups in the yard before I came in,' he said.

'Great …'

His shirt joined his tunic, neatly folded on the chair. The hair on his stomach, where it fanned out from his navel and down to his waistband, was slightly matted.

'So, stand with your fists up.'

'Hang on. What about these?' He picked at the rough blue material of his trousers.

'You can leave those on. We'll shoot from the waist up.'

'And miss my lovely legs? Bollocks to that.' He bent down and unlaced his boots, his back flaring out from his narrow pelvis, the vertebrae easy to count through his skin. He kicked off his boots and dropped his trousers. Now he was wearing only standard-issue pants and socks.

'God, I can't photograph you in those.'

'Ah! Wait and see.' He fished around in his trouser pocket, and produced a small bundle of white fabric. Two tiny triangles of elasticated cotton joined at the corners.

'What the hell is that?'

'I sent off for it from an advert in *Health and Strength*.'

'You read *Health and Strength*?' I'd assumed that only people like me read it.

'Course I do. I'm a bodybuilder, ain't I?' He flexed his arms beside his head; the muscles popped impressively.

'Right. Well you'd better … slip them on.' I turned away and fiddled with my light meter.

'Bloke in London sells them,' he said, 'mail order. All the muscle boys wear them. Supposed to show it off to its best advantage. What do you think?'

The garment barely contained him. I tried to sound professional, but just sounded prissy. 'Well, you certainly look the part.'

'Too much for RAF Reville?'

'It might be.'

'I've got my boxing clobber as well.'

'Perhaps that would be best.'

'Okay. But I want some shots in these too. I didn't pay eighteen bob for nothing.'

'Eighteen bob? Christ.'

'And I wanna get my money's worth.'

'So much for so little.'

'Yeah. But it's what's inside that counts.' He struck a pose, thrusting his hips forward, then winked and laughed and produced his shorts from his kit bag. 'Right. Oil time.'

I'd borrowed the record player from the library, loaded with a stack of 45s that Wright had borrowed from Gladys, as well as his prized copy of 'Jailhouse Rock'. I switched it on, and the first record dropped on to the turntable. 'You Send Me' by Sam Cooke. Wright smeared palmfuls of oil over his shoulders, arms, torso and thighs.

'You going to do my back for me?'

'I can't. I'll get the camera all greasy.'

'Oh, come on, mate, give us a hand. You can wipe 'em clean.'

I dabbed a little oil on to my fingers, hardly daring to touch his skin.

'Just bloody rub it in, Michael, for God's sake.'

'Seems a bit weird.'

'So?' Wright did a Mr Hyde voice. 'Maybe I am a bit weird.'

I ran my palms over the huge slippery expanse of his back. The classroom smelt like a chip shop at frying time. I wiped my hands on my trousers.

The next record dropped on to the last – 'Que Sera Sera', Doris Day.

'Your Gladys has got very soppy taste in music.'

'She's not my Gladys,' said Wright, 'she's everyone's. Anyway, thought you'd like Doris Day. *When I was just a little girl I asked my mother …*'

'That's enough. You're a boxer, not a singer, thank God. Get the shorts on. We'll do the others at the end, if you want.'

'You're the boss.' He stepped into his silk shorts, one foot after another. The waistband came up high.

'Stand over there.'

He positioned himself in front of the old black backdrop, shook out his arms, rolled his shoulders and stretched his neck, an athlete preparing for contest.

'Put your guard up, like you do in the gym.'

'Like this?'

'Perfect.' Behind the camera, away from the heat of his body, I felt safer and more confident. I took the first shot.

'Now look down towards the floor, and turn your eyes up to me … that's it.'

'Do I look lean and mean?'

'You look like trouble.'

'I am trouble.'

'Okay. Now clasp your hands above your head as if you've just knocked the other bugger out.'

'Winner!' His armpits were damp with sweat, the hair forming little curls. 'What next, boss?'

I went through the repertoire of familiar poses from the magazines. 'Put your hands behind your head, and stretch your torso up.'

'Like this?'

'Good. Now turn at a slight angle.'

'Can you see my abdominals?'

'In great detail.'

'Good.' He ran a hand down his greasy stomach. 'Very proud of these, I am.'

'Do that again. One hand behind the head, the other running down your stomach. Good.'

'Looks pretty sexy, doesn't it?'

'Oh, hot stuff, baby.'

'How about the back?'

'Face the curtain. Now look back at me. Shows off your trapezius.'

'I've got a lovely trapezius.'

'And throw a right jab. One, two, three and bang!'

'I'm working up a sweat here. These lights are bloody hot.'

'Looks more authentic.'

'Got what you need?'

'I think so.'

'Right. Fun time.' He bent over, pulling his shorts to his ankles, backside sticking straight at the camera. I pressed the shutter. 'Oi! You cheeky bugger!' His face was red as he looked back at me.

'Send that one home to the folks.'

'Oh yeah. She'd love that, my nan. Here I am flashing my arse in the RAF, love, Mervyn.'

He tossed his shorts to the floor. The brilliant white of the slip seemed to draw all the light in the room.

'Hope nobody's peeking.'

'It's all right. The blinds are down.'

'Good job. Right. How do you want me?'

The cover of the latest *Man's World* showed a model sitting on top of a pillar. 'Just perch on that. Don't put any weight on it.'

'Hope the bloody thing doesn't slip up my arse. What with all this oil and everything.' He managed the pose, thrusting his groin forward, which was the desired effect.

'Now, how about kneeling.'

'Ay ay, what's that all about?'

'You know, like a fallen gladiator, all that malarkey.'

'Oh, right. I know the drill.' He dropped to his knees and raised his arms in supplication. 'This sort of thing?'

'Don't overact. Relax your arms. There.'

He moved into a reclining pose, propped up on one elbow. 'Come on, let's get some sexy ones while I'm down here. Come on, baby, see what Daddy's got for you …'

I snapped away, my finger slipping on the shutter release, sweat and grease mixing on my skin.

'Time to change the film.'

'Okay. Just as well. I'm starting to get a bit … you know.' And he was: the fabric was noticeably stretched. I reloaded, while he did fifty press-ups on the floor.

'Ready when you are.'

'I'm ready, boss.' His muscles were pumped and gleaming, his hair falling into his eyes, damp with sweat. 'What now?'

'Let's just get a few natural poses.'

'Okay. Snap away.'

He moved like a dancer, raising his limbs, letting them fall, bouncing around in little boxing steps, feinting punches at the camera, getting into the rhythm of the shutter. Film flew past the lens.

'One more to go.'

'Come on then. One for nan. Are you ready? One …'

'Wright!'

'Two …'

'You can't …'

'Three, ready or not!' He whipped the fabric to one side, and out sprang his cock, well on the way to being hard. I released the shutter just in time.

Wright whooped, ran for his clothes and started dressing in a hurry, laughing his head off.

'You show that to anyone and I'll fucking skin you!'

'I show that to anyone,' I said, 'and we could both end up in the Glasshouse.'

We didn't speak for a while after that. We were both so busy – that was the 'official' reason. I had mountains of filing to do, he was either doing his pilot training or his boxing training, and that left very little time for me. 'Had a row, have you?' hissed Kelsey into my ear one day in the dinner queue. He seems to notice everything.

Then a week later Wright burst into my office again. 'Come on then, Cecil Beaton, where are these bloody pictures?'

'I need to book the darkroom. It's been busy.' This wasn't true.

'Well just bloody get on with it. Come on, Michael, I want to see them. I've got loads of orders already.'

'What for?'

'Prints, man! Ten by eights! A shilling a shot, nice little earner we've got here. Three dozen I've sold.'

'Who to? Who wants pictures of you in your pants?'

'You'd be surprised. The AOC has ordered ten.'

'Well, that covers the costs of the paper and the chemicals, then.'

'And gives us enough for a good weekend on the piss in Blackpool.'

I booked the darkroom, and left a note for Wright with the date and the time. He was waiting for me. He'd even coerced one of his little fans to mount a guard on the door. 'Don't want some dozy fucker barging in and spoiling everything.' I fitted the blackout round the door and turned on the red light.

'Snug as two bugs in a rug,' said Wright, lighting a fag in the sleazy glow. 'All we need now is a band playing, moon in June and all that crap.'

I'd learned the basics of photographic processing at college, but I was out of practice. I rolled the film out of its canister, on to the spool of the developing tank, praying that I wouldn't fuck it up, that I wouldn't fog or altogether obliterate the negatives. Wright smoked, keeping up a stream of banter, mostly about his chances in the ring, and his chances with various birds. He seemed to have birds all over the place – around the camp, in the village, and swarming over Blackpool, not to mention back home in London.

Time was up, and I unloaded the tank, pulling the wet film off the reel. It was clear, as clear as could be. Too clear. The dazzling triangle of Wright's posing briefs stood out as an aggressive black arrow – the kind that convicts wear. I hardly dared look at the final shot. But it was there.

'Think of it, Mikey, my photo all over the camp. I'm sending it out to the other bloke's camp as well. Get the wind up him, when he sees what he's up against, eh? I reckon that one with my guard up, looking at the camera, that's the best, isn't it? I checked it out in the mirror. I like it. My forehead's all furrowed up like Tony Curtis.'

He danced around in the fiery darkness as I laid out the paper, loaded the negatives into the enlarger.

'And those other ones, you know, in my scanties, we can send them off to the magazines. *Man's World.*'

'I suppose you realise what sort of people buy those magazines?'

'Yeah. I do. You do.'

'You know what I mean.'

'Course I do. I wasn't born yesterday. My nan ran a theatrical boarding house – I grew up with that sort. They're all film producers and playwrights and fashion designers and that, aren't they? When they get a load of me – Bob's your uncle.'

'Yeah, and Fanny's your aunt. You want to watch yourself.'

'Jealous?'

'Fuck off.' This was the first time Wright had made any allusion to the fact that I might like him in that way. He ruffled my hair, carried on smoking.

'Now shut up and stay still, or you'll shake the enlarger.'

'Yes, boss.'

I lay the paper in the enlarger, lowered the masking bars and took a deep breath. 'One for the money …'

'Two for the show …'

'Three to get ready.' I flicked the switch, pressed the button on the stopwatch, and held my breath.

'Go man, go,' whispered Wright.

The seconds passed, and I whipped the paper into the bath of developer.

'Let me see! Let me see!' He was jumping on my back, craning over my shoulder. 'Fuck! Nothing's come out! It didn't come out!'

'Wait.'

Gradually, the first grey smudges appeared, darkening and spreading across the paper as if unsure which way to go, what image to form, then suddenly taking a decision, resolving themselves into the recognisable form of Mervyn Wright, Aircraftman First Class, standing against a black background, naked but for a pair of baggy satin boxing shorts, his fists up, his brow furrowed, eyes glinting through his absurdly long eyelashes.

He whooped. 'Give us it!'

I grabbed his wrist, stopped him from snatching the print,

and transferred it carefully from developer to water, from water to fixer. We gazed at the image, his body against my back, in the dark, red silence.

'Put the light on, please! I wanna see it!'

I sealed up the bags of papers, put them away in drawers, and turned on the light. We were both dazzled for a moment.

'Christ.' Wright stared at his image, lost for words – for once.

The image was spectacular. I knew he was beautiful, from the first moment I saw him in the Freedom from Infection parade. But in two dimensions, in flat monochrome, he was something more. Distanced, framed, a composition of lines and planes, an anatomical study, an object, a statue. Like the pictures in the magazines.

'Well,' I said, when I felt I could speak without squeaking, 'that came out better than I thought.'

'It's fucking fantastic! I want to kiss you!' He grabbed me round the neck in a wrestling hold, and planted a big smacker on top of my head. 'Pyeaagh! You taste of Brylcreem!' He ruffled my hair. 'You're a fucking genius, Aircraftman Medway!'

My knees were shaking. 'Put the light out, and we'll get on with it. How many copies?'

'Bugger the copies, I want to see the other pictures! The dirty ones!'

We returned to the red gloom. Minutes later, another image swam to the surface – Wright in his posing slip, leaning on the cardboard column, a half-smile at the corners of his mouth, arms hanging by his side, crotch pushed forward.

'Oh yeah. Very tasty indeed.'

His genitals were clearly visible through the fabric. 'I think we might have to touch that one up a bit for public consumption.'

'Don't you touch anything! I'm fucking lovely.'

'You're a fucking tosser.'

'I am! I feel like tossing myself off right here and now!'

This was getting far too close to the script of one of my

imagined scenarios. 'If you can control yourself for a few more minutes, then you can go to the bog.'

I loaded another image, from the shadow-boxing routine: balletic, modern, Martha Grahamish. Arms raised to shoulder height, knees slightly bent, the quadriceps huge.

'Right then,' he said, when the print was floating in the fixer. 'Cock shot.'

'You must be joking.'

'Come on! We've got to have that one!'

'What for?'

'Don't you want to see it? I bloody do!'

'I ought to cut if off the end of the film and destroy it.'

'You bloody dare! That's me in my prime, that is.'

'For God's sake, Wright, have you got any idea of how much trouble …'

'Loosen up, for fuck's sake,' he said, but his voice was lowered, mindful of the guard outside the door. 'You can't live your life worrying about what's going to happen if you get caught. Christ, we'd be wrapping ourselves in cotton wool if we did that.'

'And what's the alternative? Do whatever you want, and damn the consequences?'

He lit a fag. 'Yeah. Maybe. That's exactly what you should do.' He sat on the edge of the table, smoking, looking at me. I couldn't meet his eyes, even in the darkness.

'Okay, I'll do your bloody picture, but if you promise me, Wright, promise me that nobody else will see it.'

'Ain'tcha gonna do one for yourself?'

'I …'

'Go on. In memory of a beautiful friendship.'

'But if someone finds it …'

He pulled back his fist, ready with a right jab.

'All right! All right! I'll do it. I must be fucking crazy.'

'We're all crazy. Now come on. I want to see my willy.'

04

This morning I lock myself out of the flat and I'm standing freezing my tits off on the landing cursing Stuart for taking so long to do whatever it is he's doing, and my own stupidity for lending him the keys. I was supposed to be going straight out to work and then he was going to come back, let himself in, have a shower and meet me in town tonight and hand over the keys, but I put out a bag of rubbish and the door blew shut. Normally I would have the keys in my hand whenever I leave the flat but not of course on this occasion, so I'm standing there in my shorts, no shirt, no shoes, no phone and more importantly no keys, and I'm due at my desk in half an hour. I look out from the balcony in the vain hope that I'll see Stuart coming to the rescue but he hasn't said what time he'll be back, or even where he's gone, so I'm in trouble.

I'm cursing and swearing, I can't even call work to tell them I'm going to be late, and then I think that I could actually ask a neighbour for help. The only neighbour I know to talk to is Michael downstairs, and he's always in, and I don't imagine it's the first time he's seen a young man in a pair of shorts, so I tiptoe down the cold concrete steps, holding my hands under my armpits because it really is quite cold despite the advancing spring, and knock on his door.

'Oh I say, is it my birthday?' he says, standing in the doorway with a big smile on his face. I explain that I've locked myself out and ask if I can use his phone, and he says, 'That's the oldest one in the book,' and then goes into the kitchen chuckling to himself while I call the office. I don't tell them all the gory details, because

I can do without the piss-taking, but I do tell them that I've lent the keys to a friend and I don't know when he's coming back.

Michael's standing in the kitchen doorway with two cups of coffee. 'So has he moved in, then?' he asks, handing me one.

'Not officially.'

'He's here a lot though, isn't he?'

'Quite a lot.' I'm slightly disturbed by the fact that he knows so much about my private life, and hope that he doesn't hear too much banging through the floor. The coffee is disgusting instant stuff, but I'm grateful for the warmth.

'I'm very pleased for you. He seems like a nice lad.'

'He is, thanks. Very nice,' I say, wondering if that's actually true. Stuart is many things – sexy, funny, optimistic, energetic, spontaneous – but I'm not sure if 'nice' is one of them.

'You get a ring on his finger as soon as you can.'

'It's a bit early to be thinking about that,' I say.

'That's what I kept saying,' says Michael, 'and look where it got me. It's always a bit early, and then all of a sudden, it's too late.'

'But I've only known him for two months,' I say, hoping that he's not going to start crying.

'Sorry,' he says, 'here I am boring you with my worldly wisdom and you're standing there without a stitch of clothing on.' His eyes travel from my face down to the floor, back up to my groin, up, down and finally up again. I laugh nervously, and cross my legs like a girl.

'I think some of his things might fit you,' he says, disappearing into the bedroom. 'If you don't mind wearing a dead man's clothes.'

This was what my mother always used to say when I came home from college wearing stuff from charity shops. It didn't bother me then, so I can't really change my tune now.

'He was about your build,' Michael says, coming out with a couple of shirts and a pair of trousers, 'perhaps a little bit taller.

Kept his figure right to the end, you know. Very proud of that, he was.'

The clothes are horrible, of course, but I'm in no position to quibble. I put on a light blue shirt – it's clean and ironed, I notice – and a pair of dark brown slacks with a sharp crease up the front, and turn-ups. If Jonathan sees me, I'll never hear the end of the turn-ups.

To my astonishment, the clothes actually do fit quite well. There's a faint odour of mothballs, but that aside, it's not a total disaster.

'I suppose you need shoes and socks.'

'Well …'

He looks at my bare feet. 'Size eight?'

'Nine.'

'Big feet,' he says, rather longingly, and I half expect him to come out with the old line about men with big feet, but instead he goes back to the bedroom and comes out with a pair of well polished brown brogues and some dark grey socks.

'I hope these will do. Now, do you need money?'

'What?'

'To get to work. Unless you keep your bus pass where the sun don't shine.'

'Oh. Right. Well, if you don't mind.'

He gives me twenty quid from a jar on the hall stand. I can see a big roll of notes inside, and I feel rather uneasy looking.

'We used to call it the Emergency Trade Fund,' he says, with a smile.

I pocket the money. There's an old dry-cleaning ticket in the trouser pocket – pink, with a safety pin through it.

'I'm glad I didn't throw all his stuff away now,' says Michael. 'Stephen's been going on at me for weeks. Says it's time to move on.'

'That must be hard,' I say, hoping this isn't going to take long; if I hurry, I can get to work almost on time.

'It is, Robert. You've no idea. So much to do.' He shudders. 'Horrible.'

I say, 'Yes,' but I realise that I have no idea what you have to do when someone dies.

'Still, I'm lucky,' he says. 'We left everything to each other. They won't be chucking me out on the streets just yet.'

'I'm glad to hear it.'

'Are you? That's very kind.'

There's a moment's silence, and I have a horrible feeling that he's about to pounce.

'Now, there's a jacket that goes with those trousers. And do you need a tie?'

'No, really, this is fine.'

'Good lord, you can't go out without a jacket. What is the world coming to?'

The jacket is really the worst part of the ensemble, a loud brown and white check that makes me look like a sales rep. I put it on – it fits perfectly across the shoulders, and tapers at the waist – and he brushes a speck of dust off the shoulder.

'There,' he says, 'you'll do. Can't send you off to work looking like a scruff. What would they say about me?'

'Thank you, Michael. You've been very kind.'

'Not at all, lad, not at all. You've made my day.' He winks, and sees me off the premises, like a proud mother.

People are looking at me from the moment I walk into the office. My 'trendy' wardrobe has become a standing joke, particularly on a Friday, as it is today, when I tend to dress inappropriately, because I can't be bothered to take my going-out clothes in my gym bag. So even though I've taken off the horrible check sports jacket, I'm still looking like I've stepped off the pages of my mother's catalogue. Anna laughs openly when I get to the desk and says, 'Don't tell me, naff is the new chic,' so I just sneer and say 'bite me' or something, because I can't quite bring myself to explain that I'm wearing my neighbour's dead partner's clothes.

To my horror this would have to be the day that New Boy, who is no longer new but has got stuck with the name, decides to come into the office to do something to the fire doors, he's the health and safety officer and his job seems to be to bore us to death with memos about how not to electrocute ourselves or have fatal accidents with staplers. He smiles and comes straight over to my desk, ignoring the fact that Anna is going apoplectic with mirth behind her screen, and says, 'You look very smart today. What's the special occasion?' I can't think of an answer at first, because if this is his idea of 'smart' then he is even more of a dead loss than I thought when I discovered that he really does buy his suits at Next.

'Oh,' I say, trying to sound dismissive but not completely hostile, 'nothing, I just fancied a change.'

'Well, it suits you.'

'Thanks.'

Anna looks as if she might have an aneurysm.

'Did you want anything?'

'No, no. Just doing my … Is she okay?'

'She's fine. She's under a lot of stress at the moment,' I say. 'Women's problems.' Anna has to get up from her desk and go to the toilet quite quickly.

'Oh well,' says New Boy. 'I'd better …'

'Okay.' My phone rings; it's Anna. I pick up, and New Boy walks off.

When he's out of earshot, I just say 'fuck off' to Anna and put the phone down. It suddenly occurs to me that he might have heard me, and thought I was talking to him, and I feel terrible, but not that terrible, and then Anna comes back into the office and it looks as if she's been crying, but I know it's only with laughter.

'You look smart,' she says, in a flat, nasal, froggy sort of voice, but I don't reply because my phone rings again and it's Stuart.

'Change of plan,' he says, 'I'm not going back to yours, I'll pick you up at the gym tonight at seven.'

Shit, I realise that I haven't got my gym kit, it's in my bag that's locked in the flat, and I need to go home at lunchtime and get it – and change my clothes.

'Where are you?' I say. 'I need my keys. I locked myself …'

'Sorry, Rob, can't help you, I'm out and about all day.'

Stuart does some work for a promotions company and keeps very irregular hours, but under the circumstances I think he could arrange to drop the keys off, so I sound slightly annoyed when I say, 'Well you'll have to.'

'Sorry, lover, got to go,' he says, and hangs up on me.

Nobody else has keys to my flat, so I'm stuffed.

I phone Jonathan, because he's borrowed so many of my clothes that half my wardrobe must be at his place. We haven't spoken for nearly two weeks but he picks up the conversation as if nothing had happened.

'Did you read about it in the paper?'

'What?' I ask, wondering whether, as frequently happens, some major catastrophe has failed to register on my radar. I'm often the last to know about earthquakes, plane crashes or tsunamis.

'He's come out.'

I say 'Who?' although I know perfectly well who 'he' is, Jonathan's talked about nothing and nobody else for months.

'Lukas of course. He's publishing an autobiography …'

'He's even younger than we are!'

'… and apparently it's all in there, about how he was abused by an uncle on holiday, and had a mental breakdown when he was fifteen, and how he's not been able to hold a relationship together because of the pain.'

'Jonathan …'

'It's in the *Mail* today, quite a long extract, and some really yummy photos.'

'I need to …'

'I'm going to get him to give me a copy and sign it next time I see him.'

'Next time?'

'Yeah, he's always round Hadley's.'

'Look, are you at home?'

'Why?'

'I need to come round at lunchtime and get some of my clothes back.'

'Oh. No. I'm not.'

'You're not, or you won't be?'

'Whatever. I saw your Stuart down at Straight the other night.' Straight is a club I've never been to, and I didn't know Stuart went either. It's at the sleazier end of the spectrum.

'Oh yeah, he told me he went,' I lie, 'and he said it was really funny.'

'Hmm,' says Jonathan, who always likes to be the bearer of bad news, 'well it didn't look like he was laughing from where I was standing.'

'Can I just come round and …'

'Oh for God's sake, Rob, I'm busy. If you need clothes, do what everyone else does. Go out and buy them.'

He hangs up.

Later on I get an email from New Boy asking me what I'm doing for lunch. I tell him that I'm going out to a client meeting. I must be more careful about what I wear to work in future. In two years of dressing sexy and stylish, I have never once been asked on a date, and now I turn up looking like an 80s geography teacher I'm beating them off with a shitty stick. I suppose that answers one question which has been exercising Anna and me for the last few weeks, i.e. 'Is New Boy gay or straight?', because I don't notice him asking her for lunch dates. I am simultaneously elated (at being asked at all) and embarrassed (because it's him), so I don't start bragging to Anna, but just delete the email. Then I have to borrow money from her in order to go shopping.

I have to sneak out of the office at lunchtime to avoid being seen by New Boy. Not that I care about turning him down, as he is so far from being my type that he might as well be a woman, but because I don't like lying. Or, to be more accurate, I don't like being caught out. I must look very furtive as I sidle along back streets towards Covent Garden. Store security guards watch me with more interest than usual. I obviously look guilty.

Anyway, this is a great excuse to buy new clothes, and within half an hour I've put together an outfit that won't completely shame me in front of Stuart and his friends. Obviously it's based around the shoes, which I can't afford to buy new, but fortunately brown brogues are timeless and this pair has the advantage of looking quite well worn. The new pairs that I'm seeing in the shops come ready scuffed and creased, which never looks convincing, like those ready-ripped jeans that Jonathan bought last year and has never worn. I've got a nice tailored shirt from Zara, and a pair of pleat-fronted trousers from H&M, and I'm congratulating myself on the fact that the whole outfit has cost less than £100 when I realise that I've basically bought the exact same clothes that I borrowed from Michael, the only real difference being the turn-ups on the trousers. I console myself with the fact that, at least, I won't have Stuart glaring at the bottom of my legs all night, and then I see a really attractive, well-dressed guy walking towards me WEARING TROUSERS WITH TURN-UPS, and my heart sinks, I've just spent nearly a hundred quid to look unfashionable.

To complete my misery I bump straight into New Boy on my way into the office, and he looks at my H&M and Zara bags and says, 'Good meeting?' and walks off with a scowl on his face.

Oh well, at least he won't be troubling me with unwanted attentions any more, that's something. His name is Simon, I noticed when I was staring at my shoes trying to think of something to say and saw it on the ID card he wears clipped to his belt.

Jonathan emailed me in the afternoon to say that I was invited to a private view at a gallery in Hoxton at six p.m., and when I phoned him to ask since when he was interested in contemporary art, he said it was Hadley's gallery, and that he's promoting new artists, and that Jonathan is hoping to get a one-man show in there later in the year, and that I should come with him and check out the space.

I email Stuart to tell him that I too have had a change of plan, not to meet me at the gym but to pick me up at Hadley's gallery. He doesn't reply so obviously he has his phone switched off.

The outfit I've bought is suitable for all occasions and so I won't feel out of place at a gallery show, or at dinner with Stuart, or at whatever club we're going to tonight, where I will take the shirt off anyway and then nobody will be looking at my trousers, turn-ups or no turn-ups.

Hadley's gallery is almost exactly the same as his flat, a huge empty space in a disused warehouse in east London, white walls, wood floor, pillars, girders, the usual gang of black-shirted gypsies handing out champagne, and of course no food. The 'art' that we've come to see is a series of huge blow-ups of photographs of shoes, empty takeaway wrappers, plastic forks and pigeons, and in the middle of them all there's an enormous out-of-focus photo of an erect cock that looks like it was taken with a mobile phone and then massively enlarged.

The artist's name is Nicolae Vladimirescu, and judging by the quality of the work he has a great relationship with someone at KwikPrint. There's a huddle of people in the centre of the room, from the middle of which I can see a shock of highly-processed black hair sticking up, and when I jump up in the air to get a better look I am not surprised to see that it is Hadley's friend Nico.

'Oh didn't I tell you?' says Jonathan, looking slightly embarrassed. 'Yes, he's a really famous artist in his own country, and Hadley's launching him over here.'

'I see.'

'Don't say "I see" in that tone of voice, I think he's amazing, and he's really brave.'

'Brave?' I say, 'well he's certainly got a lot of nerve showing this pile of ...' and then I feel a hand squeezing my shoulder, and of course it's Hadley.

'Robbie! Glad you could make it!' he says, looking even more leathery than usual. His eyes are tiny and twinkling, but the flesh around them looks dead. There's a weird flush on his neck, against which the hair follicles stand out as white dots. He does not look healthy, despite the huge muscles.

'Thanks for having me,' I say, and immediately regret it.

'I haven't ... yet ...' he says, very close to my ear, and letting his hand slide down to the small of my back. He's almost feeling my arse, and I'm beginning to wonder if this is why I've been asked to come.

'I was just telling Jonathan how much I like the photos,' I say, stepping away.

'Aren't they great?' says Hadley. 'They're such an incredible expression of the plight of asylum seekers.'

'Are they? Right. Yes, I see that.'

'All the garbage of Western life, blown up to ridiculous proportions, really thrust in our faces.'

'And the cock?'

'It's ... the ... the commodification of sex, as the only form of economic power that people in Nico's position have.'

'Ah,' I say. 'That's just what Jonathan was saying, isn't it?'

Jonathan looks daggers at me, but daren't say anything because Hadley is stroking my arm again.

'He's a very talented young man,' murmurs Hadley. 'I like talent.'

'Me too,' I say, far too brightly, then I guzzle the rest of my champagne. Hadley is almost nuzzling my neck, and if I play my cards right I could have a one-man show by the end of the evening.

We're interrupted by the artist in person.

'Hey, Hadley,' he says, 'I need you to talk to this person.'

There's an old, very drunk man wobbling around at Nico's side. 'He's from a newspaper or something.'

'Great,' says Hadley, jumping away from me as if he's just been stung. 'Hi. Great to see you here.' And he's off. Nico, or Nicolae Vladimirescu, remains, looking as if someone has just farted under his nose. He's wearing some of the most repulsive clothes I've ever seen, all appliqued slogans and frayed seams, with his waistband even further down than normal.

'Hi Nico,' says Jonathan, 'great show.'

'Yes,' says Nico. 'The creative power of the universe flows through me.' He makes a gesture with his hands – very large, hairy-backed hands that would be more at home wrapped round a pickaxe.

'How did you make them?'

'It's a very long complicated process,' he says, 'based on the theories of Ferdinand de Saussure. I write thesis on him at university.'

'Wow,' says Jonathan. 'I did a thesis too. Mine was about …'

'The art world at home … pffff.'

'Oh yes,' says Jonathan, 'it's so hard to get shown …'

'So I come to England and here I find wealthy collectors.'

'Fascinating choice of subject matter,' I say. 'The pigeon, for instance.'

Nico shrugs. 'I hate fucking pigeons,' he says, and walks off, as if mortally offended.

'He's very moody,' says Jonathan, looking starry-eyed. 'The other day he and Hadley had the most dreadful row.'

'Are they … you know. Lovers?'

'God, you're so shallow,' says Jonathan. 'Hadley is promoting Nico's work …'

'Because I got the distinct impression that Nico was an escort.'

'Oh you just see the worst in everything.'

'Not least because I've seen his photograph in the back of a magazine, with a black bar over his eyes and the words "nine inches, thick".'

'How do you know it's him?'

'Well, it says he's thick …'

Jonathan storms off to the loo to take drugs, so I pace around the walls trying to look interested in the 'work'.

'Brilliant comment on the ubiquity of the photographic eye,' I hear someone say. 'Subverting accepted notions of photography as an art form by using the cheapest mobile phone camera and re-contextualising it in the gallery space.' From this I assume that Nico downloaded a few random snaps from his SIM card and got them enlarged at Hadley's expense.

Stuart comes bounding across the room, places two hands on my shoulders and practically leapfrogs over me. He's so full of energy he makes me feel exhausted already.

'Hello,' he says, then grabs my tits. 'You didn't go to the gym. You're all flat and saggy.'

'Hello,' I say. 'Where have you been all day?'

'Studio. My God, these pictures are fucking awful.'

'Can I have my keys?'

'Sure,' he says, but he's got nothing in his pockets and no bag, so God knows where the keys are. 'What the fuck are you wearing?'

'You like it?'

'Come on, there are people I want you to meet.'

He drags me across the room, where there are four guys who look, basically, just like Stuart. They're all about thirty, they're all wearing Abercrombie and Fitch and they all have the same body. Four pairs of eyes look down at my shoes, then up to my face, down to my crotch, up, down and up again, the exact same look that Michael gave me this morning. The gay look.

'Everyone, this is Rob, who I was telling you about.'

'Aah, the famous Rob,' says one of them, shaking my hand. They have not been introduced at all. 'So, how's the world of high finance?'

I look to Stuart for some kind of clue, but he's just grinning and working his jaw muscles, which gives his face a diamond shape.

'I say,' says another, 'tell me that Hadley hasn't asked you for any money.'

'No.'

'Because he's going around trying to sting everyone for a couple of hundred quid to invest in this pile of shit.'

'Why?'

'So they can get a proper gallery show, he says.'

'Whatever you do,' says Stuart, 'never, never give Hadley money. Unless it's for drugs.'

As we're leaving I see Jonathan handing his brand new credit card over to Hadley, who won't look quite so pleased when he realises that none of Jonathan's credit cards are worth the plastic they're printed on.

We were supposed to be going for dinner but Stuart says he has VIP passes to Straight, and that we should get there early if we want to get 'good seats', which I don't really understand. I point out that a) I'm hungry and b) I think the idea of being a VIP in a sex club is like being on the guest list at the clap clinic, but he just laughs and ruffles my hair, which he knows I hate. In the cab he gives me a line of coke, which he says will deaden my appetite, but by the time we get south of the river I'm not convinced that it was coke after all, because I am feeling very strange indeed. For one thing, I'm snogging Stuart in full view of the taxi driver, and for another thing I've got my hand down his trousers trying to get hold of his cock.

'Cool it,' he says, laughing, as he hands the driver a twenty-pound note, then, 'Keep the change,' which is funny as the fair was exactly £20. In fact it seems so funny that I'm doubled up with laughter on the pavement, tears running down my face. Stuart drags me to the door where he does a complicated hand-shake with the door whore and we're in.

The place is already busy, and the air is thick with sex, and I'm so desperate to get off that I push Stuart up against the wall and start kissing him again, grabbing his hands and putting them on my bum. He takes my chin between thumb and forefinger and looks at me, nods and smiles and says, 'You'll do,' then we go into the main room.

Straight is in a club that's built into the railways arches, so you get an instant sense of claustrophobia, which adds greatly to the air of illegality that we all seem to crave. The main room is long and dark with a stage set up at one end in the shape of a boxing ring, complete with ropes. Stuart is greeting people at every step, kissing and hugging and whispering, he seems to know every single person in the club, and all I can think is that if this lot are straight then I don't hold out much hope for the continuation of the human race.

Time seems to have collapsed because before I know it the lights are glaring down on the boxing ring, all the seats around us are taken, there's a sound of roaring in the air and I have a very sore mouth, as if someone's been sandpapering it. Stuart too is looking a bit chafed around the lower face, and I realise that we've been kissing violently for a very long time, and we have our hands down each other's trousers, but I'm relieved to say that I haven't come, in fact I feel completely anaesthetised from the waist downwards.

A couple of young men are skipping around the ring in boots and satin dressing gowns, but there the resemblance to boxers ends, because they both have sculpted eyebrows and careful hair. The referee is a drag queen who seems to be in every club in London every night of the week, and she's doing some spiel about 'hitting below the belt' and 'getting licked in the ring' which the contenders don't seem to understand. Then someone rings a bell, the drag queen climbs out of the ring and gives us all a good view of her gusset, and the dressing gowns come off and, surprise, surprise, they're naked underneath. There's a loud cheer and they start dabbing at each other with their boxing gloves, like kittens. The drag queen is running around squirting baby oil into the ring, and soon the boys have slipped over and are wrestling on the floor and having sex.

This doesn't interest me greatly, although Stuart seems quite keen, so I go for a walk to clear my head. Whatever drug he gave me in the cab is wearing off, and I feel restless and anxious. In the adjacent arch, the lights are out and the music is at ear-splitting volume. I step inside, and there are hands all over me, drawing me in, and I feel a couple of penises brushing against my hands.

I step out smartly and go to the toilet, but I can't pee because I am still erect, although I really don't feel at all horny now. There's a guy at the urinal next to me, wanking away furiously, glaring at me with a horrible hunger in his eyes, and I recognise Sauna Slut from the gym, but he doesn't recognise me because he has that glassy, unseeing look that you get in a dying rabbit.

I put everything away, wash my hands and go back to the boxing match.

Stuart, of course, is nowhere to be seen, and so I spend the next two hours wandering from room to room trying to find him, getting more and more angry and upset, because I'm convinced that he's in the orgy room.

I spend some time on the dance floor with my shirt off, which is good, because even though I haven't been to the gym tonight, my abs are still impressive, and I'm so hungry and dehydrated that everything is looking really cut. Eventually I get lifted up on to a podium so I dance around there for half an hour or so, looking down at my shoes and laughing, because when Michael lent me his dead partner's clothes first thing this morning, he probably didn't imagine that the shoes would be doing this at two a.m., or whatever the time is.

Then I see Stuart watching me from across the room, his arms folded and a very ironic smirk on his face, so I jump down and put my shirt back on and run over.

'Having fun?' he says.

'Where the hell have you been?'

'I was at the bar, talking to Joe.' Joe is the promoter of Straight and half a dozen other sex-and-drugs nights around town. 'Time we were off.'

I've been ready to leave for hours, but I say, 'Oh, and I'm having such a good time.'

'Okay, so stay,' says Stuart. 'I'll call you tomorrow.'

'Wait! I'm coming.'

'No, really, it's okay.'

This goes on for quite a while, and then I remind him that he's got my keys, and for that reason alone (it seems to me) he agrees to come home with me. I want to get the night bus, which goes directly to the end of my street, but Stuart insists on a taxi because, he says, 'I'm not really a bus person.'

When we get home, he cuts out another two lines of whatever it is, and offers me one. I'm not sure, so he takes his and he's immediately all over me. I'm tired, and not really in the mood for sex, I was hoping we might actually talk and/or sleep, but no, he's ripping my new shirt off, the buttons are popping all over the floor, so I think, 'If you can't beat 'em, join 'em', and do the line while he's sticking his tongue up my arse.

The next thing I remember we're lying in bed surrounded by travel books and we seem to have decided that we're going on holiday, and when I ask Stuart to remind me what, if anything, we're doing, he says, 'Well, honey, you just paid for it on your credit card so it's a bit late to change your mind now.' So it seems that we're going to Sitges for a week, and it's a really bad time for me to take time off work, and I get so stressed about the whole thing that in the end Stuart gives me a Valium, and when I wake up around Saturday lunchtime he's gone.

Four

There is a rhythm to my friendship with Mervyn Wright. When he wants me for something, he seeks me out, he spends time with me and makes much of me, giving me packets of fags and illicit booze that he smuggles in from God knows where. He sits with me in the NAAFI, he visits me in the office, in fact he flaunts our friendship before the whole camp, even going so far as to walk about with an arm around my shoulder. He loves the fuss this causes, the cracks, the kisses blown, the whistles, the mutterings from Sergeant Kelsey, who has taken to calling us 'the Wolfenden Boys'. Wright parries it all with quick repartee, followed through with an obscenity and, in extreme cases, physical violence. Nobody messes with Airman Mervyn Wright. His prowess in the boxing ring makes him – us – invulnerable. Excitement is mounting around the camp about the regional tournament next week. The AOC has paid for posters, using my photo, which are plastered over every noticeboard. The ten by eights I churn out in the darkroom have sold better than even Wright dared hope, and adorn the lockers of about half the camp, alongside Sabrina and Brigitte Bardot.

As for those other photographs, they stay in a brown envelope inside a folder of old medical records at the bottom of a box file at the back of a drawer of a filing cabinet in the medical records office where no one will ever find them. I don't need to look at them. They're burned on my mind's eye forever, like the shadows on the streets of Hiroshima. Wright keeps his in his wallet.

Wright's interest peaks when we take photographs (we've done two sessions now) and in the darkroom, when we both seem to be caught up in a kind of fever, a whirlwind, I don't know what, when something always seems about to happen and never does. I know what it is – I've spent enough time thinking about it – and he, surely, knows too, at least if the stretching of his pants and the constant flashing and fiddling with his cock is anything to go by. I often think that he's waiting for me to make the first move – perhaps so that he can knock me back. To make some declaration, so that he can tell me not to be so fucking stupid. But I don't. I fear that if I bring this thing into the light, it will instantly die. I prefer the uncertainty of expectation to the finality of rejection. And so we press ourselves together in the darkroom, or he exposes himself in the studio, but nothing happens. The words freeze on my tongue, and my hands, which want to reach out and touch, are paralysed.

After each of these near misses, Wright cools off dramatically. Suddenly, he's busy with his mates, with his training. He's off to Blackpool at weekends, he's got a forty-eight or a seventy-two, he's visiting some bird somewhere. He talks a lot about birds at these times, and I have no doubt that he does a lot more than talk. We smile and wave when we see each other, we might even pass the time of day if we happen to be standing next to each other in the lunch queue, and perhaps no one notices the drop in temperature. But I do. And of course Kelsey does. When Wright is far from me, Kelsey starts to circle, looking for an opportunity to catch me out, to give me extra fatigues, to get me on a charge if he possibly could. I don't give him the opportunity. I am a model conscript. My boots are almost as shiny as his, my bed and locker textbook tidy. There's nothing for him to criticise. God knows what would happen if he found this diary – but it remains well hidden, unseen, unread. I make very sure of that. The case is locked at all times, the diary well concealed in the lining, along with those dog-eared copies of *Health and Strength* and *Man's World* and *Male Classics*. As for them, I might as well throw them away. I am so familiar with the images that I don't need to see them again, I have only to close my eyes. I dream sometimes about sending off for the 'private photos sets' advertised in the back pages – '20 dynamic poses! Natural, uninhibited!' – but that would be suicidal folly. Our post is monitored. It's one thing to display a picture of Mervyn Wright, 'the Reville Rebel' as he is now billed – in a pair of satin shorts. It's quite another to get pictures of unknown young men in posing pouches and less from PO Box addresses in London. That would confirm what many, I'm sure, suspect – that I am queer.

Am I queer? Stephen certainly thinks I am, and tells me so whenever I let him. I haven't yet denied it, so I suppose he is right. But am I like him? I like men, and I don't seem to be interested in women. I feel something towards Wright that is not just lust. I want to 'be with him', whatever that means. I daren't think it through to its conclusion. And what about Wright? Does he want to 'be with me'? And if he does, is he queer too? And what does that mean for all of us? A lifetime of hanging around the West End in brown shoes? Dodging plainclothes policemen in public toilets? Getting nabbed like Montagu and Wildeblood and doing eighteen months? Or living in secret, getting married, giving Mum the grandchildren she wants, hiding muscle mags at the back of my desk for the rest of my life?

There's always suicide, I suppose. That seems to be a popular course of action, at least in books and films that touch on the subject. Stephen talks about it often enough. He steers clear of me when Wright is around, but in my solitary spells he seeks me out. He still looks ill. He's badly underweight – he's lost about two stone since we arrived – his arms and legs are so thin they look as if they could snap. He's frequently on sick parade, in and out of the wards with one chest infection after another. Nobody visits him, and I suppose he likes it that way.

He cornered me in the library the other day. We call it 'the library' but in fact it's just a small, unused room above the NAAFI with a couple of bookcases containing medical texts and detective stories. There's a record player and a few dusty old records – a partial recording of *Madam Butterfly*, a few 78s of sentimental Irish tenors. Downstairs, they listen to Elvis Presley on the jukebox, and read the *Dandy* and the *Beano*. You can be pretty sure of being alone in the library. It's warm, and there's a good view across the fields to the estuary. I sit up here and sketch, or read, or just smoke and think.

'Thought I might find you here.' Stephen stuck his beak-like nose around the door. 'What's the matter? Lovers' tiff?'

'Hello Stephen. How are you?'

'Nothing a bullet wouldn't cure, thanks.'

'Oh come on. It's not that bad.'

'Easy for you to say, dear.' He came in, draped himself over an armchair, a Beardsley drawing in air-force blue. 'You've got friends.' He said the word with undue emphasis, which I ignored.

'If you just knuckle down and get on with it …'

'Oh yes. Jolly hockey sticks and all that. Play the game. I was never any good at all that, I'm afraid. Terrible at sports. Too sensitive, that's what they used to say at school. Every year on my report: "Stephen is sensitive."'

'I was "artistic".'

'Hmm …' He narrowed his eyes and looked at me, wondering, I suppose, if I had just told him something. I wondered too.

Silence fell for a while, broken only by distant shouts from the playing fields, and the occasional caw of a rook.

'It would be ever so easy to get out, you know.'

'Would it?'

'Yes. Friend of mine turned up on parade one day wearing eye make-up, lipstick and scent. Whisked off to the CO's office faster than you could say Gina Lollobrigida. They asked him what he thought he was doing and he said, "You ain't seen nothing yet", dropped his trousers and he was wearing women's knickers. He was out before sunset.'

'Yes – carted off to the loony bin, then a dishonourable discharge. Not a very good start in life, is it?'

'Bugger that. Who cares? We'd be out of here. That's all that matters.'

'And what are you going to do on civvy street, with that on your records? What kind of a job are you going to get?'

'I don't care about bloody jobs, dear. I can always get a job. Turn my hand to all sorts, I can.' He managed to make this sound very wicked.

'Why not just make the best of it, keep your head down, you'll be out in eighteen months.'

'Eighteen months?' He practically shrieked. 'I'll be old by then. Look at me! Crow's feet and saggy skin and I'm not even twenty yet. It's so unfair. I should be in London, with my friends, having fun.'

'Well you're not. You're on a godforsaken marsh somewhere in the north-west of England, and you might as well accept it.'

We both stared out of the window, watching a line of trucks making steady progress towards the camp gates. A new intake, ready to be shorn, hosed down and kitted out, just like us.

'I told them I was queer, you know. At the medical.'

The word landed with a plop, and the ripples spread out for a while.

'That was either very brave, or very foolish.'

'I thought it would automatically get me off. But they just laughed at me. I told them I had terrible eyesight, so they tested it and said that I'd never be a fighter pilot but I was fit for ground duties. Then I told them I had asthma, and flat feet, and that I wet the bed, but they said that National Service would make a man of me. I even thought of joining the Communist Party.' He ran his long fingers through his hair. 'But that was going a bit far, even for me.'

'And so here you are. And here you'll stay.'

'Not if I can help it. I'm getting out before they kill me.'

'Stephen, the only person who's trying to kill you is yourself.'

'Oh, you don't know what it's like.' His voice turned bitter. 'You can pretend to be one of them, can't you? You can hang around with your big buddy Wright and they leave you alone. They all know you're queer, of course, but you play the game and so they tolerate you. For all I know, you might even be having a bit of fun. I mean, they're randy enough to fuck anything, aren't they? As long as it doesn't rub off. But they're scared of me. They hate me, Michael.'

'Stephen, don't work yourself up.'

'Do you know what it's like to be completely and utterly alone? To know that everyone, every single person, hates you and wants you dead?'

'That's not true.'

'Oh, I suppose you're going to say that you don't hate me, is that it? That you'd like to be my friend if only I wasn't such a dead bloody giveaway. You're not denying it, I notice. Well I'm sorry, but I just can't seem to fake it like you can. I can't talk like you, and I can't walk like you, and if I try to act butch I just look like a lesbian. It's not fair.'

He was crying now. I suppose I should have comforted him, but someone might have walked in.

'Oh God,' he said, blowing his nose. 'Red eyes and a red nose to add to all my other problems.' He looked at himself in the windowpane, reflected against the darkening sky. 'I used to be known for my complexion, you know. Like the lady in the Camay advert. Now look at me.'

He took a compact out of his tunic pocket, and dabbed a little powder on his face.

'Stephen! For Christ's sake!'

'I've shocked you.' He snapped the compact shut, put it away. 'Don't worry. Your little secret's safe with me. You keep hiding, you'll be fine. You can hide for the rest of your life.'

'And I suppose your way is better, is it? Lonely, unhappy, with no future to look forward to?'

'*Au contraire*, my dear, I look forward to the future very much indeed.' He smoothed down his eyebrows, adjusted his dress. 'Times are changing, in case you don't read the papers. The world is turning. Our world. They can't keep us down forever. One day we'll be able to live free and open.'

'You're being ridiculous,' I said, but my heart was hammering in my chest, making my voice tremble, betraying me.

'And when that day comes I'm going to be ready for it. Are you?'

He ran down the stairs with a lighter tread.

'Hey, hey, hey, look at this!'

Wright burst into my office this morning with a movie magazine in his hand.

'I don't want to look at Diana Dors's tits at this time of day, thank you very much.'

'No, dummkopf. Look, here.'

He slammed the magazine down on top of my ledgers. There was a quarter-page ad circled in red pen.

ACTOR WANTED

Athletic young actor sought, age 20 to 25, over 5'8", chest normal 45", handsome and capable of performing acrobatic and dangerous feats, to play Hercules in a film to be shot later this year. The applicant must be able to speak perfect English. Send letter and photograph.

'It's me, isn't it? Mervyn Wright *is* Hercules!'

'I thought Steve Reeves was Hercules.'

'Yeah, but I'll be the British one. Come on, we've got to send them those pictures.'

'Are you serious?'

'Course I am.'

'You can't just bugger off and become a film star.'

'Why not?'

'In case it had escaped your attention, you've got another year and a half of National Service to do.'

'I'll get out of it.'

This was starting to sound familiar. In fact, the whole of Reville buzzes with the latest ideas about how to get out. Stephen's, on the whole, is the most practical.

'Don't talk daft.'

'I mean it, Mike. I'll do anything. Think of it. The cars, the birds, the lovely, lovely money.'

'It's probably some little studio in Soho turning out blue movies.'

'Bollocks. You're jealous.'

'Oh yeah? Of what?'

'You don't want me to leave here and become a star.'

'Believe me, Wright, nothing would give me greater pleasure.'

'Come on, Michael, we've got to do it! You've got to write the letter for me! Help me choose the picture. Or we can do some new ones. You'd like that, wouldn't you? Please, mate. I can't let some other bastard steal this from me.'

The thought of doing more photos got me interested despite my decision to play it cool, and Wright knew it.

'I'll get some new gear. And I've been thinking up some new poses.' He leaned over the desk, his mouth close to my ear. 'Sexy ones. We should send 'em off to the muscle mags. Make a bit of cash.'

I closed my eyes so that I couldn't see his face. But I could still smell him, the soap, the Brylcreem, the tobacco. The flesh.

'Big day for you tomorrow,' I said, suddenly needing to get up and go to the filing cabinet.

'Yeah.' He danced around on his toes, jabbing his fists in the air. 'That other cunt won't know what hit him.'

'You're confident.'

'Course I am! He can't touch me. So what do you say, Mikey?

Write me the letter, will you? You're better at that sort of thing than I am.'

'I'll type it for you if you like.'

'Good lad.'

He hung around, shadow-boxing.

'Wright, I've got to get on. The CMO will have my guts for garters if I don't get this done today.'

He wasn't listening.

'When's your next forty-eight?'

'What?'

'Weekend leave. When is it?'

'I don't know. I don't really …'

'Well find out, you silly wanker. Christ. Not knowing when your next forty-eight is.'

'What's the big emergency?'

'We're going to Blackpool.'

'Who are?' I had visions of some ghastly group outing, a pub crawl followed by a spot of whoring.

'We are, bollockhead. You and me. Wright and Wrong.'

'What for?'

He paused for a second. 'To celebrate.'

'What, exactly?'

'I don't know, Mike. My victory. Getting the part of Hercules. Surviving another day in this shit hole. There's always something to celebrate, if you put your mind to it.'

And of course, he did win. The whole camp converged on the sports hall, the largest covered space at Reville, converted for the occasion into a boxing ring with a hundred seats for officers and guests, and room for another four or five hundred standing. Those who couldn't get in clustered around the doors and windows. Wright's image was plastered all over the walls. The 'other cunt' had lost before he even stepped in the ring. He lasted two rounds before Wright KO'd him. Just long enough for them both to work up a good sweat. Wright was carried out of the hall on his comrades' shoulders, and Reville gave itself over to fiesta.

I watched it all with butterflies in my stomach and a hard-on, which kept getting pressed against the arse of the airman in front of me, one of the new flight, a lad called Miller who's caught my eye once or twice and always seems to have a ready smile. He tried to follow me out of the hall, but I gave him the dodge and walked off to the perimeter for a smoke, as far from the celebrations as I could get.

I smelled Stephen before I saw him. He must have doused himself in enough perfume to sweeten all the working girls of Blackpool, with enough left over to dab behind the ears of Lytham St Anne's. It was dark out there, by the fence, between the lights, but the quickly dampening night air carried the scent far and fast.

'Hello Johnny,' came a voice, low and insinuating and heavily accented. 'Looking for love?'

A match struck in the darkness, illuminating Stephen's face. In the yellow flare I could see that he was wearing make-up. His eyes were darkened, his cheeks and lips were rouged, his hair seemed to be glittering.

'Stephen! Are you drunk?'

'Maybe a little, darling. Are you going to take advantage of me?'

'Drop the Dietrich impression.'

'Cigarette?'

'I'll have one of my own, thanks.'

'Let's walk,' said Stephen, putting an arm through mine. I shook him off.

'For Christ's sake!'

'What's the matter?'

'Someone will see us.'

'I know a place …'

'This has gone far enough, Stephen.'

'Oh come on.' He squeezed my arm, then broke off, danced a few steps ahead. 'I'm irrrrrre-SIST-ible!'

'Keep your voice down! The guard …'

'Bugger the guard, dear. Although you'd probably quite like that, wouldn't you?'

'Stephen, you're being ridiculous.'

'I'm ridiculous, you're ridiculous, we're both ridiculous. Rrrrrri-DIC-ulous!' He pranced and posed by the chainlink fence. 'Ridiculous for being here, ridiculous in these awful drab uniforms, mincing around on the parade ground with all the naffs, trying to fit in and pass for normal when we should be OUT THERE IN THE WORLD! Being OURSELVES!' He was shouting now.

'Please, Stephen. Someone will hear you.'

'That's the general idea. I don't want to stay here ONE MINUTE LONGER!'

'And how exactly do you plan to manage that?'

'I'll show you.' We were exactly midway between two of the perimeter lights. Stephen stopped abruptly and kissed me full on the mouth. His lips were soft, and tasted sweetly chemical. I felt winded.

'There. That wasn't so bad, was it?'

'I …'

'When did you last kiss a man?'

'I never …'

'Come on.' He grabbed my arm and we ran. I felt disorientated. I didn't see the rusty old ambulance parked out by the fence until I skinned my shin on the fender.

'Here?'

'Yes. Isn't it marvellous? Think of all the trade you could drag out here.'

'Trade …'

Stephen opened the back door of the ambulance. It made a dry, grinding sound.

'As good as a suite at the Savoy.' He sat on the edge, then reclined in a movie-star pose. 'There's room for two, you know.'

'I can't.'

'You bloody well can.' His voice was no longer languorous. He pulled me down on top of him, on to his open lips. I sank into the kiss with a queasy feeling of freefall. This was not what I had imagined, in my bed after lights-out. Stephen, of all people, was not the one. But the softness of his mouth and the eagerness of his caresses were like a drug. I came to life suddenly, as if a switch had been flicked. I'd always been dead, cold and paralysed with Wright – but now I was on fire. I ground into him, and he returned each thrust. His hands worked down my back, pulling me in.

There was a crash and a crunch and the flash of a light. Stephen broke the kiss and screamed loudly.

'Now,' he whispered. 'Run. If you want to.'

There was a blanket beside him. I threw it over my head like a bridal veil, and blundered into the darkness, until the shouting and the screaming were barely audible.

When I got back to the barracks I was sick. I cleaned my teeth till my gums bled, trying to wash away the taste of vomit and Stephen's lipstick. Stephen would be in the guardhouse by now. How would he behave under interrogation? Would they hurt him? Would he reveal the name of his … accomplice? Would there be a knock at the door in the middle of the night?

But the men snored, the pipes clicked and gurgled, somewhere an owl hooted, the camp slept.

In the morning I woke with a bang, the sheets wet with sweat, my mouth dry as an ashtray. We all pissed and washed and shaved as normal. Nobody said a word, and we went about our work.

Kelsey cut off my path on the way to the SSQ.

'Your little friend was up to no good last night, Medway.'

'Who's that then, sir?'

'Princess Margaret. Who do you fucking well think?'

'I don't know what you're talking about.'

'And what we all want to know, Medway, is who was the man with the blanket over his head?'

'Is there anything you need from the dispensary this morning, sir?' I asked, opening up the office with shaking hand.

'I reckon it was you, Medway.'

'I need to open the office, sir.'

'It was you, wasn't it?' whispered Kelsey, his neck roll quivering. 'You fucking queers.'

Wright lurched round the corner, his eyes red and puffy, his hair uncombed, obviously hung over, possibly still pissed.

'Michael!' He right wheeled towards us. 'Fuckin' 'ell, Medway, that was a heavy night, wasn't it? Morning, sarge. You look chipper.'

'I wasn't boozing, was I?'

'We were, weren't we, Airman Medway? We were on a right bender.'

'Well someone was,' said Kelsey, who could sense his prey escaping his jaws.

'So I hear,' said Wright. 'Good for little Stephen, eh? At least someone's getting laid in this godforsaken place.'

Kelsey looked as if he was about to burst.

'Had your breakfast yet, Mike?'

'I couldn't eat a thing.'

'Course you can. Come on, let's go to the NAAFI and treat ourselves to a nice big fat sausage.'

Kelsey stalked off, looking for others to accuse.

'Thanks, Wright.'

'So where the fuck were you last night?'

'I went to bed.'

'You what? You should have been there to help me celebrate.'

'You were with your friends. I didn't want to …'

'I wanted you.'

We stopped, halfway to the NAAFI.

'I might just make a cup of tea in the office. I don't think I could face breakfast.'

'Was it you, Mike? The Man in the Blanket?'

'Don't be daft.'

'Right.'

We stood in silence.

'Poynter's got guts.'

'What?'

'They say he was wearing make-up and women's knickers.'

'Oh.'

'Fucking away with some other sod in the back of one of the old ambulances.'

'Right.'

'Perhaps you hadn't heard.'

'No.'

'You don't sound surprised.'

'I'm not. He mentioned that he was going to try … something of that sort.'

'Would you do it?'

'What?'

'To get out.'

I said nothing. I met his bloodshot eyes for a second, then looked down.

'You should have been there last night, Mike.' His voice was low. 'It would have been good.'

'Yeah. Sorry.'

'Still,' he said, adjusting his beret, 'thank God for good old Gladys. Speaking of which, chow time for me. Sure you won't?'

'Sure, thanks.'

'Suit yourself.'

He was absorbed by a gaggle of admirers and swept into the warm, steamy fug of the NAAFI.

05

Remind me never to book a holiday when I'm on drugs again.

Everything about Sitges was horrible and I'm not even sure that I'm going out with Stuart any more, if 'going out' really describes the mixture of chemically enhanced sex and hours in nightclubs that have made up our relationship so far.

I get home this morning at ten o'clock after travelling for fourteen hours, the final disaster in a disastrous week. I'm so tired that I don't even pick up the post, I just drop my bags and throw myself on to the sofa and groan very loudly and feel like crying. My eyes hurt, my stomach hurts, I haven't had a proper shit for about three days after having had diarrhoea for four days, I feel like I'm starting a cold and to cap it all it hurts when I pee.

I drift into an uneasy sleep full of stupid dreams about flight announcements and security checks and when my phone beeps I wake up without the faintest idea of where I am. It takes me a good five seconds of looking around and blinking before I recognise this room as my own home, the sofa as my sofa and the phone as my phone.

It's a text from Jonathan, and for the first time in ages I'm genuinely glad to hear from him, it's really thoughtful of him to remember I'm coming home today, and I hope I can see him later. I open the text and it's a joke about Madonna that I first heard about four years ago, it hasn't got my name anywhere in it and I assume that Jonathan just sent it to everyone in his address book. He spends a lot of time and money doing things like this these days, he's constantly hunched over his phone, his thumbs a blur, cackling and grunting. Jonathan used to be articulate to the point of being quite annoying, but this new withdrawn Jonathan is taking a bit of getting used to. Maybe it's part of his new 'urban' phase. I hope it doesn't last long. Jonathan's phases seldom do. His wardrobe would tell quite a story, if he didn't throw everything away. Currently he's sporting hoodies with extremely loud geometric designs, and it actually hurts to look at him.

I don't reply for a while, because he's obviously forgotten that I was due back from my holiday, in fact he's probably forgotten that I went on holiday at all, and instead I concentrate on opening my post. Most of it goes straight into the recycling, the rest is shoved into the 'important but boring' box for later filing, when I'm feeling less ill/anxious. There's only one letter with a handwritten address, and that just says 'Robert', no address or stamp. I can't think of anyone who would write, rather than texting, emailing or phoning me, so I'm quite curious.

It's from Michael downstairs, and it comes as a bit of a surprise because I realise that I haven't thought about him once while I was away; if he had been vaporised in my absence I might never have noticed.

There's a small sheet of writing paper inside, folded in half, and it just says: 'Hope you had a lovely holiday, please pop down for a cuppa sometime, I have a favour to ask.'

I can't think of anything I could do for Michael other than lend him money or help him shift furniture, and it better hadn't be the former because the holiday has cleaned me out for the rest of the month.

'Oh, you do look well,' says Michael. 'Spain, wasn't it?' I can't remember even telling him I was going on holiday, let alone where, but I suppose he heard Stuart and me talking/arguing about it before we went. 'No need to ask if the sun was shining. How nice to see a bit of colour in your cheeks.'

I'm feeling pretty grey, actually, but I'm not immune to compliments, and this cheers me up quite a lot. He looks older than I remember.

'So, how did you get on?' he asks, and I'm on the point of pouring it all out when suddenly I feel quite ashamed of the hash I've made of my holiday and I just say, 'Great, thanks, it was great.'

'I bet it was,' he says. 'We had some lovely holidays in Spain.' I remember the Spanish lady doll in the living room. 'God, the men are gorgeous.'

I didn't actually see very many Spanish men in Sitges, because it was full of all the people that we see in the London clubs all the time.

'So, you wanted to ask me something,' I say.

'Oh …' He sighs. 'You got my note, then.'

'Yes.'

'I just wondered if you wouldn't mind storing a few bits and pieces for me.'

I say 'of course' without thinking about it, but then start wondering what he's on about.

'It's just that I won't have too much space in the new place, and I'm very reluctant to just chuck it all away. It's only a couple of cardboard boxes. Well, three, actually, but they're not huge. I know it's a big imposition because I'm sure your place is full as it is.'

I realise that Michael's never been up to my flat since I moved in. Perhaps he was familiar with it from previous tenants.

'No, really, that's fine, I've got loads of room.' Looking around, I notice for the first time that pictures have been taken off the wall, ornaments removed from shelves. 'You're not moving,' I say.

'I'm afraid I am.'

This upsets me for some reason, and I feel quite wounded. 'You never mentioned it.'

'Well, it's all happened rather suddenly. Come in and sit down.' He moves a pile of books off the sofa.

'What has?'

'The sale.' I must be looking particularly stupid, because he adds, 'Of the flat, you see,' in the sort of voice you'd use with a four-year-old child.

'You've sold the flat?'

'That's right.'

'Why?' I sound like a four-year-old child as well.

'To pay the taxman, I'm afraid. When my partner died, he left the flat to me. It was always in his name, although we paid for it together, but back in those days you didn't just swan in and ask for a joint mortgage. He had a bit of money from his grandmother and he could afford the deposit, so it was his. We always meant to do something about it, but you know what it's like … Lawyers and all that … We'd made wills, and we thought that would be enough. But of course when it comes to it, I have to pay inheritance tax on its current market value. And that, I'm afraid, is far beyond my means, thanks to the way property prices in this area have gone up.'

I feel guilty, as if that's my fault.

'We paid the mortgage off years ago, and I thought I was safe and sound. Never thought about the taxman. Well, there's no way that I can afford the amount of money they're asking me for so I have to sell up and move into something smaller and cheaper.' He shrugs, stares out the window. 'Much smaller.'

'But that's ridiculous,' I say. 'They can't throw you out of your own home.'

'That's what I said, but you can't argue with the taxman. Mark my words.'

'There must be something you can do.'

'There was. We could have got married. But, like I told you, we never quite got round to it. I mean, when you're our age, and you've been together for as long as we had, it's not something you feel the need to rush into. Stephen was always nagging us, but we used to laugh at him and say he just wanted to wear a bridesmaid's outfit. Well, turns out he was right. We should have got married. No inheritance tax for civil partners.'

'Oh God. So when's it going on the market?'

'It's gone, Robert. Sold within a week.'

'Sold ...'

'Yes, to a very nice couple.'

'Gay?'

'Straight.'

'When?'

'Next week.'

'Just ... just like that?'

'Just like that. Better than hanging around, I suppose.' He looked round. 'I thought I would leave here in a box, but that's not what was meant to be.'

I can't think of anything to say. I don't understand why I'm feeling so upset. I stare at the carpet – that horrible, swirly carpet that, next week, will be rolled up and sticking out of a skip somewhere.

'I wish you'd told me,' I say in the end.

'Oh dear,' says Michael. 'There's been so much to do. And, you know, you haven't really been around much. And when you are ... well, I don't like to interrupt when you're entertaining.'

'You should have said something.' I realise how stupid this sounds as I'm saying it.

'No doubt, no doubt,' says Michael. 'Now, these boxes.'

I stand up, suddenly feeling that I'm going to cry. 'I'll come down for them later,' I say. 'I've got to unpack first.'

'And I've got to pack,' he says, seeing me out. 'Funny old world, isn't it?'

I need distraction, because what Michael has just told me is making me feel very anxious indeed, and so I phone Jonathan and propose lunch. We used to have great long boozy weekend lunches, then teeter around the West End doing a bit of shopping, usually ending up in a bar or two or three. It's exactly what I need right now. I need to tell him about Stuart and the holiday, and about Michael. Jonathan is supposed to be my best friend, and whatever his shortcomings, I need a best friend at the moment.

We meet up in Old Compton Street, the usual launch pad for these space shots, and at first I don't recognise Jonathan, he's leaning against a wall with his hood up, thinner than I've ever seen him, his legs in tight black trousers like spent match-sticks, his head nodding to music in his earphones. He's grown a scrappy little beard and he's wearing shades. He looks exactly like the other drug dealers that haunt the street.

I have to go right up to him and peer into his hood before he recognises me. But instead of smiling and taking out the ear-phones and pulling down the hood and removing the shades, he grabs me by the arm and marches me down the street towards Soho Square. He doesn't stop till we're in the park. Then, finally, he unmasks a little.

'Have you got any money, Robbie?'

'What? Lovely to see you too.'

'I need money.'

I've got some money, because I've just been to the cash point, but I'm not sure how much he has in mind.

'Are you in trouble, Jonathan?'

'No ...' He's looking around nervously, as if enemies might be hiding behind the trees.

'What do you need this money for?'

'I just owe someone a few quid, that's all,' he says, bad tempered.

'Well you owe me a few quid if it comes to that,' I say, 'but you've never seemed quite this eager to pay me back.'

He sticks his hands into his trouser pockets, which isn't easy, they're so tight, and looks around the square.

'How much is it, Jonathan?'

'It's not that bad ... God, I mean it's not like you're my mother.'

'How much?'

'Five hundred.' He mumbles.

'Five hundred? Fuck. What happened? Did Selfridges change their returns policy?'

'It's not funny, Robbie. I'm in trouble.'

'Yeah, I kind of got that impression.'

'Can you help me?'

'I'll see what I can do. Come on. Let's have lunch.'

'Yeah, but not round here. It's too ...' He shrugs, and we walk north, eventually finding a Greek restaurant on Charlotte Street that seems to be sufficiently off the beaten track to suit him.

'So,' he says, before we've even looked at the menu, 'the money.'

I've said I'll help him, and I will, even though a) I'm broke after the holiday and b) I know that lending money to Jonathan is tantamount to flushing it down the toilet, because you'll never see it again. But if I ask for a sub on Monday, I'll be able to give him what he needs and, incidentally, pay a few of those bills that I chucked into the 'important but boring' box.

'Don't worry about it. We'll sort it out next week.'

He leans across the table and grabs my sweater. 'Now! I need it now!' He's pale and slightly clammy, and the waiters are giving us suspicious glances. They must be used to druggies abusing their hospitality, and I don't want to be thrown out.

'Will you calm down, sit back, take your hoodie off and try to act like a human being,' I say. Jonathan sits and sulks and looks at the menu.

'There's nothing here I can eat.'

'What?'

'You know perfectly well that I'm vegan.'

I know nothing of the sort, but I get the waiter's attention and order a big lamb stew for myself and a plate of plain boiled rice for him.

'It's not organic,' he says when it arrives.

'So don't eat it.'

We don't exchange a word while I eat my stew and he pushes rice around his plate. He does manage to drink well over half the bottle of wine I've ordered, and I'm pretty sure that's not organic either.

'Let's go,' he says, as soon as my plate is clean. I pay the bill and the waiter glares at us as we leave.

We walk west in a big loop, and it suddenly occurs to me that we're heading for Selfridges – I don't think this is a conscious decision, Jonathan just has a sort of homing instinct. When I mention this he stops dead, looks at me as if I've just called his mother a whore, and bursts into tears.

There's an anonymous looking pub on the corner so I bundle him in there and get a drink in front of him as quickly as possible.

Then it all comes pouring out. He's been spending more and more time with Hadley and started working for him as a delivery-boy-come-debt-collector, flitting around the West End with a cycle courier's bag full of padded envelopes, some containing 'the goods', others containing money. His payment for these services is an entrée to Hadley's inner circles, and all the drugs you can eat, sniff, smoke or shove up your arse. Jonathan has developed a pronounced taste for crystal meth, and discovered that, with a little help from Tina, he has the confidence to 'get boyfriends'.

'I'm having more sex than I've ever had before in my life,' he wails, bursting into fresh tears. 'It's fantastic.'

I don't interrupt, just hand him a tissue.

'There's this one guy, right, he's a friend of Nico's, he's really gorgeous, his name's Toma, and I really like him, I mean really like him, and we've been seeing each other and it's been great, I mean really great, I mean really, really great …'

He's looking at me with strange goggling eyes, which I take as my cue to say, 'Wow, what have you been doing?'

'Barebacking,' he whispers, and then looks very pleased with himself. 'It's amazing.'

'Barebacking.'

'What?'

'You're barebacking.'

'Yeah. It's okay. He's been tested.'

'Right. Tested.'

'Oh you think you know it all,' he says, and launches into a long rambling tirade about how little I understand 'the lifestyle'. I don't really listen, because I'm feeling quite anxious myself, having been less than a hundred per cent careful with Stuart on holiday, especially when under the influence of drugs. But there's a big difference between Stuart and some dodgy connection of Hadley's …

'… with the right medication. I mean it's not a death sentence any more.'

I suddenly snap back into focus. 'What are you telling me?'

'Oh God here we go. If you're going to get pious on me I'm off.'

'What about that five hundred pounds?'

He sits down again.

'It doesn't give you the right to lecture me,' he says, sticking out his lower lip, and I suddenly feel quite sorry for his parents, because he must have been a hideous teenager.

'Let's calm down. You'd better tell me what you need this money for.'

'It's none of your business.'

'Goodbye, Jonathan.' I stand up and start putting my sweater on.

'Sit down, for fuck's sake.' Jonathan knows as well as I do that this isn't just one of our playground tiffs, this could be the end of a beautiful friendship. 'Look, I'm in trouble and I need help. Just don't … tell me off, or anything.'

It turns out that Jonathan has been helping himself to the takings, on the grounds that Hadley isn't actually paying him for his services and therefore he is entitled to a 'commission'.

Unfortunately he failed to mention this to Hadley, who quickly realised that the figures weren't adding up, and gave Jonathan forty-eight hours in which to make up the shortfall. Needless to say Jonathan failed to meet this deadline, for reasons which he thought entirely sound, and so Hadley negotiated an extension with interest. The first instalment of which, £500, Jonathan has failed to raise.

I have often mentioned to Jonathan that if he would only bite the bullet and work for a living, e.g. on the checkouts at Tesco, he would have money in the bank and less opportunity for spending it, but the idea is abhorrent to him and he is always looking for alternative revenue sources that don't involve actual work. Miraculously, he's scraped by ever since we left college, but now I think his luck may have run out.

'How many further instalments are there?'

'Flfffmfff.'

'Sorry?'

'Five, right? Five.'

'So you actually owe him three thousand pounds.'

'Yeah.'

'Shit, Jon-Jon ...'

'Don't call me that!'

'Where are you going to get three grand from?'

'I don't know.' He says it with a rising cadence, as if it's a question, as if he's throwing the ball back into my court.

'I don't suppose your parents ...'

He looks at me with disgust. Jonathan does not get on with his parents.

'So what are you going to do?'

'What else can I do? I'm going to have to work.'

At last – the message has got through. 'Great. I'm sure you can find a job easily enough. In a shop or a bar. Perhaps not a bar, but, you know, somewhere.'

'I don't mean a job, stupid. I mean ... work.'

'I don't …' I say, but then suddenly I do. 'Oh no. You're not.'

'I am. I've already got my commercial profile up.'

'You're going on the game.'

'Fuck off. You make it sound like I'm standing around Piccadilly Circus waiting for some fat old businessman to come and pick me up.'

'Well? Aren't you?'

'It's not like that any more.'

I haven't got the heart to say it, but if Jonathan is going to work as a prostitute, his clientele is going to come from the lower end of the food chain. Compared to the gorgeous, chiselled Brazilians who populate the back pages of magazines and the commercial areas of networking sites, Jonathan is, shall we say, an acquired taste.

'It's going to take you quite a while to clear three thousand pounds profit, Jonathan.'

'Rubbish. I'll do it in a week. Five jobs a day, a hundred quid a go, that's five hundred quid a day, three thousand in six days.'

'And on the seventh day he rested.'

'Something like that, yeah.'

'Have you considered whether you can actually do it five times a day?'

'I won't have to do much. Just get the money and then get them off.'

'And do you think there's sufficient … demand?'

'Course there is, with the pictures I posted. They'll be queuing at the door.'

'Are the pictures actually of you?'

'Very funny,' says Jonathan, but he doesn't look me in the eye.

'And do you think you're really cut out for the work?' In some ways, it's the only job he is cut out for. Jonathan would have made a great kept boy, in the old tradition, if only he'd been a bit better looking. He could have shopped and sulked in a rented penthouse, waiting for Daddy to call.

'I'll manage.'

'Jonathan, listen to me. Do you have any idea what prostitution is really like?'

'It'll be a laugh, it'll be fabulous.'

'Fat old men with skin complaints and dirty arses.'

'Fuck off.'

'How are you going to get it up for them?'

'I'll get by with a little help from my friends,' he says, tapping the side of his nose.

'And how exactly are you going to pay for your drugs? I presume escorts can't just get them on the NHS.'

'I have my contacts.'

'What, Hadley? Tell me you're not going to buy drugs so you can turn tricks in order to pay back the money you stole from the man who is selling you the drugs in the first place?'

'Oh, what do you know about anything?' says Jonathan, downing his drink in one and grabbing his revolting hoodie. 'You think you're so fucking clever but you don't know anything about what my life is like, not anything!'

He storms out of the pub and into the street. I wait for half an hour for him to come back, because he might think it worth it for that five hundred quid I said I'd 'lend' him, but he doesn't. I guess this is serious.

On the bus home, I pick up a celebrity magazine that someone's left lying on the seat, and read all about the fabulous wedding of Lukas to another talent show has-been. They look very tanned and tightened in the photographs, surrounded by other D-listers craning to get in the shot. Presumably they're hoping that their combined fame will just about keep them going for another year or so, after which they will either renew their vows or sell the story of their divorce and, with luck, custody battle.

So, suddenly Jonathan's decision to go in for prostitution seems quite rational.

I'm not nearly as drunk as I was hoping to be so when I get

home I open a bottle of vodka, and I'm thinking of inviting Michael up for a drink when the buzzer goes.

It's Stuart.

My stomach churns and tightens, and my first instinct is not to let him in, but of course I can't do that.

'What do you want?' I say when he gets to the top of the stairs.

'What do you think I want?' he says, grabbing my tits. 'You.'

'Are you high?'

He sticks his grinning face right into mine, and says, 'Course I am.'

'For fuck's sake.'

'You're not still angry.' It's not a question.

'Look, Stuart, let's just … cool it for a couple of days.'

'I don't want to cool it. I want to fuck you.' He's pushed me into the flat, and got me on to the sofa, and he's on top of me, kissing my neck, pressing his groin into mine. He's hard. He's always hard.

'I told you …' It's very difficult to say no to Stuart when he's like this, which is most of the time. I still find him as attractive as the first day we met – more so, perhaps. I'm addicted to his sex.

'I'm not in the mood,' I say, trying to work my way out from under him, but he knows he's got me where he wants me, and this show of resistance is one of his favourite hors d'oeuvres. I don't even know whether I'm doing it deliberately, because the sex will be better, or because I really don't want sex.

He's got my wrists in one hand above my head, and he's undoing my trousers with the other.

'Come on baby,' he says, 'you know you want it.'

And I do, just as I did through the tense week of our holiday, when he withheld sex unless I'd do as he asked, which basically meant picking up people for threesomes and taking vast amounts of stupid drugs like GHB. Even now I can feel, beside his erection, the hard shape of a glass bottle in his pocket. Any minute now he'll get it out, and we'll swig from it, and that will be that.

Fucking for hours on the floor, on the sofa, over the table, the bath, even sometimes in bed.

Finally it's over and he's asleep and the flat is quiet, the block is quiet, I imagine Michael downstairs thinking, 'Thank God they've finished,' and taking out his earplugs.

I never went back to talk about his boxes. It will have to wait. I have other things to think about.

Five

We borrowed a car from one of the corporals, an old Morris 10, and drove to Blackpool on Friday night. Wright was in high spirits, and kept up a monologue about birds and booze while I did the driving. When we arrived, the rain had set in. We dropped our bags at the boarding house, and didn't bother to change. Saturday would be the night for civvies, when there was a dance at the Tower Ballroom at which Don Lang's Frantic Five would be playing. 'From the Six-Five Special!' said Wright, when I looked blank. 'Off the telly, for fuck's sake. Get with it, Grandad!'

I took the precaution of finding out that there was an exhibition of French watercolours at the Grundy Gallery, and a production of *La Fille du Régiment* at the Opera House if – as I suspected – I was left to my own devices for large parts of the weekend. For Wright, as for most of the men, Blackpool means 'birds', 'pussy' etc. That was why we were here, wasn't it? Two mates on the piss and on the pull. He said it often enough.

The landlady gave us a lecture about the terrible fate that awaits anyone who brings 'unregistered guests' on to the premises. We made our way to the nearest pub and got the first pint in.

'What sort of boys does she take us for?' said Wright, wiping the foam from his mouth with the back of his hand. 'I wouldn't bring a lady back to that dump. The kind of bird I'm after will have a place of her own.'

There were no birds to be had in the Red Lion, despite Wright's assurances that we'd be mobbed as soon as they saw the uniform, so we moved on. It was raining, and the esplanade was deserted. Even the Blackpool whores didn't like getting cold and wet. We did the round of the pubs, each one 'bound to be heaving with fanny', according to Wright, and each one emptier than the last. By ten o'clock, with closing time looming into view, he was starting to look crestfallen. 'What kind of shit hole is this, anyway?' he said as he sank his fifth pint, and I sipped my fifth half.

Eventually we ran into a group of squaddies from the army base, on their way to the Crystal Club, 'the only place in town' according to one of them, 'and the pussy is literally dripping off the walls'.

'That's the place for me,' said Wright.

'But not me.'

'Come on, Mike! It'll be a laugh.' But he didn't sound enthusiastic. The soldiers were giving me strange looks.

'Your mate looks like he's had enough.'

'I have,' I said. 'Me for bed.'

'Suit yourself,' said Wright, looking cross. 'See you in the morning.'

'Don't wait up, sweetheart!' called one of the soldiers, as they led him away.

I went back to the boarding house alone, and felt the landlady's eyes on my back as I climbed the creaky stairs.

Wright stank of whisky when he got in at six a.m. He hadn't slept, and he was unshaven. He tried to creep around, but of course made more noise than usual.

'All right, Wright?'

'I'm completely fucked.'

'Wasn't that the general idea?'

'Not in the right way.'

'Oh dear.'

'I need some sleep.' He threw himself on the bed, fully clothed, and closed his eyes.

'At least take your boots off.'

'Can't …' His voice was already sleepy. I knelt at the foot of his bed and undid his bootlaces, easing his feet free. By the time both boots were off, he was asleep. I watched him until I got cold, and returned to my own bed.

Two hours later, he woke up, swore at length and started pulling at his clothes.

'How are you feeling?'

'Disgusting. I smell like a wet dog.' He was down to his underwear.

'You'll catch your death.'

'I need a wash.' He sniffed his armpit. 'Jesus. Did I die in the night?'

'Well if you did, you didn't go to heaven.'

'No, I bloody didn't. Christ, what a shitty town this is.'

'How was the Crystal Club?'

'A fucking clip joint and full of hookers.'

'Mission accomplished, then.'

'Fuck off. I've got some standards. Half of them made my nan look like Brigitte Bardot.'

'And the other half?'

'I don't pay for it, mate. If anything, they should be paying me.'

'Glad to see your opinion of yourself is as high as ever.'

'Damn right.' He went into his posing routine. 'Who could resist?' He had a hard-on in his pants, probably just the usual morning piss hard-on that causes so much hilarity in the barracks, but possibly more.

'Go and wash yourself before all the hot water goes.'

'Ain'tcha gonna scrub my back?'

I threw a towel at him, and he ran down the passage. I could hear him whistling from the bathroom. I wished I'd never left Reville. This was worse than anything.

The rest of the morning went well enough. We dressed in civvies and walked all over the town, had an enormous breakfast in a café overlooking the sea, and even managed to see the French watercolours. Wright barely glanced at the pictures, but he was impressed by the Grundy.

'This is more like it. This is a fucking palace.' The guard shushed and scowled at him. 'What's the matter, cock? Don't you allow the peasants in?'

I pulled him into the next room.

'All right! I don't know how to behave. You'll have to teach me some manners.'

'You're supposed to talk in subdued tones.'

'Ooh,' he said, in a nasal, Bluebottle voice, 'subdued tones.'

'And you're supposed to look at the art.'

'It's very pretty,' he said, peering at a delicate study of some cattle in a meadow at sunrise. 'I like a nice cow.'

'You're bloody hopeless.'

'And you love me for it, don't you?'

A lady in a raffia hat raised her eyebrows as Wright put his arm round my shoulders. 'It's all right, love,' he said, 'we're getting married.'

She said, 'Well!' and marched out of the gallery.

Wright ran out into the sunshine, laughing. 'Come on. Pubs are open. Let me buy you a pint.'

'Isn't it a bit early?'

He just looked at me, head down, brow furrowed, through his long eyelashes.

Two pints later – he 'misheard' my request for a half – we paid our pennies and strolled along the pier. The sun was out, the gulls were fighting with the wind, and the girls – all those girls who were nowhere to be seen last night – were teetering along the planks in their high heels, holding on to their headscarves while their skirts blew up to show stocking tops and suspenders. They screamed, and Wright whistled. He can whistle very loudly.

'See that one? She's undressing me with her eyes. Hello darling! Fancy a RAF sandwich?'

The pretty brunette stopped and whispered in her dumpy blonde friend's ear.

'They'll come over now. Watch me reel 'em in.'

I felt sick, and wondered if it was the beer.

'Lovely day, girls. Cigarette?'

The dark-haired one, with a Jacqmar headscarf and a thin spring coat, allowed Wright to give her a light. Her short, plain, bespectacled friend waited for me to do the honours.

'You're from London,' said the brunette. 'You talk funny.'

'No, love, you talk funny. Eeeh, aye, eh, oop.'

'Glahss, bahth, grahss.'

'That's the Queen's English, my girl. Isn't it, Aircraftman Medway? You've met the Queen, haven't you?'

'Oh yes. And the Queen Mother.'

'We know all the queens, don't we?'

'Absolutely.'

'You're mental,' said the girl, and started walking away. Wright skipped into step with her; I brought up the rear with the sidekick.

'Don't run away, gorgeous! We were just saying, me and my mate here, that we needed to find two beautiful young ladies to accompany us to the dance tonight.'

'Oh, were you indeed.'

'And when we saw you, we said to ourselves, "There's a pair of smashers."'

'A pair of smashers, eh?' She giggled.

'Yeah. Nicest pair I've seen for ages.'

'Oh, you …'

'So how about it, baby?'

'We haven't got tickets.'

'No problem. We'll see to all that, won't we, Mickey?'

'Yes, of course.'

The girl beside me muttered 'Thanks' and looked up at me. She was a good nine inches shorter. When I smiled, she blushed, and looked down.

Wright was laying it on thick about his boxing prowess, his flying, and how he was 'auditioning for a movie'.

'Are you at Reville?' asked 'my' girl.

'Yes.' There didn't seem to be much else to say.

'My name's Valerie.'

'How do you do, Valerie. I'm Michael.'

'You sound as if we're going to shake hands.'

'Perhaps we ought.'

'Ought! That's funny.' She stuck out a plump, mauve-gloved hand. I shook it. 'Me and my friend were out for a walk,' she said.

'So I see.'

'It's a nice bright morning.'

'Yes.'

'Not like last night. Last night was shocking.'

'Yes. Very wet.'

We walked along in silence until I tripped on a raised board. 'Oops a daisy,' said Valerie, flatly.

Wright was arm in arm with his girl now, and pulled her over to a candyfloss stand. We waited for them.

'What's your friend's name?' I asked, to break the silence.

'Gerry. Geraldine. I suppose you fancy her.'

'No, not at all.'

'Really?'

'Truly.' I didn't have the heart to say why.

'Oh,' said Valerie, brightening. 'Most boys do. I think it's because she's got such thick hair.'

'Perhaps. I'm not that bothered.'

'That's nice.' She patted her own thin tresses. 'Mine's not dyed, you know. I'm a natural blonde. Not like those movie stars.'

'Would you like a candyfloss?'

'I thought you'd never ask.'

'Come on, then.'

It was so easy, picking up a girl. Men do it all the time. I handed over the stick with a flourish.

'Thank you, kind sir,' she said, curtseying, and stuck her face right in.

Wright and Geraldine were whispering and giggling.

'We could go for a drive,' I said. I had to get off that pier.

'Hear that, Gerry?' shouted Valerie. 'They're going to take us for a drive!'

'Bags I the back seat,' said Wright.

'Where are we going?'

'I don't know.' My heart was in my boots. 'Calder Fell is nice.' We'd been up there on exercises once; it was full of skylarks and harebells. I wished I could go there alone, rid of Wright and the girls and the leaden feeling of beer and fried food in my stomach.

'Ooh,' said Geraldine, 'romantic.'

The trip was not a success. It started raining again as soon as we left Blackpool, winding along the A road, and by the time we got to Garstang it was pissing down. Valerie sat chastely by my side in the front, occasionally commenting on the scenery. I stole glances at Wright in the rear-view mirror. He was petting with Geraldine, running his hands up her thighs, kissing her on the neck, but when he tried to touch her breast she smacked his hand and said she was not that type of girl. His eyes were glazed, his lips swollen.

'I can't go on like this,' I said, meaning the weather. 'We'd better stop.'

'Yes,' said Geraldine, primly, 'I think we'd better.' She fastened a lock of hair in place with a Kirby grip. There was a mark on her neck.

'Just park somewhere,' said Wright. 'The windows will steam up nicely.'

'I'm not sitting in a steamed-up car with you, you brute,' said Geraldine, sounding like Joan Greenwood. 'Hands all over the place. What are you? An octopus?'

'A donkey,' said Wright. 'Want a ride, little girl?'

'Oh, you disgusting man.' Geraldine opened the door and got out. Wright followed, adjusting his pants.

'Let's all have tea.' She took Valerie's arm, and they trotted off to the tea room, whispering conspiratorially.

'Fucking prick tease,' said Wright. 'Let's dump them and go back to town.'

'That's not very gallant.'

'I'm not gallant. I'm fucking horny. I've got blue balls.'

'Come on,' I said, 'let's go and buy them some cakes. That usually cheers girls up.'

'Cakes. Christ.'

I made most of the conversation as the girls nibbled their way through a selection of over-iced cakes and mushy sandwiches. We drank two pots of tea, until Wright announced, 'I've got to piss,' and disappeared into the gents.

'Your friend's got no finesse,' said Geraldine, looking down her nose.

'Don't be too hard on him. He comes from a broken home. Never knew a mother's love.'

She looked curious for a moment, then changed her mind. 'Well it shows.'

We drove back to Blackpool just in time to see the sun break through the clouds in a dazzling blaze at five o'clock.

'Pick you up at eight, and don't be late!' shouted Wright as we drove off, then, 'Thank fuck for that. What a waste of fucking time.'

'You complained about the whores last night, and now you're complaining because a girl won't drop her knickers in the back of a car. What do you want?'

'I don't fucking know. But I don't want her.'

'They'll find us at the dance tonight.'

'Fuck the fucking dance.' He kicked a pebble up the street. 'I'm not in the mood any more. Let's just get pissed.'

We went straight to the nearest pub. Wright ordered a pint and a whisky chaser and disappeared into the toilet. When he came out, his hair was freshly combed, his eyelashes still wet from splashing water on his face.

'Fucking bitch,' he said, and drank his pint in silence.

After the second pint – it was still not six o'clock – he started talking again.

'I fucking hate Blackpool. It's a two-penny shitheap.'

'Well I admit it's not the Riviera …'

'Stupid little virgins.' He adopted a silly, singsong voice, and a bad attempt at a Lancashire accent. 'Oooh, don't touch my titties! Oooh, get your paws off my drawers! Oooh, that's disgusting that is, I'm a nice girl I am!' He knocked back a whisky. 'Bollocks to that.'

'It's not like you to give up so easily,' I said. 'What with your blue balls and all.'

'What do you know about my balls, other than bloody staring at them every chance you get?'

I wanted to cry. 'That's not …'

'You don't have a fucking clue what it's like for me. I'm like a caged animal up here. Surrounded by cunts in the camps, dozy little tarts in Blackpool who haven't got a fucking clue …'

'They seemed like nice girls.' I sounded like my mother.

'Nice girls! You can keep your nice girls. Oh, fuck this.' He got up and walked towards the door, just as Geraldine and Valerie came in on the arms of two Reville airmen. Wright pushed past them.

'Charming!' said Geraldine, in a loud, slightly drunken voice. I caught Valerie's eye, and we both looked away, ashamed.

'What's the matter, Medway?' shouted one of the airmen. 'Had a row?' His mate sniggered.

'Those two,' said Geraldine, 'are not what I would call gentlemen.'

'No, love,' said the airman, 'they're proper ladies, they are.' He took a few dolly steps around the bar, flapping his wrists. 'Well known, they are … Whoooooff!'

Wright's fist connected with his solar plexus, and the boy doubled up, unable to breathe.

'Anything else to say on the subject?' said Wright, rubbing his knuckles. The other airman backed away, and trod heavily on Geraldine's toes. She screamed.

'Come on, Mike. We're leaving.'

I followed him out. He was halfway up the street when I caught up.

'What was all that about? You don't mind what they said, do you?'

'Why should I? I've been called worse.'

'Okay.' I thought it was best to change the subject. 'So, what time are we going to the dance?'

'Oh Christ, Michael, we're not going to the poxy dance.'

'I thought you wanted to see Don Lang's Frantic Five.'

'Are you taking the piss?'

'At least you've got a smile on your face.'

He laughed. It was like the sun breaking out from the clouds. 'You're a wanker.'

'Thanks a lot.'

He put his arm round my shoulder. 'Still, at least you're my wanker. Let's get another drink.'

We toured the pubs again, and when we'd done them all, we started again. By nine, we were plastered, but happily so. We ate fish and chips out of the newspaper, burning our fingers as we walked around the Tower.

'Some Saturday night,' I said. I was waiting for him to make his excuses and go pussy-hunting again.

'What's wrong with this? The bright lights, a bellyful of beer, some decent grub' – he licked the salt and vinegar from his fingers, balled up the paper and lobbed it neatly into a bin – 'and my best mate by my side. That's good enough for me.'

'I'm touched.'

'Play your cards right, and you will be. Come on,' said Wright, running towards a brightly illuminated stall. 'Ten shots for a penny. I'll win us a teddy.'

He hit every target, and won a huge pink teddy bear, which he handed to a wide-eyed little boy, and a goldfish in a bag, which I had to prevent him from releasing into the sea.

'Poor little fucker,' he said. 'He wants to be free.'

'We'll put him in the pond in the park.'

'Nah. We'll fry him up for breakfast. Come on, Goldie. You're going to be lovely on a piece of toast, ain't you?'

When we got back to the room at eleven-thirty, I filled the water jug and released the fish from its bag.

'You soft sod,' said Wright.

'There's no point in being cruel.'

He hung his jacket up carefully, and unbuttoned his shirt, whistling 'Don't Be Cruel', occasionally singing in his best Presley vibrato.

'Pity you haven't got your camera,' he said, when he was barechested.

'I have.'

'Go on, then, get it out, as the actress said to the bishop.'

The air seemed thicker, the yellow light from the single over-head bulb soupy and diffuse. 'It's too dark in here. I only brought it to take snaps of Blackpool.'

'Ah, go on. Give it a try. I feel like it.' He stretched his arms above his head. His ribs, and the muscles along them, stood out in neat ranks.

I fumbled with the lens cap. 'Nothing's going to come out, just smudges.'

'Yeah, but what smudges!' He ran his hands over his chest, down his stomach, hooking the thumbs in his waistband. 'Here's one for that fucking movie producer.'

'Hold still, then.' I stopped down to F2.8, selected a 1/16th shutter speed, and hoped my hands weren't shaking too much. Wright stood beneath the light, twisting and turning to maxim-ise the definition. I released the shutter.

'If that comes out, it might be all right.'

'Do some more.'

'What?'

'I want to do more.'

I felt like we were crossing a line.

'I'll do my best. No promises, though.'

He was humming softly, winding his hips in gentle figures of eight, dancing with an invisible partner, his hands running over his torso. I kept snapping. He started dancing in earnest, moving his feet, clicking his fingers.

We both knew what was coming next. He unbuckled his belt and unbuttoned his flies, opening them to a wide V. One more button, and a flash of white.

'Oh my God. You're wearing them.'

'Surprised?' His eyes were closed, and he carried on dancing. I kept shooting, caution drowned in drink.

He unlaced his shoes, pulled off his socks. His trousers fell around his ankles. He had an erection. I kept shooting. It would be easy enough to destroy the film in the morning. One quick tug in the cold light of day, the images erased forever.

'How about it?'

'What?'

'Want a piece of the action?'

'I ...'

'Come on,' he said, in his gangster accent, 'give a buddy a helping hand.' He thrust his hips forward, eyes closed, lips parted.

It would all be forgotten in the morning.

I put the camera down carefully on the bed, and squatted in front of him. His groin was at eye level. There was a small wet spot on the fabric of the pouch. Wright pushed closer.

I had a brief flash of clarity – I saw a dirty old man kneeling before a drunken airman in a cheap boarding house, about to take the step that would turn him from latent to practising.

It was a step from which there was no return.

I took it.

'Right,' said the landlady, 'where are they?' She stood at the foot of the stairs, her arms folded across her bosom, a fag in her mouth, a scarf over her rollers.

'Morning, missus,' said Wright, trying to push past her.

'I said, where are they?'

'What?'

'The tarts you had up in your room last night. Don't pretend you didn't. I told you about bringing girls back here. This is a respectable house, not a knocking shop.'

Wright said nothing, his hands buried in his pockets.

'Come on. I'm waiting for an answer.' She glared at us, as if we might produce women from our kit bags.

'We didn't have anyone in our room last night,' I said. She softened when she heard my middle-class accent.

'I heard dancing.'

'I'm afraid we were a little bit the worse for wear.'

'Hmm. And I heard … well, I heard other noises.'

'I'm sorry if we disturbed your sleep.'

'I don't sleep,' she said. 'Nobody can get in or out of this house without me knowing it.'

'Well I assure you …'

She barged past me, and up the stairs, hoping to find the 'tarts' in the wardrobe or under the bed.

'There's nobody here,' she said, sounding disappointed.

'I hope the room is tidy enough.'

'What?' She looked puzzled, as if she was trying to work out a difficult sum. 'Oh yes, it's quite all right.'

'Good morning, then.'

Wright was standing by the car.

'Breakfast?' I said. 'I'm starving.'

He didn't even look up.

'Come on. I'm desperate for a cuppa.'

'Go ahead. I'll get the bus.'

'Look, if you want a lift back, we're stopping for a …'

'I don't want a fucking lift! I don't want anything.' He stamped down the street, head thrust forward, hands deep in his pockets, his kit bag, containing his Saturday-night civvies, banging against his backside.

I suddenly remembered the goldfish. It was too late for that now.

06

I'm sweating so much that I'm actually dripping on to my keyboard. It's hot in the office, but not that hot. I keep mopping my brow but people are starting to stare. 'What the hell is the matter with you?' asks Anna, and I say I'm just hungry, I've got low blood sugar and I've probably overdone it at the gym. 'Well go and get some food, for Christ's sake,' she says, scowling. We've got a serious deadline this afternoon and I know that I am fucking it up but there's not much I can do while I feel like this. I've got an emergency packet of chocolate biscuits in my desk drawer, so I grab them and sit in the toilet stuffing my face like a lunatic. The sweat is running off the end of my nose in a stream, falling on to the uneaten biscuits, and when I eat them I can taste the salt. My light blue shirt is rapidly turning dark blue.

I keep shovelling the biscuits in and gradually I start to calm down, the sugar is getting into my bloodstream and my hands aren't shaking so much. When I've ingested the entire packet I feel desperately tired and want above all to lie down, but there isn't room in the cubicle. I could just about manage a foetal position on the floor, curled around the toilet, but I'm unwilling to accept that I've sunk that low.

Of course, this is all self-inflicted, the result of a heavy non-stop weekend, and I would like to be able to say that it was all worth it but, from the fragments that I can actually remember, it wasn't. There were a few highs – dancing around the bathroom as we came up, dancing around the club after the second or third hit, when the DJ put on something that sounded good at the time – but many lows, in particular the chill-out party at Stuart's friend Tommy's house which quickly developed into an orgy at which I witnessed any amount of unsafe sexual behaviour.

And now I'm trying and failing to hold it together at a job that I'm in danger of losing if I don't pull my socks up. Anna has been recently promoted above me, and although she still sits at the same desk, and is still my friend and likes to hear about my weekend exploits, she has changed. She is now one of 'them' and has made it quite clear that, come my appraisal, she will be looking for some constructive suggestions about timekeeping and productivity. I don't imagine she will be impressed if I return to the office with a soaking shirt, stinking that very special post-weekend stink, with chocolate round my mouth. I need to sort myself out.

I go to the sink, strip off my shirt and wash my face and armpits. That's a start. I wish I had some deodorant, but soap will have to do. Then I dry myself with handfuls of paper towels. Miraculously, my body is holding up, despite the abuse. My pecs are firm, my abs are defined, my biceps are big. Well, they should be. I'm not taking these steroids, risking my future physical and mental health, for nothing. I had better damn well look good. The only thing that's wrong is the grey pallor of my face, and the dark circles under my eyes. And a bit of acne on my back, which I can see in the mirror if I twist my head round, but it's nothing compared to the eruptions that you see in the gyms and the clubs. Other than that, I look like an exceptionally fit young man, which is just as well, because I feel about a hundred.

The only problem now is the shirt, which is not only wet but cold. I switch on the electric hand dryer and start drying it, inch by inch, under the stream of hot air. This is going to take about half an hour, but I think it's time well spent, and it's giving me a chance to calm down and come down.

The door opens – I hadn't really thought about that – and in comes New Boy Simon, head down, reading a piece of paper, heading for the urinal. He actually walks past me, then stops, stares ahead, walks backwards.

'Am I seeing things?'

'Hi Si …' I have to clear my throat. 'Simon.'

'Are you all right?'

'Yeah, I'm fine, I just had a bit of an accident with a cup of coffee and I had to wash my shirt and it's er …'

'Taking a bit of time to dry. Yes. So I see.'

He's looking at me with a half smile on his face. Well, I am half naked. He's in no hurry to move along.

'So I'm just …'

'Yes.' Another pause. A slight flicker of his left eyebrow. 'I've got a spare shirt you can borrow. If you would be seen dead in any of my clothes.'

'Oh, that's okay.'

'It's clean. In fact, it's never been worn. You can have it.'

'No, really, I couldn't,' I say, as if I'm refusing a piece of expensive jewellery.

'Stay there. I'll be right back.'

The shirt is still in its plastic wrapper. It's from Marks and Spencer. But it's white, and there's nothing obviously wrong with it. I put it on. It's a bit tight across the shoulders and the chest.

'There. Looks better on you than it would on me,' says Simon, brushing a possibly non-existent thread off my back.

'Thanks, mate,' I say. 'You've saved my life.'

'All in a day's work,' he says, and he goes to the urinal. I tidy my hair and brush the crumbs off my trousers while his piss drums against the metal.

'You know,' he says, as he's putting himself away and I'm about to leave, 'you should take care of yourself.'

'What do you mean?'

'Well, you know. You're out there every weekend caning it …'

'No, I'm not. I've hardly been going out at all recently.' I'm embarrassed even to say these words, because it's well known that 'I've hardly been going out at all recently' is gayspeak for 'I've been spending more time in clubs than in my own home'.

'Sorry. I just don't like to see you ... like this.'

'Like what?' I'm getting aggressive, which is no way to behave to someone who's just given you a shirt.

Simon puts his hands up and backs away. 'Okay. Okay. Forget I said anything.' He leaves the toilet.

'Fucking idiot,' I say, but I'm not sure if I mean him or me.

The afternoon is more or less a disaster because it's painfully clear to everyone in the presentation meeting that I haven't got a clue what's going on, that Anna has done the whole thing and when she asks me to fill in some of the finer details I mumble and grope for words and promise to get a spreadsheet in everyone's inbox first thing in the morning. Anna just looks at me over the top of her glasses, like a schoolteacher, and makes some excuse that we haven't been sent that information yet, but Robert's on top of it, even though we have and I'm not. My heart swells with gratitude but I know I'm in for a bollocking when we get out.

It doesn't come. She just says, 'Sort yourself out, Rob,' and goes home. Gone are the days of quick drinks after work that go on for hours, of shared confidences and smutty jokes and giving nicknames to our co-workers.

I go to the gym. At least here I can forget about my problems, and work some of the toxins out of my system. And I see Andy so I get my steroids as well. Then I have a sunbed, because it's good for the acne on my back. When I come out my skin feels tight. I rub a lot of moisturiser into my face until it's shiny. I check myself out in the mirror, and I'm still looking good. Then I put my shirt on – the shirt that Simon gave me – and I feel bad about being so rude to him. That makes me cross, and now I feel angry with him. I guess you could say that I'm experiencing mood swings.

I need a night in, if only to be able to say that I'm not out every single night of the week, and so I go home via the supermarket and make myself a healthy dinner of stir-fried chicken breasts, broccoli and carrots. I drink two pints of water and watch a

DVD. The phone doesn't ring. Stuart hasn't been in touch all day. I think we must have ended the weekend with a row but I don't remember it, and I doubt he does either. I half think of calling Jonathan just to see if he's still alive, but then I remember that I vowed that he would have to make the first move.

There's so much noise coming from downstairs that I'm having difficulty concentrating on the TV. Since Michael moved out, the new people have been causing a great deal of nuisance around the place. They play loud music all the time, they hang out on the balcony smoking and talking, or rather shouting, in incredibly loud voices, and they seem to work very strange shifts because there are doors slamming and feet pounding up and down the stairwell at all hours of the day and night. The smell of their cooking seems to come up through my floorboards. They haven't introduced themselves, and when I pass them they look straight through me. I don't know if this is an African thing, or a homophobia thing, or just that they're bloody rude, and I'm trying to work myself up to a confrontation that will seem neither hostile nor racist. I'm cross with Michael for selling the flat to people like this, and then I realise that I sound exactly like our neighbours at home, who complained when an Asian family moved into the street.

I've got three boxes of Michael's stuff cluttering up my bedroom, I don't know what I'm supposed to do with it, it's probably a load of kitsch ornaments and tasteful coffee table books of male nude photography, which really ought to be chucked. He wasn't very coherent when I last saw him, on the day he was moving out, and didn't make any arrangements about collecting them. Nor did he mention them in the card he sent from his new address, to which I remember I haven't replied, as he has neither email nor mobile, and I haven't got writing paper or stamps.

The film ends, it's only nine o'clock and I'm working myself into a real temper about the noise from downstairs. I could go out, but I've promised myself that I won't. I don't know what to do with myself. I can't read. I can't work. The only thing I can think of is going to bed. I take my usual Valium but it doesn't do a thing so I take another and I suppose I sleep because the next thing I know the alarm's going off and it's time to go to work all over again.

Six

A letter from Princess Mary's RAF Hospital, Halton, Bucks, otherwise known as the loony bin. The envelope had not been tampered with.

> Dear Michael
> I am allowed to write one letter from here where I am 'under observation' which means lots of tests and interviews with the doctors and 'art therapy' we do pottery and drawing and so on which beats bull and drill any day.
>   I will be here for a couple of months and then return to civvy street which means London for me yippee. If I may I will send you from there my new address when I have found one as I would very much like to hear your news. Do not write to me here I am not allowed to receive letters but will be a better correspondent when once I am set up in town.
>   Hoping all is well with you
>
> Stephen Poynter

That covered four sheets in Stephen's curly scrawl. I read it twice, looking hard between the lines for some assurance that he had not dropped me in the soup, for an apology for using me in the way that he did, then shredded it and dumped it behind the cookhouse as usual. It wouldn't do for that to fall into the wrong hands. Although speculation has finally died down about the identity of the Man in the Blanket, any hint that I was corresponding with Stephen would be enough to make it flare up again. My position at Reville is difficult enough without that.

Wright hasn't spoken to me, or even acknowledged my existence, for four weeks, not since Blackpool. He's been promoted to Aircraftman First Class, and will soon be a Leading Aircraftman, they say, so proud is the old man of his prize fighter. He's putting in his flying hours, training hard in the gym, and spending his leisure time with the Mervyn Wright Fan Club, who surround him at all times. I don't get a look in. I have to make do with my memories of a Blackpool boarding house and a set of photographs that I dare not look at. The pictures I took that night are still in the camera, undeveloped.

I spent those weeks at work in the SSQ, the evenings at lectures or in the library, the nights awake, feverish. I didn't take any leave. I can't face going home, and I can never go back to Blackpool. What else is there?

One morning, I caught Wright's eye across the canteen.

A week later, he waved and smiled at me across the parade ground.

This morning, nearly six weeks since we last spoke, he was back in the SSQ, hanging around outside my door, glancing in, nervous, fidgety. When I looked up and saw him, he smiled and strode in.

'All right, boss?'

'Fine. You?'

'Great. Great.' He paced around the room as if he'd never seen it before, taking in every detail, like a prospective tenant.

'You ever hear back from those film people, Mike?'

'Me? No.'

'Shit. Me neither.'

'I expect they had a lot of ...'

'Fucking bastards. That should have been my job.'

'Perhaps the others were more ...'

'I bet the movie's crap, though, eh?'

'I'm sure it will be.'

'But … Fuck, this is so frustrating.'

'What's the matter? I thought you were the old man's Golden Boy.'

'Oh, that.' He waved his arm, dismissing Reville, his boxing triumph, his fan club, the AOC. 'I want to be famous, Mike. Not just some cunt in a RAF uniform. I want to get … out there.'

'Only another year to go.'

'Yeah, and then what? The fucking dole queue. Not for me, mate.'

'You could sign on as a regular. They're crying out for them.'

'Don't make me laugh.'

'Then what?'

'London. The bright lights. Fame and fortune.'

'I've heard the streets are paved with gold.'

'Yeah, and why not? Once they get a load of this …'

We were back on familiar territory, and any minute now he would ask me to get my camera out again. Who knows, this time we might take things a little further. He might allow me to take care of myself, perhaps, and then we wouldn't speak for another six weeks.

'Can we talk about this later, Mervyn? I've got a lot of work to do.'

'I want you to send them pictures off to the muscle mags.'

'What?'

'Come on. I'm better than any of 'em.'

'Okay. And then what?'

'I don't know. Modelling. Bodybuilding contests. It's a start.'

'We'll talk about this later, Wright.'

He scowled, opened his mouth to bark out orders, then thought better of it. 'All right. Beer later. My shout.'

The photographs duly went off to six magazines: *Health and*

Strength and *Physique Illustrated* (boxing shorts only), *Man's World* and *Male Classics* (a selection of shorts and pouches), *Man Alive* and *Muscle Boy* (pouches, and one rear-view nude). Every day, Wright came to my office to see if there were any replies. There never were. He became moody and withdrawn. There was no suggestion of further photographic sessions, and certainly no renewal of intimacy. He's never suggested, by a hint or even a look, that what happened that night really happened. He gives the overwhelming impression that, somehow, I've let him down – by not making him into a star, by being queer, maybe by not being queer enough. Does he want me to initiate things? Does that make it better for him? I don't understand. I'm losing sleep and losing weight and starting to look like Stephen did before his dramatic exit.

Another letter arrived, this time with a typed envelope and a London postmark. It had not been tampered with. The note-paper was headed MUSCLE BOY, the return address was a PO Box number. But the large, girlish handwriting was familiar.

Dear Michael

Well isn't it a small world! I think you will be very surprised to hear that I am writing to you in my new capacity as the art director of *Muscle Boy* magazine. Little did I think when they were doing tests on me at Halton that I would walk straight into such a cushy number which as you can imagine suits me DOWN TO THE GROUND.

Anyway I see you have been busy with your camera taking those lovely pictures of Airman Wright that you sent us which we will be very happy to feature in the spring number which is coming out in about Feb or March depending. I did not know that you read muscle mags but I suppose I should not be too surprised!!! We don't pay for pics that have been sent in by readers but I will make sure if you want that it gets a full page, usually they only get a half or a quarter but I will do it as a favour and besides which it is a good shot mmm I think the readers are going to love it. Please let me know how to credit it and if you want an advert at the back you know that is how they make their money from the small ads at the back selling pics mail order but I won't go into that now we will talk about it.

Come and see me on your next leave I am well set up and can even offer you a bed for the night no not mine in case that's what you are thinking. I had better not do any more camp talk you never know whose reading. Give my love to everyone at Reville especially my boyfriend Sargent Kelsey.

Anyway I will send you a couple of copies of the mag when it comes out.

Stephen

When I told Wright the good news – omitting to mention the identity of the 'art director' in question – he whooped with joy, ran around the parade ground punching the air, returned panting and flushed, his eyes shining.

'I knew we'd do it! I knew it! What a team! You've got the brains and I've got the muscle. We can have it all!' He put his arm round my shoulder and started walking in the direction of the NAAFI. 'This calls for a celebration. Cocoa and buns!'

'Don't get your hopes up too high. It's only a page in a little mag.'

'Yeah, but a page! A full page! Fucking fantastic!'

'And it's not one of the really big ones …'

'I don't care if it's the parish newsletter, mate, it's a start! We just have to get a foot in the door. Once they see what we can do, they'll be all fucking over us.'

Suddenly everything was 'us' and 'we'.

'We've got to do more, Michael. Supply and demand, mate. We've got to be ready for it. I need new trunks. I've seen them zebra striped ones in *Man's World*. I want some of them. Or tiger.

Or leopard! How about that? Can you see me in leopard skin?'
He snarled and extended his claws.

'Down, boy. One thing at a time.'

'Fuck that. I want it all. I want it now.' He leaned forward, the
steam from the cocoa wreathing his face. 'I'm hard.'

'What?'

'You heard. I'm fucking stiff as a post.'

'Go on.'

'Don't believe me?' He grabbed my hand under the table.
'Cop a feel.'

'Wright, for Christ's sake! Someone will see.'

'Great. The sooner we get out of this dump the better. Let's
give 'em something to talk about.'

I got up, cleared the table. Wright followed. He hadn't been
lying. Thank God everyone was concentrating on their food and
drink.

'I haven't forgotten, you know.' I was pacing fast across the
parade ground, back towards the SSQ. Wright was keeping up
with me.

'What?'

'You know what. That night.'

'Oh.'

'What's the matter, Mike?' He grabbed my elbow, stopped
me, spun me round to face him.

'You ... you just don't know what ... I mean, all these weeks
and now, suddenly ...' I didn't know what to say. If I started
telling the truth, where would it end?

'I do know,' he said, quite calm now. 'And I'm trying to
understand.'

'Right.'

Kelsey came strutting towards us, fatter and angrier than ever.
Wright went to meet him. 'Sarge! What a treat. I was just telling
Airman Medway, we don't see enough of your handsome face
these days.'

I made my escape, and fled to the sanctuary of the files.

I wrote back to Stephen, with details of my arrival at Euston.

London is not entirely strange to me. My parents used to take me to art galleries as a child, and I once spent a week with an aunt in St John's Wood. I've visited several times on my own since the age of sixteen. I know the basic geography, and I can manage the Tubes. I've read Waugh and Galsworthy and Woolf, so I'm familiar with Mayfair and Bayswater and Bloomsbury, at least in theory. I read the Sunday papers, so I know that Soho is a haunt of vice and that Chelsea is full of queers. But beyond that, I have very little idea of the sort of life that London might offer to a demobbed national serviceman, and it's time to find out. Which is why I'm on a train headed south, finally using one of my seventy-twos to take a holiday in the bright lights.

As the train pulled out of Crewe Junction, a couple of soldiers, who had been sitting quietly reading newspapers and doing crossroads, got up and walked to the lavatories. Fifteen minutes later, they emerged, transformed. The uniforms had gone, replaced by soft open-necked shirts in lavender and lemon, the boots exchanged for brown suede loafers. Their hair had doubled in volume, and they left a whiff of sandalwood in their wake. One of them turned, looked back at me and whispered to his friend. They both looked, and giggled.

Stephen was waiting on the platform at Euston. In the months since I've seen him, he's been transformed. His hair is longer, of course; everyone grows their hair out after demob. But Stephen's wasn't just long – it was *done*. It curled up in a lustrous golden quiff, it was cut into the back of his neck, and when he saw me looking he proudly patted it. His face glistened, his high cheekbones catching the light. His eyes were dark. A herringbone scarf was tossed over one shoulder. His shirt was pale green, his sweater salmon pink. He wore blue jeans – real, genuine blue denim jeans – and the same brown suede loafers as I'd seen on the train. That myth was based on fact, then. As soon as I opened the carriage door, he raised his arms in a double-handed wave.

'Michael!' Heads turned. The two young queers stared and whispered. I stepped down, and made sure my suitcase was between me and Stephen, in case he tried to take my arm.

He started talking immediately. 'Oh, there's so much to tell you! I can't believe how much has happened! Well of course getting out was the best thing I ever did, you should have seen their faces when they found me lying there like Theda Bara in the back of that old ambulance, screaming my tits off.'

'Yes. I want a word about that.'

'Wasn't it marvellous? Oh, hello boys, what's a nice girl like me doing in a dump like this. I thought they were going to ravish me, my dear!'

We bought Tube tickets and descended the escalator.

'You might have warned me of your plans.'

'If you'd played your cards right, you could have been out by now as well.'

'I have no desire to be "out", as you put it.'

He pursed his lips and looked at me. 'You'll change your tune soon enough. Here's our train. Westward ho!'

I sweated all the way round the Circle line, convinced that people were staring. We made an odd couple: me in my uniform, Stephen in his. I shuddered at every flap of his wrists, every crossing and re-crossing of his legs, every emphasised sibilant. But nobody stared, nobody even looked. A handsome older man in a sports jacket, perhaps forty, caught my eye and smiled, but got off at Edgware Road.

Stephen kept chattering. 'You'll love my flat, it's quite bijou. Room for us both, and room for a friend if it comes to that. Oh, I've had some marvellous parties already, we can really let our hair down. And of course it's convenient for everything, the Serpentine, Earl's Court, Chelsea, and I mean if the handbag's empty you can practically walk everywhere, and you always bump into someone you know, or if you're lucky, someone you don't!'

We got out at Bayswater.

'Welcome to Fairyland!' said Stephen. 'Now, let's get you out of that ghastly uniform.'

The flat was in an elegant redbrick block, with a carpeted lobby and a lift. I wondered how much Stephen was earning as the art director of *Muscle Boy* magazine.

He waltzed around the living room. 'Isn't it divine?' Two large windows looked down on to Queensway, there were two red leather Chesterfields and an awful lot of *objets d'art*.

'Lovely,' I said. 'Where am I …?'

'In the guest room, of course. Unless …' He posed seductively in the doorway. 'No. Thought not. Well, you can't blame a girl for trying. Here we are. All the comforts of home.'

There was a divan, an armchair, and a dressing table with a vase of chrysanthemums on it.

'It's very nice. Thank you for the flowers.'

'I'm blushing! Now get out of that ghastly drab and get yourself zhoozhed. We're going out.'

When I emerged ten minutes later, he looked disapproving. 'Oh dear. Oh very dear.'

'What's the matter?'

'We're going out. We're not going to church.'

I was wearing flannel trousers, a navy blue blazer, a white shirt and a plaid tie.

'Please don't be offended, but would you mind if I just …' He loosened my tie, undid the top button of my shirt. 'No, not quite. Let me see …' He removed the tie altogether, and rearranged the shirt collar outside my jacket. 'Better. I don't suppose you'd consider a cravat?'

'No, I would not.'

'Shame. Well, one more button.'

'I can do that for myself, thank you very much.'

'Oooh, Airman Medway, I'm not trying to undress you!'

We walked through Hyde Park, where a few determined sunbathers soaked up the last rays of the afternoon. 'I say,' said Stephen, gazing at a particularly tanned young man who was getting dressed as slowly as possible, 'isn't he bona?'

As we proceeded along Piccadilly, he got bolder.

'Look! There's Vauxhall Vera! Oooh-ooh! Vera!'

A figure in a loud check jacket lurched out of a doorway. 'Hello Stevie, dear. Who's the trade?'

'This isn't trade, dear. Allow me to introduce my good friend Michael. Michael, this is Vera, the biggest queen this side of Buckingham Palace.'

'Charmed, I'm sure,' said Vera, extending a hand weighed down with bangles, the nails perfect ovals, French polished. 'My, what a strong grip. First time out, dear?'

'I suppose.'

'Well watch her.' He nodded towards Stephen. 'She's notorious.'

'Oh!' Stephen pulled me away. 'We're not listening to another word!' We proceeded on our way, arm in arm. 'Honestly. She's such a wicked bitch. Talk about the pot calling the kettle beige.'

I disentangled myself. 'Please, Stephen. That's enough.'

'You've been in the RAF too long. Time to relax.'

'It's just so ... effeminate.'

'Well? I am effeminate.'

'I didn't mean to offend you.'

Stephen walked on. 'I'm not offended. I know what I am. The doctors at Halton told me often enough. I am an effeminate homosexual, an invert, a path ... What's the word?'

'Pathic.'

'A pathic. That's right. I'm one of them and all. What are you?'

We stopped outside Simpsons and looked at the windows. 'I don't know.'

'Let's go and find out, then.' He squeezed my arm again.

'Look at those lovely cream leather gloves. Oh, let me buy them for you, Michael, please.'

'Absolutely not. Come on. Wherever we're going, let's go there.'

He marched me along the street towards Eros.

'Emerald City is closer and prettier than ever!'

'Where are we going?'

'Here!'

From the outside, it looked no different from any other West End pub: etched glass windows, a bit of dirty red carpet under the worn doormat, a grimy sign that announced it as The Standard. The bar was almost empty, a few couples sipping halves of bitter or gin and tonics.

'Follow me!' Stephen opened a door on to a staircase. Laughter, music and smoke poured down. The couples cringed, and looked at the floor. 'Up you go.'

The upstairs bar was crowded with men, some in business suits, some in casual jackets, a few in colourful sweaters and a smattering of military uniforms. Stephen was greeted on every side with shrieks and laughter, even a few pecks on the cheek. Bangles jangled and eyes rolled. From the jukebox, Connie Francis asked 'Who's Sorry Now?'

I was. I would have backed out, but there were others coming up behind me.

'Come on, let me introduce you to some interesting people. Look over there! That's him off the telly!'

I recognised a familiar face. 'What on earth is he doing here?'

'That soldier, by the look of things.'

We fought our way through to a space between the bar and the window, and I stood with my back to the wall. I had already been touched half a dozen times.

'See over there?'

'Oh my God.' Squeezed into a tight white T-shirt and a pair of blue jeans was a body that I recognised from the pages of *Man's World*. 'He's not ... is he?'

'If the price is right he is. That's that film bloke he's talking to. Casting-Couch Carol, we call her. Don't stare.'

'Jesus!'

'What? Is she here too?'

'I've just seen someone I was in basic with.' I shielded my face, hoping the young man in question wouldn't see me.

'Oh, they all come in here. I've met no end. You'd be surprised. Even the butchest ones.'

'Why?'

'Is he in uniform, your friend?'

'Yes.'

'Then he's on the batter.'

'The ... batter?'

'The game. The rent.'

'He can't be. He was always talking about girls.'

'They're the worst, dear. Bore you to death on the subject, even while you're ... Well, you know.'

'But you don't ... do you?'

'What? Pay for it? No, dear, not me. I can't afford those fancy prices. I say, look sharp! Off they go!' The television personality was leading his new uniformed friend towards the stairs. 'He's got rooms in Half Moon Street, I believe. Oh, if walls could talk!'

'But it's so dangerous.'

'Not really, as long as you have an understanding landlady and you don't pick up a blackmailer.'

'Blackmail? Oh my God.'

'Doesn't frighten me, dear. I'm beyond blackmail. I mean, who are they going to tell? My family? My employer?'

'The police.'

'Oh, them. But if they tell the police, they'd be in trouble too, wouldn't they? Because I'd stand up in court and tell them everything. Everything! Ooh, I'd make their eyes water.'

'You could go to prison.'

'Can't be worse than National Service.'

I wanted to run. Any minute now I expected to see coppers swarming through the door.

'Relax, Michael. You look as nervous as a kitten. I prescribe gin. Large ones!' He signalled to the barman, a made-up little chorus boy with a disappointed pout. We drank, and I felt better, or at least numb.

'So, how are all my dear friends at Reville? How is that gorgeous creature Sergeant Kelsey? Does he miss me terribly? My dear, there's a closet case if ever there was one.'

'He's a pain in the arse, as usual.'

'What a disgusting thought.'

'But I can put up with him.'

'Strikes me you put up with altogether too much. You should just get out.'

'That's what Wright says.'

'Oh yes, the lovely Airman Wright, with his bedroom eyes and his dining room lips. They've been swooning over him at *Muscle Boy*, I tell you. He could make a fortune down here.'

'I'm not sure if that's quite the career he has in mind.'

'Well you tell him from me that he'd be living in the lap of luxury if he shows his pretty face in London.'

'That's what I'm afraid of.'

'Jealous, are we? I did wonder. So, you finally got him, did you?'

'For Christ's sake, Stephen. The way you talk.'

'I'll take that as a yes.'

'I just don't want him falling into bad company. He's so impressionable.'

'Oh please. Rita Wright? She's about as impressionable as a rhino.'

'You're wrong. He thinks the streets are paved with gold.'

'And for the likes of him, they are.'

'He's not a whore.'

The barman heard the word, gasped theatrically and put a hand to his collar.

'Look, Stephen, you've got the wrong idea. Wright is normal. He's just … well, he gets …'

'Frustrated? Don't tell me. He was so randy, and the women were all bitches, and he was drunk, and the next morning he didn't remember a thing.'

'It wasn't like that.'

'What was it like, then?'

'What is this, Stephen? The Spanish Inquisition?'

'No, dear. I learned my interrogation techniques at Halton. They know how to worm a girl's secrets out of her.'

'Thankfully, I don't know anything about that.'

Stephen looked over the top of his gin. 'Yet,' he said, and took a swig.

The next port of call was in Gerrard Street, another tatty doorway with the words 'The Captain's Cabin' painted in jaunty white lettering with a few nautical motifs on a blackboard. A steep, narrow staircase led up to a heavy wooden door. It took a good shove to get it open. Again, there was a gust of noise, but this time it was immediately hushed, as a dozen pairs of eyes turned towards us. There was a second of silence – the jukebox had chosen that moment to change records – and the volume rose again, along with the voice of Tommy Edwards, 'It's All in the Game'. There was the same mix of civilians and servicemen, the majority of them sailors, and, to my surprise, a number of women.

'Girls from the local brothels,' said Stephen. 'They come in for a rest. Well, they're not going to be bothered, are they?'

He led the way to the bar, where a tubby little man was wiping glasses.

'This is Max, the most celebrated landlord in London.'

'I don't want any trouble tonight, Stevie. Is that clear?'

'Trouble? Moi? The very idea.'

Max poured large slugs of gin into two glasses. 'Who's your friend?'

'This is Michael. He's still in the RAF.'

'Bad luck, dear.' He pushed the drinks towards us. 'On the house.'

We clinked and drank. The gin was neat, but quite possibly watered down.

'Has Tony been in, Max?'

'No. And if he does, I warned you ...'

'All right. Keep your hair on.' We sat at a table. 'What's left of it.'

'Who's Tony?' The gin was starting to hit me.

'He's my ... publisher.'

'Ah. Maybe I could meet him. Talk about photography.'

'Yes. You'll meet him, I expect.' He scowled.

'What's the matter?'

'If you must know, we've had a little ... difference of opinion.'

'You've not lost your job, have you?'

'Nothing like that. If you must know, I told him I wanted him to leave his wife. There's no need to look so shocked. People do have wives, you know.'

'But he's your ...' I didn't know the right word. Lover? Boyfriend?

'Oh dear. You've got a lot to learn. Tony is a very respectable married man. Well, he's Italian, at any rate. He has a lot of business connections, and he's terribly successful, and it wouldn't do for them to know that he's screwing me on the side.' He slammed his empty glass on the table. 'But I'm sick of his respectability! If he loves me like he says, he should bloody well want to be with me all the time!' Heads were turning.

'Stephen, please, lower your voice.'

'Oh, let them stare. I don't give a damn. Let's have another drink.'

'Shouldn't we get something to eat?'

'What? And ruin this sylphlike figure? Max! *Encore deux gins, s'il vous plaît.*'

Max brought the drinks, and shot a warning look at Stephen. I tried to steer the conversation back into safer waters.

'So, it must pay well, your job. Judging by the flat and everything.'

'That comes with the position.'

'Do all employees get a place to live?'

'It's Tony's flat. He's sort of … installed me there.'

'I see.'

'He has quite a lot of flats.'

'And does he have people … installed in all of them?'

'Aren't you full of questions? If you must know, he's got tarts in most of them.'

'You're not by any chance a tart as well, are you?'

'Certainly not.' He rearranged his scarf. 'I'm an art director. There is a difference.' He drank. 'Just about.'

A short man with long grey hair sticking out from under a dirty maroon beret was toasting us from across the room.

'Who's that, Stephen?'

'What? Where? Oh, Christ. Gerald.' He raised his glass in return. 'Hello, Gerald. Oh no, she's coming over. Watch your family jewels, dear.'

'Gerald?' The name was familiar from the muscle mags: Photo by Gerald, Studio Gerald. 'The Gerald?'

'In person,' said the little man, extending a hand with a gold signet ring. The accent was hard to place, possibly American.

'Gerald, allow me to introduce my dear friend Michael Medway, a very promising young photographer. You may recall the pictures I showed you of that dolly bit of rough in the posing pouch.'

'Ah, what exceptional talent.' I wasn't sure if he was referring to me or the photographs. 'You have the eye.' He held on to my hand. 'You could go far, my boy.'

'All right, Gerald. Hands off. He's mine.'

'Come and see me some time.' Gerald pulled a dirty, creased card from his wallet, which was bulging with banknotes. The card bore an Oxford Street address. 'Now if you will excuse me, I have a little business to attend to. See you later!'

'And we know what sort of business that is, don't we?' said Stephen, as Gerald resumed conversation with a uniformed sailor. 'That one will be out of his bell bottoms before the night is over.'

'Really?'

'I don't know how he gets away with it. He's going to end up in prison, or worse.'

'Why?'

Stephen lowered his voice to a whisper. 'Because, my dear, he does dirty pictures.'

'You mean nudes?' I thought of those photographs stashed at the back of the filing cabinet in faraway Reville.

'And more. You know. Sexy stuff.' He made a delicate masturbatory gesture. 'Sometimes twos and threes.'

'Oh my goodness.' My cheeks were burning, and not just from the gin. 'And he sells them, right there, out of his studio. I've seen them. I've been round to collect pics for the mag. He's shown me. My dear! It would make your hair curl.'

'But you don't print nudes.'

'Oh no. That's for private customers only. You know, reply to the ad at the back of the mag, send off your postal order, get the catalogue, and if you can read between the lines of all that crap about uninhibited natural poses, you pop along to the studio with a wallet full of cash and *voilà!* All the cock you can eat.'

Gerald was lining up more drinks for his new discovery.

'Look at him! Look at the money! My God, he's as rich as Croesus. I wish I had a bit of that. I'd have a dinky little car and holidays in the south of France and dinner at posh restaurants and a nice husband to keep house for.'

'Is that what you want?'

'Yes, dear. Are you available at all?'

'I'm afraid not.'

'Oh well. Some day my prince will come.'

'And you'll live happily ever after?'

'Why not?'

'That doesn't happen for people like us.'

'Oh! Like "us" now, is it?'

'You know what I mean.'

'I certainly do, dear. And why shouldn't it? Why shouldn't we get the same chance of happiness as everyone else?'

'I don't know. But we never will.'

'Well I think we will.' His voice was getting loud again. 'Maybe not in our lifetime, but one day.'

'Look around you, Stephen. Is this your brave new world?'

'Yes it is. The freaks will inherit the earth.'

'If you believe that, you're a fool.'

'Who's the fool, dear? Me or you? At least I'm being honest.'

'And I'm not, I suppose.'

'No. You're not, and you know it. You're living a lie. You're pretending you're normal because you're scared to death of being one of us.'

'I'm not one of you. Not … this.'

'You're a coward, Michael. I'm going to stand up and be counted.'

We were both drunk by now. 'And you'll be rounded up and sent away to prison.'

'I'm not frightened.'

'Then you should be.'

'For God's sake, Michael, you're an intelligent man. Don't you read the papers? We don't live in Russia, you know. People don't just disappear. We have laws here.'

'Laws that forbid our very existence.'

'Yes dear,' said Stephen, laying a hand on top of mine, 'but laws can be changed, can't they?'

07

Another card from Michael this morning inviting me to come and visit him, nothing about the fact that I haven't responded to any of his other cards, just saying 'I know how busy you are', which I am of course. I don't really know why he's so keen to see me, I hardly know him, and I don't know why I feel so bad about not visiting him either, much worse than I feel, for instance, about not visiting my parents or my sister. The truth is that I'm finding it hard to face anyone outside my immediate circle because I just don't think they would understand what I'm going through and to have to explain would be even more exhausting than living it in the first place.

Stuart calls me at work and tells me where we're meeting tonight. This is the usual routine now. I don't know until the afternoon if I'm seeing him at all, and if I am seeing him, what we're doing, except that it's always the same thing, we go to a party of some sort, then we go to a club, then we go back to my place, where Stuart spends five nights out of seven. The other two nights he spends at his place – or perhaps it would be more accurate to say he spends them 'not at my place', because I have no proof that he goes home, it's just a convenient thing to believe. We never spend the night together at his place. We did it once, and he was so jumpy we couldn't even watch TV. When he's with me, he's relaxed and horny and even sometimes affectionate, that is when we're not arguing or he's not storming downstairs to shout at the neighbours. Stuart has taken it into his own hands to escalate a minor neighbour dispute about noise and cooking smells into all-out war. He can't stand noise, unless he's making it, and so when the door slammed once too often he flew down the stairs, cornered some hapless African woman and laid into her with a stream of invective. She gave as good as she got, and it has made matters much, much worse. I will wait across the road before entering the block if I see them outside the flat, and will hide in my flat until they've gone before leaving. I can't sleep without Valium now, I'm so wound up by every single bump or footstep or gurgle of the water pipes. If Stuart's here, I'm terrified that he'll charge downstairs and start World War Three again. If he's not here, I feel anxious and vulnerable. I wish Michael had not left.

So, where was I? Oh yes, tonight. Stuart calls me at work and tells me where we're meeting tonight, and I'm rather surprised to learn that it's at Hadley's. I haven't been to Hadley's since the party where we met, and my first thought is that I might run into Jonathan, which will be embarrassing because we still haven't spoken since that night he walked out of the pub. It's our longest ever split, and I guess it's terminal, which means we'll either have to avoid each other, or make polite small talk, or have a big public row, which at least might lead to a reconciliation. I am missing Jonathan far more than I'm prepared to admit. The only person I've got to talk to is Stuart, and he's no good because the thing I really need to talk about *is* Stuart. Jonathan is a terrible listener, but talking to him is one step up from talking to myself, which I'm doing far more than is healthy. Sometimes I even do it at work. The new person who sits opposite me at Anna's old desk gives me very funny looks and I realise that I'm muttering.

Hadley's parties really aren't what they used to be, because this time there are no waiters, and no champagne, just a table covered in bottles and plastic glasses to which we are invited to help ourselves. The boys who used to serve the drinks are now guests, which either means that they're doing well and climbing the social ladder, or that Hadley is slipping down it and is obliged to socialise with 'the help'. Either way, there are a lot of them, they all look like Nico-variants, and are possibly from the same village/gene pool. They wear the same horrible designer clothes and have the same interesting hairstyles, in any colour as long as it's black.

Even though I arrive a bit late, Stuart is not there.

'Ah,' says Hadley, lumbering into my path, 'it's the Robster. Good to see you, mate.' He never could keep his hands off me, but this time it's more to steady himself than to molest me. I'm shocked at his appearance. He's still huge, but his cheeks are sunken and his eyes, which used to be buried in puffy, over-tanned flesh, are protruding.

'Hey, Hadley. How's it going?'

'Yeah, fine, fine, fine ... Never better, mate ... Wow look here comes Stuart.'

And here does come Stuart, beaming and swaggering and chatting to everyone he sees. At this rate it will be at least ten minutes before he traverses the five yards that separate us.

'Have you seen Jonathan, Hadley?'

'Who?'

'My friend Jonathan. Oh, er, Nathan. Nate.' I nearly add 'the one who owes you several thousand pounds' but think better of it. Perhaps they have come to some kind of agreement. I shudder to think what.

'No,' says Hadley, and suddenly has to take a call. He turns his back on me and crouches over his phone. All the black-haired boys are watching him for some kind of sign.

'Stuart.' I touch him on the shoulder, with a smile on my face that I don't really feel. He barely turns his head, acknowledges me with a little wave of the hand and carries on talking to some grinning musclebound lummox that I recognise from the clubs. I wait, like a 1950s wife at a cocktail party. No attempt is being made to include me in the conversation, which is about people I don't know, although every so often the lummox looks at me over Stuart's shoulder. He has pale blue eyes and blond hair, and quite frankly he looks shifty, if sexually attractive.

I'm bored of being ignored, so I go over to the bar and help myself to a large glass of white wine. I actually hate white wine, and would only ever drink it with a meal if someone insisted, but it's all there is apart from beer, and beer is even more full of unwanted carbs, so wine it is.

'You are Rrroberrrt.'

It's one of the black-haired boys, possibly the one that was with Hadley when I first ever met him, possibly his brother, cousin or uncle.

'Yes. Hi.'

'You are Stuart's friend.'

'Guilty as charged.'

'Tell me,' he says, standing too close, 'how does it feel?'

I'm about to ask him what he's talking about when suddenly Stuart is at my side, an arm round my neck in a wrestling hold, his fist rubbing my scalp – this is one of his favourite greetings, and a sure sign that he's high.

'Robbieeeeeee!' He pulls me away from the bar. 'What are you doing over here? Come back and join us.'

'I was just getting a drink. Who was that?'

'Who? That? One of Hadley's boys. I don't know. They all look the same to me, luv,' he says in a northern club comedian voice.

'He was about to ask me something.'

'Oh Christ, he didn't ask you for money, did he?'

'No, he said …'

'Robbie, this is Matt.' All Stuart's friends have names like Matt, or Jake, or Guy. Straight names.

'Robbie.' It's the lummox. He's got his thumbs hooked into the belt loops of his jeans, pulling them down so I can see underwear. His lower stomach is flat and tanned and covered in a light dusting of golden hair.

'We thought we might go somewhere,' says Stuart, shifting from foot to foot like an athlete warming up for a race.

'Right. Where?'

'Yours?'

'What, now?'

'Yeah,' says Stuart. 'Why not?'

'I don't want to go back there. I'm sick of the fucking place.'

I see Stuart and Matt exchange a glance, as if they're dealing with a troublesome child.

'Come on, Robbie. It's nearest.'

'What's the big hurry? I thought we were going out.'

'We are out. But sometimes staying in is the new going out.'

Stuart's grinning, and Matt is concentrating on smouldering, and I'm in no mood for either of them. I want to go out dancing, take drugs, listen to deafening music, show off my muscles and forget about everything, my neighbours, my job, my sleep problems, my acne, my debts, Michael, Jonathan, Hadley, the weird black-haired guy and whatever it was he was trying to ask me. I want to forget about Matt. I want to forget about Stuart. I want to forget about sex, which is the last thing I feel like at the moment, and certainly not with a complete stranger.

'No,' I snap. 'You two do whatever you want. I'm going to Vacuum.'

They look at each other again – positively a conspiratorial glance – and I see Matt giving the tiniest of nods.

'Actually,' he says, 'Vacuum could be fun.'

And so we leave Hadley's, and go to Vacuum – in a cab, of course. I'm staring out the window, watching the orange street lights against the darkening sky, wondering what the fuck that guy meant when he asked me 'how does it feel?' Stuart and Matt are making small talk, apparently to coax me out of my sulk.

'Well that wasn't exactly the party of the decade,' says Stuart.

'I've had more fun at funerals,' says Matt, with a giggle. I don't doubt that this is true.

'Still,' says Stuart, 'it's quite exciting in a way, to see which one gets Hadley first. The law, or the cancer.'

'What?'

'Oh, didn't you know?' Stuart and Matt exchange a pitying look. 'The police are busting all the dealers. Hadley's number is up. When they find out about his little business model ...'

'Which is what, exactly?'

'Like a pizza delivery company. You get your basic piece of trade, most of it to a traditional Eastern European recipe, with or without a variety of toppings that include cocaine, Viagra, GHB.'

'Mozzarella, anchovies, spicy sausage,' adds Matt, still giggling. 'And the cancer?'

'Oh, that,' says Stuart, as if he's already bored of the subject. 'Yeah, he's dying. Everyone knows that.'

I did not know that. How could I know that? Stuart is looking at me with a little smile at the corner of his mouth, one eyebrow half raised, as if to say 'beat that'.

'That's awful,' I say, but we've arrived at Vacuum and now we're fumbling for money. Before I know it, Matt has paid and the cab is driving off. He puts an arm round my shoulder, an arm round Stuart's, and we walk into the club as if we (or at least he) own the place, which for all I know he does.

Vacuum is your basic black box with lights and music, and it's open pretty much twenty-four hours a day, seven days a week, and here the concept of time is much more simple than in other clubs. In Vacuum, whatever the time and whatever the day, it's always Friday night. There is no bar, just a very large cloakroom at which you check as many of your clothes as you possibly can. There are large ice buckets dotted around the edge of the room, containing plastic bottles of water, but rumour has it they've been opened and refilled with tap water, possibly spiked, so people either bring their own or go thirsty. There are drug dealers stationed at the four corners of the club, doing a brisk trade in GHB, crystal meth, cocaine and ecstasy. You are, of course, searched at the door, to make sure you're not bringing any Class As on to the premises – but this, I presume, is to protect the domestic trade. Everyone is gurning and sweating and dancing, and the music is ear-splittingly loud.

Despite this, Matt and Stuart seem able to carry on a conversation from which I am completely excluded; perhaps they can lip read. We hit the dance floor, and Stuart comes up behind me and lifts my shirt over my head. Matt is dancing in front of me, doing something complicated with his hips, his arms held out in front of him as if his shoulders are paralysed. He has a big, stocky, muscular body which I ought to find attractive, but there's something about him I don't like. Perhaps it's the way he's staring at me as if he's watching a porn video. He comes closer and starts 'bumping pussies' as Jonathan used to call it. I'm unable to retreat because Stuart is grinding into me from the rear, and I realise I'm the filling in a 'mandwich'. Stuart engineered a few threesomes when we were on holiday, and hasn't stopped going on about it since, despite the fact that I've made it quite clear that I don't like sharing, or being shared.

We dance for about half an hour, then sit it out for a while, and Matt passes round water. Normally I would only drink my own supply in a place like this, but Matt is a friend of Stuart's, and Stuart's drinking it and putting the bottle to my lips, so I guess it's okay. I quickly realise that it isn't, when the familiar rush of GHB kicks in and instead of going back to the dance floor, we're piling into a cab that seems conveniently to have been waiting for us at the door.

The cab ride is actually the sexiest part of the evening. Matt and Stuart have got their shirts back on, but I seem still to be without mine, lying across their laps, with Matt paying a great deal of attention to my tits. He's pinching them and squeezing them and sucking them, keeping up a stream of porn dialogue like 'Yeah baby' and 'You like that, don't you?', which under normal circumstances would be a complete turn-off but, under the influence of G, it works. Stuart is grinning, his eyes hooded, and I'm abandoning myself to the situation. The driver doesn't give us a second look.

I don't know where we're going until I recognise my own street. I assumed that we were going back to Matt's, wherever that may be, but no, here we are in front of the old familiar block, climbing the stairs, slamming the doors, rolling around on the hall floor before crawling like a six-legged, three-backed beast into the living room.

Matt cannot take his hands and mouth off my tits, and keeps whipping out his mobile phone to take pictures of me, and what he's doing to me, as if the memory is going to be more important to him than the actual experience. I'm still feeling super-horny, but I'm recovering because I'm beginning to think that Matt is ridiculous again, whereas twenty minutes ago in the back of the cab I thought (and kept telling him) that he was 'fucking hot'.

Stuart meanwhile is coming in from the rear, and has wrestled me out of my jeans and shoes so that I am naked while he and Matt are clothed. Obviously this appeals to my sense of vanity, and we go with the flow for a while, and before I know it Stuart is sticking a load of lube up my arse and is about to fuck me. Matt is slobbering over my chest, and my nipples are actually getting quite sore now.

Stuart manoeuvres me into a kneeling position and slides his cock into me; I haven't even checked whether he's got a condom on. He's taking a big hit from a bottle of poppers which he then sticks under my nose, and I inhale. There's a huge rush as he starts fucking me, and then Matt gets back on to my tits like a pig returning to the trough, and we carry on like this for a while, banging away. The neighbours must be furious, I think, and that's when I know that the drugs are really wearing off and I'm actually not enjoying this at all.

Somehow the entire show has now moved to the bedroom – I

don't remember getting here – and now it's Matt who's getting fucked while burying his face in my chest. I'm feeling like garnish. Stuart's eyes are half closed, only the whites visible, and he looks more than usually mask-like. He's been banging away for what seems like an hour, and shows no signs of finishing. Occasionally he slaps Matt's arse, or grunts out some obscene monosyllable.

Suddenly I'm revolted by the whole scenario, I want these people out of my house, out of my bed. I push Matt's face away from my chest and extricate myself from the various limbs.

Stuart's eyes flash open.

'Where you going?'

'I've had enough. I'd like to be alone.'

'Go on, then. Suit yourself.'

Matt is so out of it that he doesn't seem to notice I've gone, and carries on licking the air where my tits were. Stuart keeps mechanically fucking him.

'No,' I say. 'I mean, I think you should leave.'

'Fuck off,' says Stuart, and that's it. His eyelids come down like shutters, he grips Matt's hips and carries on pumping.

I go to the living room, and lie on the sofa. I don't have a spare duvet or a sleeping bag, so when I start feeling cold I pull the rug up off the floor and wrap myself in that. I can hear Stuart and Matt at it in the bedroom, I can hear the downstairs neighbours crashing around and shouting into their mobile phones, and as I drift into sleep I can hear voices and music in my head, as if I'm still in the club.

I get up for a piss around first light, and peep through the door into the bedroom. Matt is fast asleep in Stuart's arms. They look very peaceful and happy. I feel as if someone has stuck a butcher's knife in my stomach and is twisting it.

I go back to the sofa, but I can't sleep again. I listen to every sound. Eventually I hear lowered voices from next door, the toilet flushing, the front door opening and closing. Then footsteps pad back to the bedroom.

Stuart has the duvet pulled over his head.

'Hey.'

'Go away,' he says, 'I'm tired.'

'We need to talk.'

'Not now.'

'Yes,' I say, pulling the duvet off him and feeling sick when I see his naked body, 'now.'

He sits up with a face like thunder.

'What? Go on. What do you want to say to me?'

I don't know what to say, I'm too close to tears.

'You expect an apology or something? Well forget it.'

'Who is Matt, exactly?'

'What do you mean, who is Matt? You know perfectly well who Matt is.'

I don't, actually, but I let it pass. 'I mean, what is he to you?'

'He's a good friend.'

'A fuck buddy.'

'Have it your way.'

I sit down on the bed, and try to sound less confrontational. The sun has hit the blinds; it's going to be a lovely day.

'I've told you before, Stuart, I don't like threesomes.'

'Well I do.'

'And I think it's a bit much bringing him back here.'

'You weren't complaining.'

'I was off my face.'

'So what's the problem?'

I lose my temper. 'What's the problem? I don't like being passed around like a piece of meat. I don't like Matt and you sniggering and nudging each other like you've discussed it all before. I don't like being treated as a walking pair of tits.'

'Oh don't you.'

'No I don't.' He's as cold as ice.

'So why do you spend so much time in the gym, then, pumping them up?' He grabs my tits and squeezes them hard.

They're sore from last night, and it hurts. I push his hand away.

'Fuck off.'

'Yeah,' says Stuart, pulling on a T-shirt. 'I think I will.'

He's dressed and out of the door in seconds.

'Wait!' I shout after him. 'Don't go like this! We need to talk.'

I hear his footsteps echoing down the stairwell, watch him striding out across the road, the sun in his hair.

'Stuart!'

He doesn't look back.

Seven

I am writing this in the form of a letter to myself because the diary is no longer in my hands. I packaged it up in several layers of brown paper and a lot of thick string and sent it to myself care of my parents, marked PRIVATE AND CONFIDENTIAL. I posted it in the village, and I will do the same with this letter. I don't trust the post at Reville.

Things moved fast after my trip to London. Wright ambushed me the moment I got back to the camp.

'So? When am I going to be famous? I bet their bloody mouths are watering!'

I was hung over from another night on the tiles with Stephen, followed by tearful farewells at Euston and an exhausting journey in an overcrowded Sunday train.

'Give me a chance.'

'Did you see them?'

'Who?'

'The editors, the producers, the casting people, the agents.'

'Yes, but …'

'What did they say? Do they want me? What were the clubs like? Did you go to the 2 Is? How's Poynter? Did he make a pass at you? What are the birds like? How are they dressing these days?'

He was all over me like an eager puppy. 'I need to have a shit and a shower, Mervyn. Can you wait that long?'

'No, I bloody can't!'

'Well unless you want to join me in the shower, you'll have to.'

We met in the village pub, which was quieter than anywhere on the base. Wright was still full of questions.

'Look, Mervyn,' I said, 'there's no point in getting so worked up. We've still got months to do here.'

'Fuck that. I'll get out.'

'And what will you do for a job?'

'I won't need a job. I'm going to be a fucking star, mate.'

'Even stars have to eat.'

'I won't be short of people to buy me dinner.'

Of that I was sure. 'Do you know what sort of world you're getting yourself into?'

'Yeah. Queers, mostly. Is that what you're saying?'

'Yes. But not just that. It's a shady business ...' I thought of Gerald, his wispy grey hair, his filthy beret. 'You've got to watch out.'

'You're just worried someone will take me away from you.'

'Don't be ...' I had to swallow. 'Don't be silly.'

'Look, Mike, I'm sorry. While we're here, you're my best pal and you're the only cunt in the place I can talk to. But it's not enough. Out there, there's a lot of opportunities. I've got to grab 'em while I can.'

'Don't be so bloody patronising.'

'What?'

'Like I'm some lovestruck girl that you're giving the brush-off.'

'Why not? You're acting like one.'

'God, you have a high opinion of yourself.'

'You're pretty keen, from what I remember.'

Our eyes locked. It all seemed so hopeless, him and me, Stephen's world in London, the future. 'So I'm just a stepping stone, am I?'

'That's not what I meant.'

'I'll do, till something better comes along.' I was in pain, and I wanted to hurt him back.

'Oh, fuck this,' said Wright, draining his pint and pushing back his chair. 'If I want to be nagged, I'll get a fucking wife.'

He walked out of the pub, combing his hair.

This time we didn't speak for nearly two months. I lost sleep and lost weight. Wright was more popular than ever. He won another big boxing match, which I did not attend, and was given a gala dinner in the officers' mess. He was off the base every weekend. He seemed to get as much leave as he wanted.

One night, we were both down for guard duty together. I tried to get the rota changed, but no go.

Hours passed with nothing but the essential exchanges. We took it in turns to walk around the perimeter, check the out-buildings, avoiding being together in the guard hut. Finally, towards three a.m., when the sky was pitch black and the rest of the camp as quiet as the grave, Wright came in, put his feet up on the table and lit two cigarettes. We smoked for a while without talking.

'I'm off to London soon,' he said, 'did you know?'

'I did hear.'

'Big fight. National title. Honour of the camp and all that jazz.'

'Good luck.'

'Thanks.'

We smoked a little more.

'You want to come?'

'What?'

'To London, wanker.'

'Why?'

'I don't know. Show me round. Protect me from perverts.'

'Fuck off.'

Cigarettes finished, he filled the kettle and lit the gas ring.

'I'm not coming back, you know.'

'What?'

'From London. I'm not coming back here.'

'What are you talking about? You can't go AWOL.'

'Watch me.'

'You'll end up in the slammer.'

'They'll have to catch me first.' He put a mug of tea in front of me, lit more cigarettes. 'Shouldn't be smoking, really. I'm supposed to be in training.' He handed me the burning tobacco. 'But then, we do a lot of things that we probably shouldn't, don't we?'

'I suppose so.' He was watching me as I sipped my tea.

'What are you going to do, Mike? When I leave, I mean.'

'Cry my eyes out for a few weeks, then get on with my life, I suppose.'

'No, but really.'

'That's it. Really.'

'Come to London.'

'Okay. It's easy enough on the train.'

'I don't mean for a visit. I mean for good.'

'What's the point, Mervyn? There's nothing for me there.' He carried on looking steadily at me. 'Actually,' I said, 'I'm thinking of signing on as a regular.'

'Fuck off.'

'Why not?'

'Because it's a fucking prison sentence.'

'I'll manage all right without you.'

'You stupid cunt,' he said, pacing around the room. 'You can't live like this. You'll go mad. You'll fucking kill yourself.'

'What are you talking about?'

'You know perfectly fucking well what I'm talking about. Blackpool and that.'

'Oh, that.' It was the first time either of us had referred to it.

'Yeah. That's what you're … like, isn't it?'

'Is it?' My heart was beating fast, my mouth dry. I took more tea.

'You could get out of here just like that, Mike.' He snapped his fingers. 'Just go along to the old man and tell him.'

'What sort of future would I have, with that on my record?'

'There's always a reason with you, isn't there?'

'That's none of your business.'

'Yes it is. You are my business.'

'Why, all of a sudden? After you've ignored me for the last God knows how many weeks?'

'I was confused.'

'And now you're not?'

'No.' He stood over me. 'I'm not. I've made up my mind. You're the best mate I've had in the last stinking year of my life and I don't want to throw that away.'

'Throw what away? Our great love affair?'

'Oh fuck off.' He threw his cigarette butt to the floor, ground it out with his boot. 'You've always got some fucking clever little remark, haven't you?'

'Look,' I said, standing up. 'I'm glad you've got big plans. I want you to succeed, and I think you will. But I can't live like this, not knowing from one day to the next how things stand between us. One day I think you care about me, the next day … It's like torture. Look at me, Mervyn, for fuck's sake! Look at me! I'm a fucking wreck! You've done this to me.'

'Then let me make it up to you.' He took me by the shoulders and kissed me on the mouth. I stood rigid. 'For fuck's sake, Michael, this is where violins start playing and you melt into my fucking arms.'

'I can't do this. We can't do this. It's not fair.'

I ran out of the guard hut, and the cold night air hit me like a fist to the gut. I didn't start crying until I got to the perimeter fence.

We didn't speak again before Wright left for London. I watched from the library window as he was carried to the bus on the shoulders of his fan club. He was taking half a dozen of them to London – including Sergeant Kelsey, who had become his number one fan. Perhaps Stephen was right about him, too. The bus drove away, as I listened to the final act of *Madam Butterfly*, scratched and jumping, on the old record player.

I carried on as best I could, not sleeping, not eating, not knowing what was wrong with me, avoiding questions, avoiding company, even the padre when he made a few well-meaning enquiries.

Then I fainted in the office and was carted upstairs, a patient now. They gave me sleeping pills and antibiotics and tried to get me to eat. After three days, I was discharged, because the doctors could find nothing wrong with me. Then I collapsed in church, and was taken back in. The CMO came to see me, and asked if there were any personal or family problems. I said no, and they discharged me again. This time I collapsed in the shower block and hit my head on the floor and got a slight concussion.

'Medway,' said the AOC, as I shuffled into his office a few days later, walking like an old man, 'you're a valued member of the team here at Reville.' The AOC is mad about sport, and talks in these terms a great deal. 'We don't want to lose you. Now, I'm very worried about these reports I've been hearing about your … harrumph, well, your health …' He flicked through a file. 'What's this all about, old chap?'

'I don't know, sir.'

'Do you need compassionate leave? That can be arranged.'

'No, sir.'

He pressed his fingertips together and looked me in the eye. 'Medway, I'm a man of the world. You wouldn't think it to look at me, but I've lived through two world wars and an awful lot of messy situations on either side of them, and nothing much can shock me any more. Do you get my drift?'

'No, sir.'

'If there was something you wanted to tell me, Medway …'

'Sir?'

'I would be … understanding.'

'There's nothing, sir.'

He played with the papers on his desk. 'We were all very disappointed with Wright, you know.'

'Sir?'

'Going AWOL. We all miss him.'

'Yes, sir.'

'Sergeant Kelsey is inconsolable.'

I laughed, quietly.

'You must miss him too, Medway.'

'Sir.'

'Do you?'

'Yes, sir.'

'You and Wright were very good pals, weren't you.'

'Yes, sir.'

'Have you heard from him, by any chance?'

I hadn't, but I'd heard the rumours – that he'd been caught in London by the MPs and ended up – as I'd so often said he would – in the Glasshouse. 'No, sir.'

'He'll be out in six months. Might as well have saved himself the trouble.'

'Sir.'

'I suppose you'll join him, eh?'

'I don't know, sir.'

'You don't know much, do you, Medway. Hmm?'

'No, sir.'

'Dismissed.'

That night I collapsed in the barracks, climbing into bed, and spent another night on the wards.

I was up before the AOC again three days later.

'Medway, this can not go on.'

'No, sir.'

'I'm going to have to sign you off.'

'What do you mean, sir?'

'Temperamentally unfit for duty.'

'I'm fine, sir. I'll be okay.'

'You will not.' He handed me a piece of white paper with a large red seal on it. 'I'm sending you for assessment.'

'Where, sir?'

'To RAF Halton. That will be all, Medway.'

I walked slowly back to the empty billet. Kelsey saw me, but ignored me, as if I had left already. I packed my few belongings, parcelled up my diary and my magazines with the prints and the negatives and went to the post office. That night I slept better than I had slept for weeks, untroubled by thoughts or dreams. It had happened, at last – happened, but not happened. I had said nothing, confessed nothing, but I was out, following in Stephen's footsteps, following the trail to London. To life. To Wright.

Nobody mentions the word 'homosexuality' at Halton, but they watch me like a hawk for any signs of it. We sit in the dayroom doing art: one day we have to paint a picture, then we make a sculpture out of plasticine, then we make a basket out of raffia. The doctors in their white coats pace up and down the rows of tables, making notes on clipboards, occasionally asking questions.

'What is that, Medway?'

'It's a tree, sir.'

'It has a very thick, straight trunk, Medway.'

'Yes, sir. It's an oak. It's at the bottom of my parents' garden.'

'And these things at the bottom … these two round things …'

'Toadstools, sir. Fly agarics, to be precise.'

'They're rather large.' He licks his lips.

'They do grow rather large, sir.'

'And what's this, coming out of the top of the tree? Shooting out, you might say?'

'A flock of starlings.'

'They're white.'

'I haven't got around to colouring them in yet, sir.'

'I see.' Scribble scribble. As far as the doctor is concerned, my little painting of the garden at home is a spurting cock with big red balls. The same thing happened with the plasticine ('you say it's a jug, Medway, but would you not also say it's a shaft?'), and

God only knows what they read into the basket. Perhaps raffia work is, in itself, suspicious enough.

I'm enjoying the art. It's ages since I've drawn anything other than pictures of Mervyn Wright naked in the shower, Mervyn Wright naked in the boxing ring, Mervyn Wright naked in a Blackpool boarding house – you get the idea. Now all that seems far, far away, like something viewed down the wrong end of a telescope, distinct but distant. I can't summon up the feelings I had, that fever of whirling confusion, the heart beating like a drum, the dry mouth and gurgling stomach. If I think of Wright at all, it's only to wonder if he's still in the Glasshouse. I don't have queer feelings about him any more. About anyone at all, in fact, although there are some good-looking lads in the hospital, some of them no doubt here for the same reason as me. But I'm not bothered. They say they're putting something into the tea to keep us calm. If that's true, I welcome it. When I leave, I might ask for some to take away.

I don't know what the AOC at Reville put in my notes, but I have a pretty good idea. My admission interview went along these lines.

Doctor: You know why you're here, don't you, Medway?
Me: Yes, sir.
Doctor: Temperamentally unfit for duty. Do you know what that means?
Me: Yes, sir. I've been fainting a lot.
Doctor: Why is that, Medway?
Me: I don't know. I was hoping you'd tell me.
Doctor: What do you think, Medway?
Me: I suppose I've had some sort of breakdown, sir.
Doctor: And what would bring that on?
Me: I don't know.
Doctor: Have you been under any particular emotional strain, Medway?

Me: No, sir.

Doctor: No 'Dear John' letters or anything of the sort?

Me: No, sir.

Doctor: No particular friendships at the base?

Me: No, sir.

Doctor: I see. (Scribbles a few illegible notes.) Are you interested in the theatre, Medway?

Me: Yes, sir.

Doctor: Dramas, Medway? Or … musicals?

Me: Anything, really …

Doctor: Do you go to the pictures?

Me: Sometimes …

Doctor: Do you like westerns?

Me: Not much …

Doctor: Ah! But you would prefer to see *South Pacific*.

Me: It's okay …

Doctor: Have you seen *Spartacus*, Medway?

Me: Not yet.

Doctor: But you would like to, hmm?

Me: Yes …

Doctor: Or *Ben Hur*?

Me: Well yes …

Doctor: (Triumphant.) Ah ha! (Scribbles.) So you like gladiator pictures, then.

For the next assessment I was required to sit in a darkened room with electrodes taped to my hands, while images were flashed on a screen in front of me. This reminded me of the Freedom from Infection parade when I first saw Wright, the images of soft chancres and missing noses that always caused someone to faint. I smiled at the memory, like something from childhood.

This time, however, the images were easier on the eye. We started off with Elizabeth Taylor in a swimsuit, then Burt

Lancaster in trunks. We had images of cute, gurgling babies, boxers in the ring, Sabrina in a negligee, Tony Curtis in blue jeans, and so on. You don't have to be Sigmund Freud to work out what they're getting at. I concentrated on my breathing, and viewed them all with indifference, even when they started to get a little more interesting: Marilyn Monroe with her tits out (so those photographs really did exist after all; I wondered where they'd got them), a physique model in a posing pouch (I recognised the picture from *Man's World*; they'd certainly done their homework). I felt nothing, apart from slight nausea, but I feel that nearly all the time anyway.

After two weeks of this sort of thing, I was called in to face a panel of three doctors who had my 'case notes' spread in front of them. They all stopped talking quite suddenly when I walked in.

'Aircraftman Medway.' I am still an aircraftman until I leave here with the relevant bits of paper. 'Please. Sit down.'

I walked to a chair. They all watched me. What did they expect? Mincing? Some of the other lads walk around the hospital like Mae West. This is known as 'working your ticket'. They would have sat down, double-crossed their legs and rested their hands on their knees. I imagine Stephen did just that. The thought made me smile.

'Something amuses you, Medway.'

'No, sir. Just thinking about a friend …'

'Ah! A particular friend, perhaps?'

And we were off again, with lures and baits at every conversational turn. Did I like Connie Francis? Was my father in any way weak and/or absent? What games did I play at school: football or hopscotch? They made me strike a match, and looked excited when I struck it away from myself. They made me stand up and pretend I had just trodden in chewing gum, to see which way I lifted my foot (disappointingly in front, rather than to the rear). They tried everything, rather than asking me outright if I was queer. What would I have answered? The truth is that I am neither one thing nor the other. I am nothing. Whatever appetites I may once have had have gone. Not satisfied – just gone.

After half an hour of this farce, we got down to business.

'Quite clearly, Medway, you cannot go back to active service.'

'Oh, really?'

'You sound disappointed.'

'I am, rather.'

'Why?' He looked genuinely surprised.

'I was thinking of signing on.'

They looked at each other in consternation. 'I'm afraid that's quite out of the question. The issue we have to decide is on what grounds you will be discharged.'

'I see.'

'Normally, in cases such as this, we would have no alternative but to put certain things on your discharge papers which would … well, limit your employment options in civilian life. Do you understand?'

'Yes, sir.'

'But in your case, we don't think you are what we would call a habitual offender.'

'Sir?'

'Hmmrrrmmph, and so we are willing to offer you a deal.'

'A deal, sir?'

'We would like you to volunteer for a form of therapy which has been getting excellent results in the United States and which we believe will return you to civvy street as a useful and balanced member of society.'

'What's that, sir? A lobotomy?'

'No, Medway, in this instance I don't think a lobotomy is indicated. But we would like to try you on a course of hormone treatment.'

'Sir.'

'Nothing to be alarmed at. Nothing at all. Just a question of realigning certain chemical imbalances in the … er … the pituitary gland which may, we believe, control … the procreative and other … impulses. You see?'

'Yes, sir. And if I undergo this treatment?'

'We'll send you out of here with a glowing report and the world's your oyster, my boy. You just report to an assigned doctor every three months to monitor your progress and any possible … side effects.'

'I see.'

'So, if you'll just sign here, here and here, we can set the wheels in motion.'

I signed.

Now I am at home, with a new notebook and all the time in the world in which to write in it. I spend most of the days in my room. Mum brings food up on a tray. I think she and Dad actually prefer me not to take meals with them, as after a while the silence is so strained that it puts us all off our food. At least I'm eating well. I'm putting on weight. I've regained all the weight that I lost during those last months at Reville, and more. I'm flabby. I can't stop eating. I think it's a side effect of the pills they made me take at Halton, and which I am still taking, twice a day. I assume that the puffiness around my chest is another side effect, the headaches, the loose bowels and the uncontrollable fits of crying when I watch *Emergency – Ward 10*.

My parents have said nothing about why I am home. I suppose someone has written to them. I don't know what the letter said. We don't ask questions. It's been put about that I am 'convalescing' but nobody says from what. Callers are not encouraged.

There were things waiting for me at home: a big brown paper parcel tied with string, addressed to me by me, and a dozen or so letters, ditto. I've put them on the top shelf above my bed, behind some of my old children's books. There was also a letter from Stephen, forwarded from Reville.

Dear Heart, it's been ages, have you dropped off the edge of the world? I do hope this finds you well and happy, please drop me a line. Life goes on much the same in the wicked city, I'm busy busy busy with all sorts of excitements which I won't bore you with. Please do think about coming up to town again, we can have another jolly night out, they all ask after you, you made quite an impression! And of course I miss you madly. Please do drop me a line just to let me know your news.

I haven't replied. I don't know where to begin. The last few months seem like a big mouthful of cotton wool. Everything has happened, and nothing. I am in a dream, in a fog. Perhaps it's the pills. Perhaps if I stop taking them, things will seem clearer. But then, will it all begin again?

One morning I stood in front of the bathroom mirror, wondering why I didn't have to shave quite as often as before, when I noticed that I had breasts. Not just a bit of puffiness from over-eating, but actual tits. I touched them. They were tender, sore. I collected up all my pills and flushed them down the toilet. For four days, I had a splitting headache, couldn't bear light, stayed in my room with the curtain drawn except when I had to run to the loo. Then I woke up and felt better than I've felt in months. I drew the curtains, looked at the trees and the birds and realised that spring was here. I clambered up on the bed, pulled aside a load of books and retrieved that brown paper parcel with the Reville Village PO postmark. I blew off a layer of dust and untied the string.

It was all there, all the stuff I've tried to forget. The diary, the magazines – *Man's World*, *Health and Strength*, *Man Alive*, *Male Classics*, the covers like familiar friends, the photographs, the negatives, even the undeveloped roll of film from Blackpool.

My hands are shaking and I can barely write this.

There is Mervyn in his boxing shorts, guard up, looking at the camera through his eyelashes.

There he is in his posing pouch.

And there he is out of it.

For the first time in months, I have an erection.

I met Stephen at Lyon's Corner House on Coventry Street. 'I would have made you lunch at the flat, but my dear, it's such a mess!' He looked older than when I'd last seen him, more nervy, constantly glancing over his shoulder, jumping at shadows. 'God, but it's good to see you, Michael. I had no idea. Oh, my dear,' he said, laying a hand on mine, 'what you must have been through! Well, don't tell me, I know. Those doctors!' He flapped his hands around his head, as if brushing away flies. 'What they don't do to you in the name of science! But the main thing is that you're here and you're well and you look, if I may say so, utterly fabulous.'

'Stephen …'

'No! Don't look at me!' He shielded his eyes. 'The wreckage of a once great beauty. Oh, when I think of it, wasting my youth on the RAF, I should have established myself with the officers and set up a nice little brothel. Hey ho. But let's not dwell, dear. Tell me everything about your plans.'

'I've applied for a job at the …'

'Oh God, don't look now, it's someone I don't want to see.' He hid behind the menu. 'Has he gone? Did he see us?'

'What's the matter, Stephen?'

'I'm afraid when a girl gets notorious in this town there's just no place to hide.'

'Are you in trouble?'

'Certainly not! I always insist they wear a condom.'

'Anyway, I've applied for this civil service position …'

'Good for you! At least someone's going to be earning an honest living. I mean what we do isn't strictly against the law, but you'd think from the way they carry on that we were selling secrets to the Russians, dear, although from what I hear some of those Russians have ways of getting a girl to talk, and you know me, I just can't keep my mouth shut when that sort of thing is on offer. Oh! Boris! What do you want to know?' He shrieked with laughter and started coughing. 'I need a drink. Come on.'

'Stephen ...'

'What?'

'Sit down for a minute.'

'Oh dear. Is it bad news?'

'Of course not. I just wondered if I might possibly stay for a couple of nights. You know, you were always saying ...'

'But darling the place is such a dump at the moment.'

'I could help you clear it up. Just while I have the interview and the entrance board.'

'Well, it's not terribly ...'

'Please? For old times' sake?'

'Oh, Michael, darling, you know I could never deny you anything. But don't get angry if you don't like what you find there.'

There was a light under the door when we got back to the Queensway flat, and the radio was tuned to a rock and roll station. My heart jumped, and I pushed past Stephen into the kitchen. He was sitting there in a vest, his hair longer and slicked back, eating beans on toast, a mug of tea beside the plate, a fag burning in the ashtray. He didn't look up at first.

'Aircraftman Wright.'

Then he looked up.

'Aircraftman Medway.' He pushed back his chair, looked me up and down. Through his vest, I could see the familiar contours of his torso.

'Aaaah,' sighed Stephen in the doorway. We both turned and glared at him. 'All right! All right! I'll leave you two together!' He went to the living room, singing at the top of his voice 'Now I shout it from the highest hill, even told the golden daffodil ...'

Wright stood up, shook his arms.

'How have you been, Michael?'

'Not bad. You?'

'Yeah. Never better.' And then some smoke got in his eyes, he rubbed them and stumbled forward and we ended up in each other's arms, breathing as if we were fighting for air.

08

The first contact from Jonathan in months, and it's typically dramatic. A text, while I'm at work. 'Please come over now I've done something stupid.' That's hardly news, and so I don't reply straight away, because Jonathan's idea of a crisis usually involves not having the right shoes. I've got to keep my head down and be a good boy at work. There have been too many days off with 'flu', too many missed deadlines. Anna is cracking the whip and I had better jump or I'll be joining Jonathan in the ranks of the self-employed.

In fact, I'm enjoying work more than I've ever done. Perhaps 'enjoying' is the wrong word – but I'm happy to be there because it offers a respite from the chaos everywhere else, including home. It's the only thing standing between me and total meltdown, not to mention poverty, losing the flat, moving back in with my parents, and suicide within six months. So really I'm quite motivated at the moment.

The time flies by and I haven't thought about my problems for hours. I'm on my way to the gym when I turn my phone on again, and there's a voice message this time. It's not Jonathan, but it's about him.

He's in hospital, unconscious, possibly in a coma, and they found my number on a note that he'd left in his flat. Please could I contact them as soon as possible.

A note? What sort of note? Like a suicide note?

I've got to go to the gym, because today is the day I do back and legs and I'm hoping to see Andy because I'm getting very low on steroids and if I don't take them I'm going to start losing bulk and what's the point of doing what I do if I'm going to lose bulk and then suddenly I realise that this is Jonathan, my best friend even though we haven't spoken for a long time, in hospital, possibly dying, and he's asking for me.

I get as far as the gym door before I can persuade my feet to stop, and even then I'm sure my kit bag is actually trying to pull me inside, but I turn around and get on a bus and I'm re-reading the text Jonathan sent me earlier, and it's obvious now that this wasn't a shoe crisis. Or at least, if it was, it was a particularly bad one.

'He called 999 just before he became unconscious,' says the ward sister, who won't let me see him until she's 'filled me in' a bit. 'He's taken an overdose of sleeping pills. Did you know that he was taking them?' She sounds like she's accusing me of something. I almost say, 'Darling, we're all taking them,' because I haven't had a night without Valium for weeks, but what comes out is, 'No, he never mentioned it.'

They've pumped his stomach and now they're waiting for him to come round. They won't know for a while what exactly he took, but whatever it was was washed down with red wine. If he comes round – I don't like the 'if' – there may be some brain damage. I can hear Jonathan saying, 'Oh fuck, does that mean that I won't be able to co-ordinate accessories any more?' and I don't know whether to laugh or cry. He's lying on a hospital bed with a ventilator mask over his face and a drip in his arm.

'I'll leave you with him,' says the nurse. 'If anything happens, just press the button.'

Nothing happens.

I sit with Jonathan for an hour, staring at him, occasionally holding his hand, looking out of the window at the amazing view of London spread out before me. It's vast and impersonal and I wonder how I ever thought I could make a home here. Night is falling and the street lights are on. I look for landmarks but the angle is unfamiliar and I can't work out where I am at all.

My phone beeps. It's a text from Stuart, with the usual arrangements for tonight. I start replying, but the sister hurries over and tells me I can't use my phone on the ward, I'll have to go outside. So I just turn it off and don't bother to reply and sit back down by Jonathan's bed.

The possibility that Jonathan might die, might have wanted to die, hits me hard, and I almost bring something up from my stomach, something cold. We have not been good to each other. I have not been good to him. He asked me for help when he was in trouble and I turned him down. For all I know he's been through hell over that money he owed to Hadley, and he's obviously been taking more drugs than are good for him, otherwise we wouldn't be here. I cut him out because I had problems of my own, and now my oldest friend is unconscious in a hospital bed and I can't help feeling that it's partly my fault. I should have been with him. We should have got each other through our troubles, taking the piss and bickering because that's the only way we can show that we care, but instead life and clubs and boyfriends and jobs became more important than friendship and I forgot what Jonathan really means to me. And why, just perhaps why, he has been such a pain in the arse in recent months.

Because he feels that I have let him down.

Because I have let him down.

I don't know when I fell asleep but I wake up slumped in the chair with dribble on my shoulder. The ward is dark and quiet, apart from the whirr and click of ventilators, the odd moan and groan and snore, the sounds of the nurses' feet pacing purposefully up and down.

Jonathan is still unconscious, still on the ventilator.

I thought I would have been chucked out hours ago, but maybe they don't have such things as visiting hours any more. I don't know. Maybe when a patient is dying …

'Should I stay?' I ask the night sister.

'Only if you want to.'

'Is he going to die?'

She smiles, and takes my hand. 'No, darling, he's not going to die. Not this time.'

I finally start crying and she takes me into the corridor and gives me a cup of tea and stays with me till I've drunk it and calmed down.

'Is he your boyfriend, darling?'

'What? Oh God, no. But he's my ...' I'm going to say 'best friend' but I suddenly have to take a big gulp of air, as if I'm trying to cure hiccups.

'You go home, my love,' says the night sister. 'He'll still be here tomorrow.'

'P-promise?'

'Oh, I promise,' she says, and gives me a hug.

I get a series of night buses home and I feel calmer and better than I've felt for weeks.

Stuart is in the living room with another guy, someone I recognise from the clubs or from Hadley's or somewhere. They're smoking a joint and I've obviously interrupted them in the middle of something. Stuart's shirt is untucked, his trousers undone, his feet bare. They look at me as if I'm in the way.

I open the window to let the smoke out. I tidy away glasses and a plate that has been used as an ashtray. It's the last piece of a little dinner service my mum gave me when I went up to college, the idea being that I should always be able to entertain friends. I don't think this is what she had in mind. A joint has been left burning on the rim, and it's marked the little floral design. I throw the plate like a frisbee, aiming it directly at Stuart's head. It glances off and hits the wall and smashes into a hundred pieces. Stuart's bleeding.

He says nothing, picks up his jacket, puts on his shoes, takes his trick and leaves.

I take a Valium, and later on another Valium, but I stop at

two because I don't want to end up in the bed next to Jonathan.

I wake up late and call the office while my voice is still woozy from the pills. I try to explain to Anna that my friend is in hospital and I'm in a bad way but she just says 'Get here as soon as you can' in a very odd way, even though she's met Jonathan loads of times and always used to get on with him.

I feel better after a shower and some toast and tea and I get into the office by eleven.

She grabs me before I even get to my desk.

'You need to come into my office right now, Robert.'

I say that I'm really sorry I'm late, that Jonathan is in a coma and I'm worried to death about him, but she interrupts.

'It's not about that.'

Derek the big boss is sitting at Anna's desk and it's quite clear they've been talking about me. He's got a load of A4 printouts in front of him and I recognise them as pages from my blog. My stomach tightens and I really need to shit.

'Robert.'

'Hi Derek.'

'Sit down.'

I sit. Anna sits. We all sit, and nobody says anything.

'Robert, do you recognise this?' Derek holds up some paper.

'Yes. It's my blog.'

'Right. Your ... blog.'

'My private blog.'

He reads out a passage that has been highlighted in yellow, something about going to a club and taking crystal meth.

'Did you write that?'

'Yes.'

There's another long pause.

'Robert, do you realise how this reflects on the company?'

'No. I mean, why should it? It's ... it's like a work of fiction. All the names are changed. I'm really careful.'

'Are you using these drugs?'

'People I know are using them.' People not exactly a million miles from where I'm sitting, Anna, I want to say.

'Are you aware of the morals clause in your contract?'

I'm not. 'Yes. Of course I am.'

'I understand that there have been some timekeeping issues. This morning, for instance.'

I'm about to explain that my best friend is hovering between life and death in a hospital bed, when Derek continues, 'And other performance issues.'

My face is burning.

'I don't see what my blog has got to do with all this.'

'Robert, I've been speaking to HR. They take a very hard line on this sort of thing.'

I want to say 'What sort of thing?' because I can't imagine that many other employees have written indiscreet online diaries about their sex and drugs shame.

'But I've persuaded them to give you another chance. Robert, you are now receiving an official warning. It'll be typed up and on your desk by the end of the day.'

'What does that mean?'

'It means,' says Anna, 'that if you don't clean your act up, you'll be sacked.'

'Thank you for making that so clear.'

'Robert,' says Anna, at last sounding like a friend rather than a manager, 'we don't want to lose you. Don't fuck this up. Seriously. Do not fuck this up.'

Derek's eyebrows are halfway up his forehead.

'Okay, Anna,' I say. 'Can I go now?'

I could walk out of the office and never go back. It would be very easy. Instead I log on to my blog, and delete the whole account. Woof. Just like that. Anything I write from now on is for my eyes only. As far as the rest of the world is concerned, I'm dead.

Jonathan is off the ventilator and breathing normally when

I get to the hospital. The ward sister says he came round for a while in the afternoon, and asked if anyone had been to see him. She says he smiled when she told him I'd sat with him all night, and muttered a 'very rude word', so I suppose he'll survive.

I sit beside him and tell him all about Stuart and work and the blog and he appears to be sleeping, but when I've lapsed into silence I feel him squeeze my hand and whisper 'cunt'.

The next day is Saturday and I really need a lie-in but someone's banging on the door and ringing the bell and although I'm doing my best to ignore it eventually I have to get up. I'm assuming it's Stuart so I haven't bothered to put on any clothes. I'm wearing a pair of white CK briefs, and my hair is sticking up like a clown's.

'Oh, you're in, then.' It's Stephen, Michael's friend, his enormous glasses glinting like an insect's eyes. He's got his arms folded across his chest, his weight on one leg, a hip thrust out at an angle – it's international gay body language for 'and what the bloody hell do you have to say for yourself?'

I rub my eyes. 'What do you want?'

'Oh yes, thank you, I will come in,' he says, stepping past me. 'Well well well, look what you've done to the old place, who'd have thought it. Right you. I want some answers.'

'What are you talking about?' I ask, although I know.

'Every day he waits, and every day he's disappointed. Do you have any idea what it's like for him?'

'I've been very busy.'

'I'm sure you have.'

'Look, Stephen, I don't know what Michael has told you, but we hardly knew each other.'

'You were his neighbour, for God's sake.'

'Yes, but … I mean, that doesn't mean …'

'And he's gay, dear, unless you hadn't noticed.'

'So?'

'So we're meant to look out for each other! We're meant to

take care of each other! What the bloody hell is the point of it all if we can't do that?' He's shouting now, and his voice sounds shrill in the confines of the hall. 'Oh put some fucking clothes on, for Christ's sake. It's like waiting at the butcher's.'

Within minutes we're in his car and driving out of London, through the suburbs, having several near misses with stationary vehicles, oncoming buses etc. Stephen is keeping up a monologue punctuated only when he lights or puffs on a cigarette.

'… and don't look at me like I've just farted, I'll smoke in my own car if I want to, God knows I can't bloody do it anywhere else and you should see the bitches' faces when I light up outside Michael's place. Open the bloody window if you don't like it although I imagine compared to what you stick up your nose a little bit of fag smoke isn't exactly going to kill you.'

We pull up outside a long low yellow-brick building with grass and shrubs outside.

Michael's flat is on the ground floor, with a view of traffic (front) and walls (back), but it's warm and clean and he's made it feel like home. I recognise a number of the knick-knacks from his old flat, and for the first time they seem not just tacky souvenirs collected by an old man with poor taste, but portable pieces of a life.

He's at the door with open arms, beaming as if I'm his long-lost son.

'Well well well,' he says, 'the mountain has come to Mohamed. How lovely to see you, Robert.' He puts a hand on each arm and looks at me. A cloud passes briefly over his face, then he's all smiles again. 'Come in! Come in! They say an Englishman's home is his castle.' He gestures around the tiny living room. 'My castle!'

'I'll leave you two young lovebirds to it,' says Stephen. 'I have things to see, people to do. There's a bus from the corner that goes straight to the end of your road, young man. Perhaps you'd like to learn how to use it.'

'Don't mind Stephen,' says Michael, when he's gone. 'He always was an interfering old busybody. But I'm very grateful to him for bringing you. I hope you don't mind being kidnapped.'

I laugh, and sit awkwardly in an armchair. There's so little room for furniture. He must have got rid of most of it.

'So, how are you, Robert? You look, if I may say so, a little the worse for wear.'

'Oh, it's nothing. Just working too hard I suppose.'

'Hmm ... And burning the candle at both ends.'

'Something like that.'

He looks at me. 'How's Stuart?'

'Fine, fine ... As far as I know.'

'Oh dear.'

'We're just ... taking a break.'

'I'll mind my own business. Well now. A cup of tea, or something.'

'That would be lovely.'

While he's bustling around the kitchen, I pick up a silver-framed photograph. It shows a handsome young man with slicked-back hair, broad shoulders and a narrow waist, a movie-star grin, shirtsleeves rolled up to show thick, muscular forearms. One hand holds a jacket slung back over his shoulder. The other is shoved into his trouser pocket. It looks as if he's deliberately plumping up his packet.

'Oh, he was a terror,' says Michael, right behind me, making me jump. 'Look at him. My God, I was a lucky bugger.'

'Is this ...' I can't remember the dead partner's name, if I ever knew it.

'Yes. That's him all right.'

'He's very ... fit.'

'Oh, my goodness! That's the understatement of the century.'

'Did he go to the gym?' I'm not sure if there were such things as gyms in those days.

'Yes, dear, he may have popped in once or twice.' Michael's

laughing at me, I think, but he's too kind to show it. 'Recognise the trousers?'

I look closer, and see the turn-ups, and realise I never gave them back.

'It's all right. You can keep them.' He pats his round pot of a stomach. 'They're no good to me.'

I put the photo carefully back down on the table. 'How did you two meet?'

'Oh, dear, that's rather a long story.' Michael sits down, pours the tea. 'I'll tell you one day, if you're really interested.'

'I am.'

'But not today, if you don't mind.' He hands me the tea; his hands are shaking slightly, making the spoon rattle in the saucer. 'I don't feel like wallowing in the past. I want to hear about you. About young people.'

'I don't feel very young at the moment.' I want to tell him about Stuart, about Jonathan, about work, but I'm ashamed.

'Nonsense,' he says. 'You've got your whole life ahead of you.'

I have a sudden flash of the next twenty years spent in clubs and gyms, fending off unwanted threesomes, struggling through the come-downs, watching my body decay and doing everything I can to disguise it, waking up one day in my forties and looking like one of those middle-aged men with shiny faces and starved bodies who haunt the clubs like ghosts.

'Yeah,' I say. 'I suppose so.'

'Youth is wasted on the young,' says Michael, putting a hand briefly on my knee. 'But try to be happy, if you possibly can. I really recommend it.'

'And are you happy, Michael? Here?'

He looks around, shrugs, lays his hands out open on his lap. 'I'm all right. I had my share of happiness.'

When I leave, after an hour, I promise that I'll come to see him more often. The bus home takes forty minutes.

Jonathan is making excellent progress, say the doctors, and

he'll be out by the middle of the week, and it's up to his friends to make sure that he looks after himself.

He's sitting up in bed with his headphones on, wearing a particularly offensive grey hoodie covered in brightly coloured death's heads and dollar signs. He's reading, or at least looking at the pictures in, a book.

'He's so much like me,' he says, pulling out his earphones. 'We were both bullied at school. We both had fathers who hit us. It's amazing.' He puts the book down, breaking the spine. It is, of course, Lukas's 'long-awaited' autobiography, simply entitled *Me*.

'Hello, Jonathan.' I kiss him, and give him a bunch of enormous chrysanthemums. He receives them like a diva taking a curtain call.

'Oh my God, thank you, thank you so much,' he says, going into Gwyneth Paltrow Oscar speech mode. 'Have my people put them in water.'

He seems well enough to answer a few burning questions.

'So, Jonathan. What the hell happened?'

'You know how it is,' he says, 'I just never know when to stop.'

'The nurse told me that you'd taken a massive overdose of Valium.'

'Oh, she's always exaggerating.'

'Washed down with red wine.'

'Yummy,' he says, without much enthusiasm.

'What was that for? Just to make sure you did the job properly?'

'I wasn't trying to kill myself, if that's what you're driving at.'

'Really?'

'No.' His face shuts down, and he starts fiddling with his earphones.

'Jonathan …'

'What? What do you want me to tell you? "Oh, Robbie, I'm so unhappy, blah blah blah, it was a cry for help, thank God you saved me, oh, you actually didn't, did you? But you've been such

| 194 |

a good friend to me, look at these lovely flowers, wouldn't they look super on my grave?"'

'I'm only trying to help. I care about you.'

'Well don't.'

The earphones are back in, he's burying himself in *Me,* and I guess visiting hours are over.

'I'll be off, then.'

'Oh fucking sit down.' He tears the headphones off and throws *Me* on the floor. 'God, you're such a drama queen.' I'm not the one lying in the hospital bed after a suicide attempt, but I don't mention that. 'As you're obviously determined to get all the juicy details, yes, I was very depressed, yes, it seemed like a good way out at the time, and yes, I'm glad the ambulance got there in time because now I'd quite like to live.'

'Pleased to hear it.' I take his hand. That was one of our fastest ever fallings-out-and-makings-up.

'Yeah, well, there's no need to make a big thing out of it.' He doesn't remove his hand. 'I still owe money.'

'To Hadley?'

'Her? God, no. I paid him off. I told you I would.'

'You never went on the game,' I asked, suddenly sick with worry, as if I'd just heard my kid sister was doing punters behind King's Cross.

'No, that's a mug's game.'

'So how did you get the money? Did you earn it?'

'Don't be ridiculous. I stole it, of course.'

'You … stole it?'

'I went up to Hadley's gallery one night and nicked a couple of pictures and sold them on eBay. Who would have thought that crap was worth so much money?'

'You're not serious.'

'I'm so serious. A picture of a pile of vomit on the pavement, and a collage of prostitute phonebox cards. Two grand each.'

'But Hadley …'

'Never had a clue. Doesn't know arse from elbow. That's the marvellous thing about cancer,' said Jonathan. 'He just took the money, said thank you and we shook hands.'

'Right.' I withdraw my hand from Jonathan's.

'You don't approve, of course, and I wouldn't expect you to understand, but there you go. Take me or leave me.'

'Don't tempt me, Jonathan,' I say, but I stay till he's tired, and when he's sleeping I put *Me* on the table and kiss him goodbye.

Two days later, I get a floral notelet in the post from Michael, thanking me for my visit. 'PS,' it says at the end, 'you asked me if he ever went to the gym. The enclosed may answer your question.'

There's a black-and-white photograph with the words GERALD OF LONDON stamped on the back, and a name written in pencil. Mervyn.

He must be about twenty-two, twenty-three, certainly no older than me.

His hair is thick and dark and slicked up into a kind of rockabilly quiff.

His eyes are big, the eyelashes long, his lips full and slightly parted. The effect might be almost feminine were it not for the big, straight nose, the heavy eyebrows and the strong jawline.

He's naked, except for a pair of leopard-skin briefs that taper to tiny straps on the hip, and just about contain him.

He's holding a bar in a bicep curl. His biceps are big. So are his pecs, deltoids, triceps and lats. The legs are great. Everything is in proportion. He has a tattoo on his left forearm; it's a bit smudgy on the black-and-white print, but it looks like it could be a bird of some sort. On closer scrutiny, it could be a peacock.

He's staring into the distance, clear-eyed, with a hint of a smile, his fists bunched around the bar like hammerheads, ready for anything.

I strip to my underwear, and duplicate the pose in the mirror. It's like a distorted reflection in a fairground mirror.

There's a round rusty mark on the top border of the print, and a hole in the middle, where a drawing pin must have gone. I find a new drawing pin and carefully tack the picture to the headboard of my bed, so he's watching over me.

I wish I'd met Mervyn. But I only ever saw his dead body being carried away in an ambulance.

Eight

Mervyn is washing dishes in a café called Carlo's off Leicester Square, which he hates. From what I can gather from remarks that Stephen has made, he is not above supplementing his income from the generosity of various 'admirers' who take him out for dinner and feed him with steak and potatoes. It's hard for Mervyn to keep his weight up, especially when he's spending every free hour training at a gym in Putney, the one where all the serious bodybuilders go. At home – either at his nan's in Shepherd's Bush, more usually at Stephen's, since they found each other wandering around the West End one night – he eats beans on toast, a sausage if he's lucky, a piece of cake. He's keen to do more modelling, he says – he 'did the rounds of the studios' when he got to London, but didn't like what he found there, and is unwilling to say more on the subject. Stephen occasionally ribs him, but Mervyn's temper is as quick as ever and he lashes out if Stephen goes too far.

We live in a strange domestic bliss in Queensway, the three of us. Stephen is out all day at *Muscle Boy*, and in the West End most evenings, but often entertains our 'landlord', Tony, at night. We know that we have to make ourselves scarce while 'Momma pays the rent,' as Stephen puts it. I slept on the couch in the living room for the first two nights, while Mervyn was in the guest room. On the third night, when Stephen was out and we were celebrating the news that I had been accepted at a very lowly post at the Treasury, starting the next day, Mervyn and I had a conversation. We had not talked about 'it' since I came to London, since that first impetuous kiss of reunion.

'So,' said Wright, 'it was all worth it, then.'

'I don't know about that. Time will tell.'

'Come on, grumpy. What have you got to look so miserable about?'

'Two months in the loony bin, a nervous breakdown and drugs that turned me into a woman. There's no need to look quite so interested, Wright.'

'Fuck off. It ain't exactly been a bed of roses for me, you know. They picked me up after three days. Three fucking days! I'd only fucked one bird! Christ, the bastards, they had my number all right. Six months in the Glasshouse, Mike. Six fucking months giving myself calluses.'

'Yes, well, we've all paid our dues.'

'And now I'm up to my fucking elbows in dirty fucking water six days a week and not making enough to keep a roof over my head.'

'Thank God for little Stephen, eh?'

'Yeah. Who'd have thought it? Although I'm sure he earns every penny.'

'You could do the same, of course.'

'Fuck off. I'm not cut out for that game.'

I poured red wine into our mugs while he lit cigarettes.

'So, did it work, then?' he asked.

'What?'

'The treatment. The what-do-you-call-it.'

'The therapy?'

'Yeah. Have they straightened you out?'

'No.'

'Right.' He looked at me. 'I'm glad to hear it.' He pressed his leg against mine, and the feelings began again – the swirling pits, the confused flicker of images before my eyes, the longing and the fear.

'I don't think I can start this all over again.'

'Come on, baby,' he said, as if he was with a woman, 'you

know what I want.' His hand picked at his groin. 'Remember?'

'Look, I'm tired and I've got a job to go to in the morning.'

He sat with his head hung, drawing patterns on the tabletop in the spilt red wine.

'So I'll say goodnight, then. If you don't mind. I need the sofa.'

'Oh don't be so fucking ridiculous,' said Wright, standing up and holding out his hand. 'You're coming with me.'

'If this is because you feel sorry for me, or just because you're randy, or something …'

'Can we just stop fucking talking and go to bed?'

He took my hand and led me into the guest room.

Mervyn didn't leap out of bed in the morning, or sulk, or pretend nothing had happened. He sat up, lit a cigarette and watched me dress, stretching out, naked under the sheets.

'Well, I'm still not sure that I'm queer,' he said, 'but that was … pretty good.'

'Thanks a lot.'

'Come here.'

'I can't, Mervyn … I've got to go to work. It's my first day.' He pulled back the sheets.

'Come on …'

I picked up my hat, aimed and lobbed it across the room, as if I was playing quoits. It landed exactly on target. 'That, mate, will have to wait till I get home.'

He jumped up, grabbed my tie and pulled me into a kiss. And then, my face tingling from his stubble, he put the hat where it belonged.

The summer is dragging on, long and hot. My office in Victoria is high up and windowless, which is a bad combination. I have a fan, and am allowed to leave the door open, which is something. I sometimes think that all I have accomplished in leaving the Air

Force is exchanging one set of filing cabinets for another – and then I remember Mervyn, and my stomach flips, and I have to bite the insides of my mouth to stop myself from grinning like an idiot.

He is not as happy as I am. Fame isn't coming fast enough for his liking, although he's doing everything in his power to meet it halfway. He's built up quite a following in the physique magazines, thanks to my efforts and those of a few other photographers around London including, I am distressed to report, Gerald, who got him to pose in a leopard-skin slip that made him look very sleazy indeed. Others have done a better job, and Stephen put him on the cover of *Muscle Boy*, which earned him a ton of fan mail that Stephen diligently brings home at the end of every day. While we're out at work, Mervyn trains at the gym, washes dishes in the café and dreams of stardom. We are together every night, on that single divan, except when the air is too hot and one of us retreats to the living room. Sometimes he is moody and distant, and I know then that I must tread carefully to avoid confrontation. For the most part, however, we jog along amicably, the three of us, in our strange ménage.

We sat one Saturday morning over our usual weekend breakfast of black coffee and cigarettes – because nobody had remembered to go to the shops for bread or eggs – while Stephen opened the post.

'Oh my God!'

'What is it?' said Mervyn. 'Cops caught up with you at last?'

'Very funny, I don't think. No. Look!' He placed a printed card on the tablecloth, avoiding the spills and ash. 'We've been invited.'

'Who the fuck is Edward Templeton?'

'Dearie me, don't you know anything? Does the name Imperial mean anything to you?'

Mervyn shrugged, but it meant a great deal to me. 'What, as in Imperial Studios?' Theirs was the name on all the best physique photographs, those that graced the covers of *Health and Strength*, beautifully lit, artistically posed, a far cry from Gerald's sleazy output.

'The very same.'

'Show me.' Mervyn picked the invitation up, surveyed the thickness of the card, the gilt edges, the thick black ink of the printing. 'Very classy.'

'Classy? I should say it's classy! People scratch each other's eyes out for an invitation to one of Lady Templeton's at-homes. My God! We've made it! We've really made it!'

Templeton lives in a large, stucco-fronted Regency house in Pimlico, 'handy for the barracks' according to Stephen, who is full of lurid tales of Edward Templeton's taste for 'rough trade'. It hasn't rained for so long that the London streets smell of piss; here in Pimlico, everything is clean and fragrant. We walked from the bus stop in our best clothes, after a whole morning of fussing and grooming. 'You look like a bloody civil servant, dear,' complained Stephen, dressed for the occasion in a camp version of cricket whites. 'Can't I just …'

'No. I am a civil servant. Leave me alone.'

Mervyn wore a tight-fitting cream shirt with short sleeves and a huge collar that he bought at Vince's in Newburgh Street; he'd saved up for it for weeks, and could still only afford it with a little help from me. His hair was brilliantined to a high gloss, his trousers like a second skin. Stephen looked him up and down, walked around him, brushed off the odd speck of dust and said, 'You'll do. Just don't sit down.'

We mounted the steps to the pillared porch, the front door flanked by clipped bay trees in brass pots. Mervyn whistled. 'Blimey, there's money in this racket.'

'Oh, he doesn't make his money from the photo business, dear. That's just a hobby. He's in the movies.'

'You're kidding!'

'I'm not. They own a chain of news cinemas, and they make

films. That got you interested, didn't it? Oh yes, very powerful man is our Teddy Templeton. Very powerful and very wicked. You want to watch your back.'

'I know all about that,' said Mervyn, slapping his arse loudly.

'So I hear, dear.'

The door was opened by a handsome, crop-haired young man in what looked like a chauffeur's uniform. Stephen whispered 'That's … him. From the magazines.'

'I know.'

'All right, Don,' said Mervyn, shaking hands. 'These are my mates, Michael, Stephen. This is Don. We know each other from the gym, don't we?'

'Go up, lads,' said Don, with a wink. 'He's expecting you.'

At the top of the sweeping staircase stood a sturdy house-keeper with a tray of champagne, her face completely impassive.

'Bottoms up!' said Stephen, getting his nose in the glass.

The main reception room was huge, stretching from French windows at the front to French windows at the back, both sets giving on to a small wrought-iron balcony. There were about forty men in the room, but it didn't look full. Someone was playing show tunes on the white baby grand.

'Fuckin' 'ell,' said Mervyn, under his breath, as forty pairs of eyes gave us the once-over, 'every fucking poof in London.'

'Ah!' said a cultivated voice behind me, 'my guest of honour!' A tanned hand shot out, followed by a dazzling white cuff, a navy blue sleeve with gold buttons. Mervyn took it and shook it.

'Pleased to meet you, sir.' He sounded nervous. Templeton turned to me. He was a tall, handsome man in his fifties, maybe sixties, his grey hair well cut, his clothes beautifully tailored. I felt very shabby. 'And this must be Mr Medway. I've heard all about you.'

'Thank you, sir.'

'A very talented photographer, I gather. I shall have to keep an eye on you, young man. Now, Mervyn.' He laid a hand on

Mervyn's elbow. 'There are people you need to meet. Come with me.'

He steered him away.

'Hello, am I invisible all of a sudden?' hissed Stephen. 'She didn't even say hello! After all the times I've put her bloody pictures in the magazine. I mean, I'm the one she knows!' He took another drink from a passing tray. 'Oh well, I'll still drink her liquor.' He mimicked Templeton's public school accent. 'Here's how.'

Don, in his uniform, was chatting to an elderly gentleman with a pink, cherubic face. Stephen followed my eyes.

'Lovely, isn't he? Even with his clothes on. Well, he was a penniless merchant seaman before he caught Lady T's eye one night at the A&B. Now he's practically living here, he drives his girlfriends around in the Bentley, he gets taken on holidays to the Caribbean.'

'And what does he do in return?'

Stephen rolled his eyes. 'Give a little, get a lot. That's the rule in this game. Officially he's Templeton's secretary, but, well, you know …'

I looked over to the piano, where Mervyn was being presented to a group of wealthy looking men of Templeton's age. 'And are they real? Or are they just after you know what?'

'Oh, they're real, all right. Men of affairs. That one, with the spotted cravat, is a very famous West End theatre producer. And that one next to him, the one with the terrible sweater, is, or at least was, Terence Rattigan's boyfriend, he still keeps him in a bijou little lattie in Cornwall Gardens.'

'And who's that, with the awful wig?'

'Oh dear. Has he got it on backwards, do you think? Well, one must allow these little eccentricities to members of the peerage, especially when they are just mad about the movies.'

He prattled on in this vein, detailing who had done what to whom and for how much.

'You seem to know everyone's business, Stephen.'

'Of course, dear. I'm like the spider in the centre of the web.'

Mervyn returned, somewhat the worse for drink, his eyes sparkling. 'Hey, Michael! They want me to do a screen test!'

'I bet they do,' said Stephen, rolling his eyes.

'A proper screen test, out at Pinewood.'

'That's wonderful, Mervyn. Congratulations.'

'This is where it begins, Mikey! The long climb up the ladder to success.'

'It's the snakes you want to watch, dear,' said Stephen. 'You may have to slide down a few. Oh, I say.' He had spotted a particularly brutish looking creature in a black T-shirt and biker boots. 'Isn't that my new husband?'

'So what do you think?' Mervyn was dancing on the balls of his feet, like he did in the ring. 'Should I do it?'

'Why not? It's better than washing dishes.'

'He says he'll put me on at Mr Universe.'

'What? You're joking.'

'Not in the competition, like. As a featured artist.'

'Doing what, exactly?'

'Dunno.' He frowned, then grinned. 'Just poncing around in my underwear I suppose.'

'Nothing too demanding there, then.'

'But, I mean, Mr Universe. Fucking Mr fucking Universe. The Yanks come over for that. They're going to laugh at me. I'm underweight. I look like a fucking plucked chicken.'

'No, you don't.'

'Why would he want me to get up there and make a fool of myself?'

'I'm sure he doesn't …'

'He says he'll get me into films. But they all say that, don't they?'

He carried on like this for a while, blowing hot and cold with alternate breaths. The party got busy, and loud, and unbearably hot. Stephen was nowhere to be seen, neither was his new husband. Every time we tried to leave, Mervyn was accosted by yet another elderly admirer.

'I've followed your career with great interest ...'

'Those marvellous pictures in *Man's World* ...'

'Well, I must say, Gerald really didn't do you justice ...'

'Dinner one day, perhaps, or drinks at my place in Albany ...'

Hands fluttered above and below, cards were given, promises made. Mervyn's smile was starting to look strained.

'For fuck's sake, Michael,' he said, 'get me out of here.'

We ran all the way to Victoria station, whooping and screaming, smoked three cigarettes on the top of the bus home and took full advantage of the fact that Stephen did not return to the flat that night.

The area round Argyll Street was choked. Those with tickets sat in cafés reading their programmes and analysing the competition. Those without set up camp on the pavements, with Thermos flasks and sandwiches, getting pally with the stage door staff in the hope that they might slip in when the show was underway. When we arrived at noon, the area was at a standstill, the crowds spilling out into Regent Street in the west and Oxford Street in the north. Around the Palladium itself they swarmed like bees round a hive full of honey.

We got out of the taxi – we could have walked in less time than it took to find a cab and negotiate the traffic, but Stephen insisted we travel in style – and while I paid, Mervyn signed autographs.

'Oh my God! It's Mervyn Wright! Mervyn! Mervyn! Over here, Mervyn!' Cameras clicked, programmes and pens were thrust in his face. Some of the younger fans actually screamed. Mervyn took it all as his due, kissing the girls, shaking the boys' hands.

I propelled him gently through the crowd, and we made it to

the stage door intact. He turned and waved like a proper movie star before we went inside.

'Fuck,' he said, breathless, 'did you see that? They fucking love me!'

'They certainly do.'

'I mean, that's just from a few appearances in muscle mags. Think what it'll be like when they've seen me in a movie.'

'One step at a time, Valentino. Let's get this show on the road.'

The backstage areas were hot and crowded, with fifty-five bodybuilders competing in the amateur and professional contests, not to mention the orchestra, the compere and a host of variety acts, the judges and other officials, the reporters and the photographers. In every dressing room, a naked muscleman stood surrounded by clothed men, some kneeling, some sitting, some standing, scribbling, taking photos. Nervous types hovered on the sidelines, catching what glimpses they could. The bolder ones were allowed to help in the oiling-up process.

I deposited Mervyn in his dressing room and positioned myself in the wings, having secured an official photography permit, and watched the auditorium filling up. Men outnumbered women by twenty to one.

The house lights went down, the band struck up the overture and the compere bounced on stage in his ill-fitting grey suit, slicked-back hair and spivvy moustache. The curtain went up and the audience gasped and the band played on. Ten girls in swimsuits were arranged decoratively on low podia, singly and in pairs, their feet encased in white high-heeled shoes. Behind them, standing against the rear curtain, were thirteen of the world's best-developed men, in trunks and bare feet. These were the juniors, all under twenty-one; I recognised a couple from parties and magazines, including a blond seventeen-year-old who, they said, was a shoo-in for the junior Mr Universe title. They paraded, the audience applauded, and I snapped away; pictures like these are money in the bank, and we need it.

A dark-haired youth in minute leopard-skin briefs bounced on from the wings and took up a pose centre stage: Paul Nash, the rising young Birmingham bodybuilder, all white teeth and doe eyes. Three thousand pairs of eyes devoured every detail of his body as he turned, stopped, posed and flexed. If mere will-power could destroy fabric, those pants would have had it.

But Nash, for all his charms, could not stop a distracted murmur from passing through the crowd. The air was full of whispering, as heads turned towards a box at stage left where a giant of a man in a black suit stood nodding and waving. It was Mickey Hargitay, the Hungarian Mr Universe and former Mae West muscleman ... and if Mickey was there, then surely ...

The compere strode on, microphone in hand. 'Ladies and gentlemen, please give a special Mr Universe welcome to ...'

She stepped into the box, her hair radioactively white, her breasts bursting out of a tight floral dress.

'Miss Jayne Mansfield!'

The audience rose and cheered. Jayne blew kisses, leaned forward and threatened to spill over into the stalls. Mickey loomed behind her.

After nearly two minutes of adulation, Jayne took her seat and the show went on. Paul Nash – whose pectoral development almost rivalled Miss Mansfield's – blew a kiss back to the box.

I felt a hand on my shoulder.

'She's here! She's fucking here!'

'She certainly is.' I reloaded my camera. 'In person.'

'Christ, Michael, she's going to see me in my knickers.'

'Lucky girl.'

'Look what she's fucking done to me!' He pulled my hand down to the front of his trunks.

'You'd better get rid of that before you go on, or there will be riots in the front rows.'

'There's plenty back there that would like to help me out, too. Don't worry, I'm saving it for later.'

The show continued with light relief from Margaret Stannett, 'the Super-strong Housewife', a sturdy young woman with Betty Grable hair and silver boots who wowed the audience with a display of dumbbell swinging. Next up were the professionals, giants of men who had been training for so long that they no longer resembled human beings. I lost interest, and scanned the audience instead. Row upon row of pale faces turned up towards the footlights, hands clasped as if in prayer.

It was time for the results. The popular American, Bruce Randall, took the honours in Class 1, and Paul Wynter, 'famed for his dusky muscular excellence' according to the programme, was the winner among the shorter men. I was so busy with my camera I barely heard the next announcement.

'And now, ladies and gentlemen, with a singular display of muscle control, please give a big Universe welcome to London's very own Mr Mervyn Wright!'

There were screams as the lights went down. The stage was dark. I heard the thump, thump of bare feet on the boards, but could see nothing.

A single spotlight lit Mervyn from above, casting deep shadows under his brows, his cheekbones, his lips. Every muscle stood out in sharp relief, catching the spot in dazzling highlights. Framed by the darkness, isolated in the spotlight, he seemed distant, unattainable, as if he was being taken away from me.

I remembered a night in Blackpool, a dingy room, a single overhead bulb.

He stood for a moment at ease, the weight on his left leg, his right leg slightly bent, like a Greek statue. And then, in time with the roll of a drum, he flexed. His fists met in front of his waist. His legs sprang to life, the thighs huge and striated, his torso a relief map of ridges and valleys. The audience gasped, and Mervyn scowled, holding the pose, exaggerating it until the veins popped out on his arms. And then the lights changed, the follow spot hit him from the balcony and he smiled. The crowd roared as he paraded the footlights like a star taking an ovation. Up in the box, Jayne's white head leaned towards her husband, whispering in his ear.

Mervyn made the most of his three-minute spot. Naturally, he overran. The orchestra finished, the compere came back on but Mervyn did not want to leave, nor did the audience want to let him. He played them like a pro, cupping a hand behind his ear to make them shout louder and then, when the compere tried to edge him off, doing an elaborate pantomime of dismay. Finally, when the compere was glancing into the wings for backup, Mervyn did a perfect handstand and left the stage upside down. It took a good minute to quell the applause.

'Did you get pictures?'

'Of course I did.'

'Did she see me?'

'I think so.'

'Pinch me, Mike. Harder! I'm not dreaming, am I? Ouch!' He rubbed his upper arm. 'Not that fucking hard. Cunt.' He threw his arms around me. 'I've got you to thank for all this,' he said, gesturing to the stage, the audience. 'Come here.' He pushed me into the darkness of the backstage corridors and kissed me.

Templeton's house was blazing with light and bursting with people. There were flambeaux on either side of the door, and uniformed footmen (recruited from the Wellington barracks, said Stephen) to hand the ladies from their cabs. Waiters circulated with drinks and canapés. It was well after midnight when we arrived; this party would keep swinging well into Sunday.

Mervyn, Stephen and I ascended the steps together. Templeton put a proprietorial arm round Mervyn's shoulders and whisked him away.

There was a jazz trio playing in the reception room, vases of red roses on every surface, the twinkle of diamonds around the ladies' throats competing with the crystal drops of the chandeliers. The men of affairs had brought their wives or, if they weren't the marrying type, had rustled up a lady friend. Half the male contestants from the Palladium were crammed into that room. The air was redolent of baby oil.

We drank and ate and Stephen bitched and drank too much.

Mervyn made an entrance half an hour later, freshly groomed, wearing on his arm a carbon copy of Jayne Mansfield. Flashbulbs popped, and he swept her up in his arms. She shrieked, threw her head back and kicked off a shoe. I wondered if this had been rehearsed downstairs.

'Pretty as a picture,' said an amphibious voice behind us. It was Gerald, older and dirtier than ever, his fingers brown with nicotine, the ever-present beret at a crazy angle.

'Gerald, darling,' said Stephen, extending a fingertip, 'how lovely to see you.'

'Like the Wicked Carabosse, always turning up where I'm not wanted.'

'Wonderful show,' I said, for want of any better remark.

'Yes,' hissed Gerald. 'Wonderful. So much one could tell if one wanted to.'

'Oh Gerald,' said Stephen, 'you always dish the dirt on everyone.'

'Take your boyfriend,' he said, gesturing towards Mervyn and scattering cigarette ash over the carpet. 'Templeton's new discovery. Oh, he snaps them up and cleans them up, doesn't he? And look at the lovely playmate. Our very own platinum blonde. Miss Maxine Trent. Well, they look quite lovely together, don't they? Quite convincing. But scratch the surface …' He wiggled his little finger, which had a horribly long and dirty nail.

Templeton was frowning in our direction.

'Oops, she's seen me,' said Gerald. 'And any minute now one of his delightful henchmen will come over and tell me that there's a taxi waiting for me at the door. I don't fit in here, you see, with all the ladies and the diamonds and the stink of respectability.

But he daren't throw me out. One little shake from me and the whole house of cards comes tumbling down.'

'Mr Gerald, sir …'

It was Don, Templeton's 'secretary'.

'Don't tell me, angel face. My carriage awaits.'

'Sir.'

Gerald poked Don in the chest. 'You're looking good, Don. Almost as good as when you posed for me. Remember those photos?'

Don's eyes flickered over to Templeton.

'Don't worry, ladies,' shouted Gerald; the room hushed. 'I won't cause a scene. The wicked fairy is leaving the party.' He shuffled towards the door, passing Mervyn. 'Hey, Sleeping Beauty,' he said, 'watch out. Just one little prick and poof! All this disappears.'

He cackled as he was escorted to the door.

09

Everyone is dying.

Jonathan says that he's a trendsetter and they're all copying him. First of all, I notice that Andy, my steroid dealer at the gym, hasn't been around for a couple of weeks, I assume he's on holiday until someone tells me that he was found dead in bed by his boyfriend. They went out the night before, took cocaine, ecstasy and GHB, came home and had sex and Andy never woke up. It's funny going to the gym now. He's just … not around any more. Oh well. That's one way to give up steroids.

Then there's Hadley. He's been getting thinner in the face, and much redder, for months, and everyone sort of knows that he's got cancer, although nobody knows of what. Now he's in hospital – private, of course – and he's had secondary tumours removed from his neck, but the main cancer is in his lungs and it's inoperable. Nobody is saying 'HIV-related' but we're all thinking it.

Jonathan wants me to go with him to visit Hadley, 'because I want a witness to make sure that the bitch is really going to die,' he says, but I think it's because he's terrified of going into a hospital on his own. Since his near-fatal Valium-and-red-wine cocktail, Jonathan has been jittery, erratic and even less reliable than usual. 'When I came out of hospital,' he says, 'I thought that maybe life was a wonderful gift and I should start taking more care of myself. Then I thought about how fragile life is, and that maybe I should just live every day as if it was my last. And then I just decided to stop thinking about it at all.'

Hadley looks terrible. His face is sunken, his eyes protruding, his ears sticking out from the side of his skull. 'Fuck,' says Jonathan, 'she looks like Gollum.' There's a long crooked wound on the left-hand side of his throat, the edges angry and pink around the stitches. He's wearing a pair of hospital pyjamas, but you can see how the skin, once stretched by his massive muscles, is hanging off him. It's only a few weeks since I last saw him, but he looks like a different species.

'Hadley, darling,' says Jonathan.

We've brought nothing; Jonathan said it would be throwing money away, that we should save it for a wreath.

Hadley opens a gummy eye. 'Hey, Nate.'

'It's Jonathan, actually,' he snaps. 'Look. Here's Robbie to see you. You always did like Robbie.'

'Aaah …' He raises a weak hand. 'The Robster. Good to see you, man. Looking hot.' He starts coughing. It obviously causes him a great deal of pain.

'You sound terrible, Hadley,' says Jonathan, casting a snooty eye over the Get Well cards that crowd the bedside cabinet. 'You ought to suck a Fisherman's Friend.'

Hadley laughs, which hurts too.

'Where's Nico?' asks Jonathan.

'Oh …' Hadley gestures with a hand that has a drip stuck into the back of it. 'He's away … Working …'

'And we all know the sort of work he's doing,' says Jonathan, but quietly, so only I can hear. Then he says out loud, 'What a shame he can't be by your side. After all you've done for him.'

Hadley's gone very quiet. A nurse comes over to change a dressing, and we leave.

'That was unnecessary,' I say, as we light cigarettes outside. 'The poor guy is dying.'

'Yes. Isn't it marvellous.' Jonathan inhales deeply. 'No more fags for Hadley.'

'You don't think he'll come out alive?'

'I sincerely hope not.'

'God, what did he do to you?'

'Oh, nothing much,' says Jonathan. 'Just a small matter of threatening to kill me.'

And so the whole story comes out, about how Jonathan's £3,000 drug debt escalated to the point that Hadley gave him a week to sort himself out, and when the week was up he sent a large man round to Jonathan's house in the middle of the night to frighten him, and that's when Jonathan decided that the only solution to his predicament was theft, and went down to Hadley's gallery to help himself to photographs of vomit. Even though I still can't fully condone Jonathan's descent into crime, it suddenly seems like a much more viable option.

'Anyway,' says Jonathan, 'I've been punished for it. I felt so bad about the whole thing that I … Well. You know what I did. Silly me.'

This is the nearest Jonathan has ever come to telling me why he tried to kill himself. He likes everyone to think that he's entirely superficial, and is embarrassed by any suggestion of depth. So am I.

To lighten the mood, we go into Soho for a drink or ten. Jonathan knows everyone in every bar we go in. There's kisses and hugs and he even pays for a round, which is a first. I suspect he's still dealing. Obviously his dark night of the soul has taught him nothing.

We end up pissed at my place, Jonathan chopping out lines of coke on the kitchen table. He's necking vodka that he's found in my fridge, and telling me some story about how he went to a club in north London called Piss, where men were lying with their heads in the trough, for everyone's convenience.

'You know me,' he says, 'I can't pee if there's anyone else around, so this was my worst nightmare, but eventually I'd drunk so much I was past caring, and if I didn't go I was going to wet myself, so I just think what the hell and stand over this old bald bloke in a rubber vest who's lying there in all the muck. And I've got it out and I'm about to piss in his mouth and he looks up at me and turns his head to one side and says "No. Not you."'

Jonathan starts laughing hysterically.

'No! Not you!' He puts on a silly old queen voice. 'No! Not you!' He knocks back a large neat vodka. 'My God,' he says, 'I've put up with a lot of rejection in my life, but that really takes the biscuit.'

I'm laughing too, but now I realise that Jonathan is crying, or at least it looks as if he might be. It's so hard to tell.

'Don't take it to heart,' I say. 'There's plenty more fish in the sea.'

We carry on drinking and doing lines and when I wake up in the morning, Jonathan is cradled in my arms like a drunken child.

I'm on autopilot at work these days. People occasionally say 'You're very quiet' but that suits me. I'm there to earn a living, not to make friends. Anna keeps her distance. Derek watches me like a hawk. Simon sometimes brings me cups of tea or stops for a chat, or sends me jokey little emails that usually end by asking me out for lunch, but I'm always too busy.

I don't have a sex life any more, not since Stuart left. I don't even wank. I go to the gym and I see people looking at me, smiling at me, looking over their shoulders as they walk towards the sauna or the steam room, but I can't be bothered to follow, and eventually the offers dry up. Even Sauna Slut isn't waving his willy at me any more. I feel like a beautifully sculpted block of ice.

Sometimes I go to a gay sauna, in an attempt to thaw myself out. There's one up the road from the flat, and it's always busy, any hour of the day or night. The minute I walk in, I'm surrounded. I'm not the only gym body in the place – there are maybe three or four of us, each the focus of a sort of feeding frenzy. I move from the changing room into the shower, from shower to sauna, from sauna to steam room, from steam room to maze, from maze to cabin, always with a school of hungry scavengers around me. I let them feed. If I take a bit of Tina, or a bit of GHB or Viagra, whatever's on offer, I can get it up, which is what they want. But I never come. When they realise they're not going to get anything out of me, they move on, to make way for others.

'Fucking Muscle Marys,' says one disgruntled customer. 'All show, no action.' I'm a shop-window dummy. For display purposes only.

I wake up one morning with a terrible headache and a temperature. I go to the bathroom and shoot about a gallon of diarrhoea down the toilet. Thank God it's a Saturday, is my first thought, and I won't have to take another day off work. I'm feeling worse on Sunday, dehydrated and slightly delirious. I ought to phone someone, because it's frightening to be ill and alone, but I don't want anyone to see me like this. I still feel like shit on Monday but I drag myself into the office, and on Tuesday, and for the rest of the week. I even go to the gym a couple of times; I've got no energy, just getting changed exhausts me, but I will not give in.

Finally I look so terrible that Anna tells me to stop acting like a child and go to see a doctor. The doctor takes one look at my yellow eyes and says, 'You have hepatitis,' and starts feeling my liver. Then I have to pee into a plastic canister and he dips a little stick in it and frowns.

'Have you been having unprotected sex?'

'No.' I haven't. Not since Stuart, anyway.

He takes blood and tells me to stay in bed for a week, eat lots of vegetables, avoid alcohol and fatty foods (as if). I tell him I can't take time off work, and he says that if I don't I am putting myself at risk of cirrhosis or cancer of the liver, the choice is mine, and he practically pushes me out of the door.

So I'm spending a lot of time sleeping, reading, watching telly, playing patience on my laptop, writing a bit, but it's no longer for public consumption and it's getting so depressing that my heart isn't really in it.

I text Jonathan a few times but he doesn't reply, and when I try to call him there's a message saying the number is unavailable. Which means that Jonathan has changed his mobile yet again, but this time he has omitted to tell me.

Simon calls from the office, and seems to know that I'm ill, even though the official line is that I'm 'working from home', and offers to bring round any shopping that I need, or books, or DVDs, but I can't face him and so I don't reply. He sends me a card anyway. Nobody else does. I haven't told anyone I'm ill, not even my parents. They'd only worry.

I sleep, sleep, sleep for hours on end, whole days at a time. It's like I'm catching up on a lifetime's late nights. Mervyn looks down at me from the bedstead, a picture of health in his leopard-skin pouch.

The diarrhoea clears up, my temperature returns to normal, and my piss, which has been a horrible dark brownish colour, runs clear. My eyes are no longer yellow. I'm better.

I go out for a walk along the river, on my own, kicking through the falling leaves and watching the children jumping in puddles, driving their mums mad, laughing and running away, giggling and wriggling as they let themselves get caught.

I go home, pour four bottles of vodka down the sink and flush my stash down the bog. I think about putting my flat on the market and moving out of London. I look on estate agents' websites to see what sort of price it might fetch. I'd like to live in a cottage looking out to sea. I'd like to have a dog.

A letter arrives from Stephen. Michael is dead.

'He passed away peacefully in his sleep,' it says. 'We had no warning, and he had not been ill. I think he was just in a hurry to join Mervyn.'

There are details of the funeral, but I really can't take any more time off work. I write to Stephen, expressing my condolences, trying to suppress any hint of the relief that I'm ashamed to feel. The thought of trudging to and from Michael's flat through the dismal outer London suburbs, watching him grow older and more needy, fills me with dismay. I can't help it.

I've still got his boxes of stuff. I don't know what to do with them. Obviously he won't be wanting them back. Perhaps the family will ask for them, the 'estate'. I can't imagine they're worth anything. And they are in the way here; Michael himself said that they would be. So he'd have understood why I've moved them out into the bin store. If anyone really wants them, they can come and get them.

Two weeks later, another letter from Stephen. A note – unsigned, no 'Dear Robert' or anything – it just says 'He left this for you'. Enclosed is a blue envelope with my name on the front. It feels quite thick. I don't have time to read it, I'm on my way to work, and I put it in the 'important but boring' box for later filing.

Nine

Mervyn and I are established in what we laughingly refer to as a 'bachelor pad' a little further up Queensway. 'You want to watch just how far up Queensway you go,' said Stephen when we left, dabbing his eye (which was perfectly dry). We have barely seen him in recent weeks, he's out so much, 'with candles at both ends' as he puts it. He doesn't talk much about his work any more, but there were strange callers in the middle of the night, whispered telephone conversations, the occasional unexplained black eye. We do not miss any of this.

It's a nice flat, large, airy and furnished, with a porter and a lift and hot water on demand and access to a roof garden. It has two bedrooms, only one of which we use unless, for appearances' sake, we are obliged at least to ruffle the sheets in the other. Or unless we have had a disagreement. There have been a few, mostly relating to Mervyn's much-publicised friendship with up-and-coming screen siren Maxine Trent, to whose well-upholstered wagon he has hitched his star. Edward Templeton says they will be the British Mickey and Jayne. Stephen says, 'Mickey and Minnie, more like,' in reference to Miss Trent's squeaky voice, which is overdubbed when she is lucky enough to get a speaking role. So far she has appeared in a handful of movies for Rank, mostly in party scenes, as a barmaid in one ('Gin and lemon, dear?') and as a gangster's girlfriend in another. Templeton plans to launch them both in a boxing picture, a sort of British *Somebody Up There Likes Me*, which has already been through a dozen different titles – *Seconds Out!*, *Put 'em Up!* And endless variations involving the world 'ring' – and as many scriptwriters. Mervyn is already focusing on the gala opening, the Leicester Square marquee with his name in lights, the dinner jackets and furs and diamonds, and Maxine Trent on his arm.

'Think of it, Mike,' he says constantly, his hand blocking the words in the air, 'Mel Wright'. I can't bring myself to call him Mel, although the studio thought Mervyn was too plebeian. It was hard enough learning to call him Mervyn. I still think of him, really, as Wright.

He spends his days at Pinewood, where there is a well equipped gym frequented by several other stars-in-waiting. Occasionally a producer swoops down and plucks one of them out to do a couple of days' stunt work on the picture of the day. Mervyn has jumped off tall buildings, fallen through plate-glass windows and plunged into freezing cold water, always hoping to be spotted and fast-tracked to stardom. Meanwhile, the script goes to and from the head office, a scriptwriter is sacked, a new director is appointed, a new title invented, and we are no nearer to a camera.

I spend my days at the Treasury, like an automaton, earning our keep. We can live in some comfort on my wages because, of course, the rent on the bachelor pad is taken care of by Edward Templeton.

One lunchtime, I came home to pick up some papers that I'd forgotten to take with me in the morning, and found Mervyn in bed with Maxine Trent. To be exact, she was bent over the bed, and he was standing behind her.

I walked out without saying a word, went back to the office, told the switchboard not to put through any calls and, when five o'clock finally rolled round, went to the nearest pub and drank myself stupid. When I got home at ten, the flat was empty, the bed made, a few of Mervyn's belongings, including his suitcase and his best clothes, missing. No note.

He could have gone anywhere: his nan's in Shepherd's Bush, Maxine Trent's (she too is kept in style by Edward Templeton), or to Templeton's himself. Or to any of the other admirers and lovers that I suspected he has. How long has this been going on? While I was at the Treasury, and he was waiting for stardom, who else has he entertained in what I stupidly thought of as our home?

I heard nothing from him the next day, or the next week. I left an empty flat in the morning, returned to an empty flat at night, usually drunk. I tried to see Stephen, to pour out my troubles over a bottle of wine, but he never answered the door. Sometimes there was a light in the window, shadows moving across the blinds, but nobody came down.

Mervyn came home late one night, or early one morning; the birds were already singing. I heard his key in the lock, as I had so often prayed to do, and woke from my drunken sleep with a bang, my heart pounding. I saw him standing in the doorway in the dim light.

'Wright,' I groaned, my voice still thick with sleep. 'What the fuck are you doing here?'

He climbed into bed, fully clothed, and held me so tight I thought my ribs would break. He was shaking. I badly needed to piss, and I was conscious that my breath stank of booze, but he would not let me go. When he was finally able to speak, he said, 'I love you, Michael, oh God I'm so sorry, I love you, I love you,' and started kissing me on the mouth, the neck, the chest.

After we'd finished, he took a shower, I had a long piss, then joined him under the hot water. We washed each other's backs, kissed, dried each other, and shaved together at the sink. I was so relieved to have him back that I swallowed the recriminations that kept rising in my throat, and waited to hear what he had to say.

In the event, it wasn't much. Trivia from the studios. The latest verdict on the screenplay. Setbacks and achievements at the gym. No clue as to where he'd been living, who he'd been fucking and what had prompted the tears and protestations of love. Knowing

Wright as I do, it must have been something very bad. He is not the crying kind.

We had breakfast, and he chaffed me about the empty bottles and dirty crockery in the sink. 'You can't cope without me, can you?' he said, adjusting my tie as I tried to leave for work. He was still dressed in nothing but his underwear, his body catching the rays of the sun that poured through the huge east-facing living-room window.

'Not really, no. I can't.'

'Off you go, tiger. You'll be late.'

'Will you be here when I get back?'

'Course.'

And will you be entertaining in my absence, I wanted to ask, but instead I squeezed his arse and walked to the bus stop with a lighter tread than I've had for some time.

When I got home, he was drunk.

'Fucking bastard Templeton, fucking cunting bastard, who the fuck does he think he is?'

The air was thick with cigarette smoke, and with the fug of Wright's anger. I went round opening windows, taking off my tie, my shoes, pouring myself a drink.

'What's the matter?'

'Calls me up today saying he wants me to drive him out to Pinewood. Me!'

'What's so wrong with that? You always said you wanted to get your hands on his cars.'

'Because I'm not a fucking chauffeur!'

'Calm down. It's not the end of the ...'

'And then when we get there he tells me to wait in the car because he'll need me later.'

'So?'

'I'm supposed to be an actor, aren't I? Not some fucking flunkey.'

'Has something happened?'

'Then he says there's been another setback with the movie, some fucking crap about raising the money, always the same fucking story about co-production bollocks and I don't know what. So I ask him how long it's going to take to sort it out and he says he can't tell, they've got a full slate of movies to make for next year and we'll just have to see.'

'Oh.'

'So I ask him what's really going on and that's when he tells me about the pictures.'

I had a horrible feeling I knew what was coming. 'What pictures?'

'Oh, fuck it. When I got out of the nick I was broke, wasn't I? I told you I went round all the physique studios and made a few quid here and there. Well, some of them paid better than others.'

'Gerald.'

'He fucking told me that nobody would see the pictures except for a few of his personal friends. That they were fucking private. He gave me ten quid.'

'That's a lot of money.'

'Ha fucking ha. It seemed like a lot of money at the time. It was the difference between eating and not eating. Or going with one of those dirty old cunts in the West End. I could have done that you know, twenty times a day, if I wanted to, but I didn't.'

'What's in the photos, Wright?'

'You know … the sort of thing …'

'Nudes.'

'Yeah, but …'

'Oh shit. Hard.'

'Yeah.'

'Wanking.'

'Yeah, all right, you don't have to fucking spell it out. You weren't so fucking prudish at one time.'

'But I didn't sell those pictures at five quid a go to anyone who came calling, did I?'

'That fucking bastard,' he said, slamming his fist into the wall, 'I'm going to fucking kill him.'

'Calm down, for Christ's sake. How far has this gone?'

'Someone sent a photo to the head of the studio.'

'What, to J. Arthur himself?'

'Yeah, that's a fucking laugh, isn't it? Here's your new boy in nothing but a pair of boots, having a good old J. Arthur.'

'Did he ask for money?'

'I don't fucking know, do I? All Templeton would say is that under the current circumstances it would be unwise to launch my career in pictures.'

'I see.'

He carried on, swearing and spitting and punching.

'Is that why you came back?'

'What?'

'This morning. Is that what made you come back to me? Templeton sacked you?'

'No, of course not.'

'Or did Maxine throw you out when she heard that you weren't going to be her leading man?'

'Fuck off, Mickey, it's not like that.'

'No. Of course not.'

'Don't you start being a cunt too.' His voice cracked. 'I can't …'

I put an arm around him, and let him sob out all his frustration, shame and broken dreams.

After a week of peace and normality, the phone rang in the middle of the night. Mervyn just rolled over, taking most of the blankets with him.

'Michael? It's Stephen. Are you all right?'

'Stephen … It's three o'clock in the morning.'

'You haven't heard, then.' He was practically whispering. I could hear traffic in the background; he must have been in a phone box.

'Heard what? Stephen, are you in some kind of trouble?'

'Me, dear? No. Not me.'

'Then what's this about?'

'It's Mervyn.'

There was a long silence, then I asked, 'What about Mervyn?'

'There's a warrant for his arrest.'

I looked over at the bed, at Mervyn's sleeping form, the blankets slowly rising and falling. 'What for?'

'For Gerald's murder,' he hissed. 'Don't tell me you didn't know.'

'Of course I didn't … But Mervyn didn't do it. For God's sake, Stephen, what's happening?'

'If I were you, dear, I'd get out of there as fast as you can, and take Pretty Boy with you.' The pips went, and I just heard Stephen saying 'Good luck' before the line went dead.

I climbed back into bed, freezing cold. Mervyn turned towards me, threw a heavy arm across me. 'Wha'wazzat …'

And then the doorbell rang.

A letter arrived from Edward Templeton, advising me that he would need vacant possession of the flat as of the weekend, as he had new tenants lined up, hoping that we had enjoyed our stay, yours faithfully. No word about Mervyn's arrest or forthcoming trial. Nothing but those few businesslike lines, signed pp by a secretary.

I packed everything, hired a car and took it all to my parents' house, piling up the boxes and bags in the spare room and the attic. As usual, no questions were asked. They watched me going up and down the stairs with fear in their eyes. I stayed for lunch, packed a small suitcase with a few necessities and got the Tube back to town, with nowhere to stay, no address, no telephone, nothing. I called on Stephen but the concierge told me he had gone. I took a room at the YMCA.

There has been nothing in the papers about the murder. I

scan them in the staffroom every day, but not a word. There are paragraphs and letters about WEST END VICE which the police seem to think they can tackle, but that is all. What little I know I have learned from the pubs and clubs, where I spend most evenings looking for Stephen, who seems to have disappeared off the face of the earth. I am afraid for him. I realise that I know nothing about his life over the last year. I haven't asked. I suppose I didn't really care, until now, when I need him. I am sure he knows something about Gerald's death. Why else would he have phoned when he did, before Mervyn's arrest?

Several different versions of events are circulating, but all agree on the main points: Gerald was murdered at his flat in Oxford Street, beaten to death with a tripod, his head so badly smashed that he was unrecognisable. There were no signs of a break-in, but drawers and safes had been broken open, and there had been a fire, whether deliberate or accidental nobody knew. Of course, everyone knows that Mervyn has been arrested, and the general assumption is that he went to see Gerald in connection with the photographs that had been sent to the studio, they had got into a fight, Mervyn lost his temper, beat Gerald to death and then attempted to destroy the negatives.

Three weeks after his arrest, I was allowed to visit Mervyn on remand in Brixton Prison. He looked remarkably well, and had obviously found his way to whatever exercise facilities exist in such places. He was thin in the face, a little dark around the eyes, but apart from that the only big difference in his appearance was the absence of Brylcreem. His hair was soft and clean and hung down over his forehead, where it irritated him. He kept pushing it out of his eyes.

We sat across a square wood table, deeply scarred with long black cigarette burns.

'Thank God,' he said, putting his hands over mine. The guards looked and sneered. 'Yeah, go on, have a good look,' said Wright, then muttered 'fucking wankers'. It was not his first time in prison, and he knew exactly how far he could push it.

'What's happening out there, Michael? Have they found out who did it yet?'

'I don't know …'

'Christ, I wish they'd hurry up. I'm starting to get ants in my pants.' He whispered. 'And I'm so fucking horny. Can't you just put your hand under the table …'

'Templeton kicked us out of the flat, you know.'

'Shit. Where's my stuff?'

'Don't worry. It's safe. And yes, thank you, I'm fine, I've taken a room at the Y.'

'That must be fun,' he said.

'Oh yeah. Orgies every night. Bit like prison.'

'Michael, I've got to get out of here. I've got to get a better lawyer. It's fucking shit, them trying to pin this on me. I didn't fucking kill Gerald.'

'Didn't you?'

He pushed his chair away from the table, and picked at his dirty nails. 'I see. It's come to that, has it?'

'What?'

'Even you think I did it.'

'Well did you?'

'If you have to ask that …'

'I'm afraid I do.'

'You don't trust me, then.'

I lit cigarettes, handed one to him. He smoked deeply, exhaled long. 'No. Fair enough. You've got no reason to. I've been shit to you, Mikey, I admit it. What can I say? I'm a cunt. I always have been, and I probably always will be.'

'Yeah, but you're my cunt.'

He laughed nervously. 'Don't let this lot hear you say that. There's enough of them who'd like me to be their cunt for the duration.' He leaned forward, lowered his voice. 'But for what it's worth, I want to say two things. First, no, I didn't kill Gerald. I'd have liked to, and I'm not sorry he's dead, but someone else got to him first. End of story. Second, I love you …'

'Wright …'

'Don't interrupt, because you won't hear this often, at least not when I'm sober. I wanted you from the first minute I saw you looking at me at that stupid fucking Infection parade at Reville.'

'I didn't …'

'You did. Your eyes, Mickey. They always give you away. I thought, "There's one that might be a bit of fun …"'

'A bit of fun. Well, I was certainly that.'

'At first, you were. I was like all the other wankers up there, chasing pussy, being the big man, king of the ring, all that jazz. And I didn't want to be queer. I still don't if you want the truth. But you were always there, at the back of my mind, and I couldn't help it. Every time we … You know, we nearly … I fucking hated you for making me that way, and I hated myself for acting like a cunt, and I kept pushing you away and you kept coming back for more.'

'Bollocks. It's you that kept coming back.'

'Because that was it, Mikey. I realised, didn't I? That this wasn't going to go away. That I was stuck with you.'

'And it's taken a murder charge to make all this clear to you, has it?'

'Maybe. I don't know. All I know is that I have to get out of here so that we can start our lives again. Start properly this time. No more fucking around. No more chasing rainbows.'

'No more Maxine Trents.'

'Yeah …' He looked wistful. 'She was the last. And fucking good she was too.'

'I don't want to hear it.'

The bell rang, and the guards started moving around, separating the kissing couples, ushering out the crying mums and dazed looking kids.

'Mickey, you've got to help me.'

'How can I? The lawyers are doing all they can.'

'Someone knows who did it. Someone framed me.'

'What can I …'

'Come on, you two, none of that.'

'Fuck you, screw.'

'Mervyn, for God's sake …'

'Please, Mickey, you've got to do something.'

'Get up, Wright. You're on governor's report.'

'I'll fucking …' He stopped himself, stood up. 'Don't let me down, Michael. Remember what I said. All that I said. Understand? All that I said.'

I stood outside the prison gates with the rest of the visitors, the wind whistling up Brixton Hill and blowing grit into our eyes.

He loved me, he said, he'd always loved me, he wanted to get out and start again. I would do anything for that, for the promise of that. And he knew it.

10

I'm losing weight. Since Andy disappeared, I've not been taking steroids, and my muscles are just evaporating, dissolving back into my bloodstream, being shat and pissed out of my body. Shirts and jackets that used to strain at the buttons and seams now hang quite normally. I am starting to look like everybody else. I'm still going to the gym, but only out of habit. I no longer feel the thrill of challenge as I step out on to the floor. I'm going through the motions with the weights, watching the others sweating and straining, grunting and grinning, spotting for each other, lifting up their vests to show their abs, talking about supplements and carbloading, whispering about steroids and hormones. I used to be the best of the lot of them, the cock of the walk, and now I'm melting, melting into the background. I don't get the envious looks in the changing rooms. I don't plan my route from the locker to the shower to get the maximum reaction. Now I just wash and dress and go home to an empty flat and watch DVDs till I'm tired enough to go to bed. Sometimes I drink myself to sleep. Sometimes, if I feel panicky, I take half a Valium. I'm eking them out, because supplies are running low, and I don't want to see the sort of people who could sell them to me.

They're out in force for Hadley's funeral. Stuart is there, which I was dreading, and Jonathan, who pounces on me and then watches my face for a reaction every time Stuart comes into view. I've been practising a detached and slightly hostile look for days, and I think I've got it down pat. It's become my default expression, which is just as well because Stuart's with Matt, both of them bigger than ever, as big as houses, like walking sides of beef from a meat warehouse, gossiping behind their hands like vastly inflated schoolgirls, looking over at me and Jonathan and giggling, which is nice for a funeral, I think.

It's a sunny November morning, not really cold, but everyone seems to have taken this opportunity to debut their winter wardrobe, so there are a lot of casually-tied scarves and pre-distressed overcoats and a smattering of absurd fur hats, which look very odd with this summer's aviator shades and sunbed tans. There's a certain amount of overheating going on, and some very red, shiny faces, although that could be drug-related. There are several Hadleys-in-waiting in the crowd, pumped up to bursting, ravaged by time and excess but still dressing like American college jocks. They tend to be radically underdressed, tight T-shirts and clamdiggers, even flip-flops, the goosepimples white against the brick-red skin.

Hadley arrives in his coffin, borne on the shoulders of escorts. We follow them into the chapel. 'I wonder how much they're charging for this,' says Jonathan. His foray into prostitution was not a success, as he only got one punter who wanted him to dress as a schoolboy and pelt him with cream horns, which was a complete disaster as Jonathan was on a strict no-dairy diet at the time. 'Six of them, at £120 an hour, say this lasts for two hours …' He mumbles through the calculations half a dozen times, reaching a different answer every time, eventually doing the sum on his phone's built-in calculator, until asked to switch it off by an usher.

Stuart is sitting across the aisle from me, and it's impossible to ignore him. His face is so wide now that his grin is like the Cheshire cat's. I give him my best detached-and-hostile, but seeing him makes my stomach cramp and flip, as if I'm about to get diarrhoea again. It doesn't feel like love. Stuart winks, then whispers something to Matt, but I'm staring ahead so I don't see if Matt turns to look at me. I don't want to see his face.

Various friends are giving speeches about what a great guy

Hadley was, what fun, how talented and generous. There's an ex-wife ('Who knew?' whispers Jonathan, very loud) who cries and laughs at the same time, and several members of Hadley's family, including an elderly mother. There must be at least 200 people in the room, and I can't help wondering if I'll do as well when my time comes. I don't suppose there were that many at Michael's funeral, to which I was too busy to go.

'Nobody's mentioning drugs,' says Jonathan. In fact, nobody has mentioned anything about Hadley's professional life. I suppose it would be in poor taste.

A good-looking young foreigner – I can't place the accent – speaks in halting English about Hadley's love of art, and his patronage of young artists.

'Who's he?' I ask Jonathan.

'Oh, he's the new Nico. He makes online installations. What-ever they are.'

'Where's he from?'

'The back pages of *QX*, dear,' says Jonathan, 'like the rest of 'em.'

The coffin eventually disappears through the curtains, and there's a lot of competitive displays of emotion from the muscle boys. Stuart and Matt are hunched over in their seats, hands over their eyes, shoulders shaking. Even Jonathan, sitting on my right, is sobbing and sniffling. 'What are you crying for?' I whisper. 'You couldn't stand Hadley.'

'I'm not crying for him,' snaps Jonathan. So I guess nearly everybody is taking this as an opportunity to feel very sorry for themselves.

When we get outside, sunglasses are clamped over faces.

The wake is in a nearby pub, where the escorts get quickly drunk and start doing noisy folk dancing, which involves a lot of stamping while one of them plays a guitar. 'Oh, Hadley would have loved this,' I hear someone say.

Stuart materialises in front of me. He's peeled off his outer layers and is now dressed for the hunt, his T-shirt so thin and tight he could be shrink-wrapped. Stuart regards all social events, even funerals, as sexual opportunities. I'm wearing a suit, not least because I have to go back to work.

He places a hand on my chest.

'You've shrunk.' It's an accusation.

'Yes, thanks, I'm very well,' I say, in a social voice. 'And yourself?'

'I don't know why you bothered to come. I didn't notice you crying.'

This is the man over whom I shed so many tears in private. I feel nothing now, not even desire.

'You're right, it is terribly sad for his mother. Well, Stuart, look after yourself.' I hold out my hand.

'See you, Rob.'

'Not if I see you first.' He grins, but I mean it.

I get to work at two o'clock. At half past three, Simon brings me the usual cup of tea. He's the only person, apart from Derek, who knows why I had the morning off.

'Was it awful?'

'Yes. But not for the reasons you might think.'

We go for a walk after work, round and round Lincoln's Inn Fields in the dark, going nowhere, just talking. Simon seems to think that I should be more upset than I am, and when I tell him about the elderly mother he actually seems to be crying a bit himself.

'Honestly, it's not that big a deal,' I say. 'Hadley was one of those people who had a death wish. I mean, really, he just got his wish.'

Simon is quiet for a while, and we complete our fourth or fifth circuit of the square.

'Why did you go to the funeral?' he asks, and I get the impression that my answer to this question might be quite important – to him, at least.

'I was asked.'

'Who by?'

'I don't know. His friends. The people who arranged it.'

'So you went … to … to show your support to them, I suppose.' It's taking Simon a good deal of mental effort to interpret my behaviour in a positive light.

'Yeah, that of course,' I say. We walk another ten steps in silence. 'And to show off this really nice tie I bought for the occasion.'

He stops, I stop, he looks at my face, down at my tie, up into my eyes again, he looks puzzled, like he's trying to make a decision. Eventually he laughs, a great bark of laughter that resounds across the Fields.

'You're too much,' he says, and I think that this is the moment to kiss him, but instead we break our circuit at the corner and head home in different directions.

There's a text from Jonathan when I get off the underground.

'Have you seen yourself? You're famous! Check out Xtube.'

I don't know what he's talking about, but he doesn't leave me in doubt for long, because the phone is ringing before I've even got my key in the door.

'Have you seen it? Well? Have you?'

'Seen what, Jonathan?'

'Are you serious? You really don't know? I mean, you didn't put it up there yourself?'

'I really don't know.'

'Oh my like God. I'm so coming over right now. I wouldn't miss this for the world. Don't do anything. Don't talk to anyone. I'm getting in a taxi now.' He is, I can hear it. He yells my address at the driver. 'Everyone was talking about it at the funeral. Everyone. Couldn't believe you'd do anything so tacky. Oh my God then who was it?'

He keeps this up till I can see the taxi pulling up outside the block. I've got money ready, but it seems that Jonathan is cash rich again. Perhaps he did some dealing at the wake.

He's still talking into his phone as he comes up the stairs, doesn't draw breath as he switches it off and puts it into his pocket.

'Get your computer on,' he says, pushing past me into the living room. It's the first time he hasn't headed straight for the drinks cupboard in the kitchen. 'You are going to fucking die when you see this.'

'I hope not.'

'Right, brace yourself.' He types the word 'gymbunny' into Xtube's search engine and waits, an evil grin on his face.

'What is this, Jonathan?'

Picture boxes have come up around the screen of men sticking metal implements into their arses, advertising GAY CHAT AND DATE 10P PER MIN and telling me to HOOK UP WITH HOT PEOPLE IN BRACKNELL, which is frankly ambitious.

There's a blank grey oblong in the middle of all this, a little daisy wheel going round and round.

And then my face.

'What the fuck.'

'Wait. Look. Here we go.'

The image is moving. It's a shaky, blurry video shot in this very room of me dancing around, taking off my clothes, showing my cock, wanking, spreading my arse, fingering myself, and sucking someone else's cock. I say 'someone else' but of course I mean Stuart, who shot this little masterpiece on his phone when we were, as they say, courting.

It lasts about two minutes and I end up with a faceful. I remember Stuart saying that it would keep him warm on the nights we weren't together.

'So I'm guessing that you didn't post this yourself,' says Jonathan.

I'm so upset that I don't know what to say. I pace around the room and swear. Jonathan watches me with an idiot grin on his face.

'I've got to get it off there. Suppose someone sees it.'

'Judging by the number of comments,' he says, scrolling down the page, 'plenty of people have already.' He reads a few out. '"Wow dude you are so hot. Hey nice one buddy fucking hot facial. Nice arse mate. I just came watching u u r wicked man. This is your boss Robert u r sacked."'

'Don't even fucking joke about it, you bastard.' I push him out of the chair and start stabbing at the mouse. 'How can I get rid of this?' I'm in a panic, I can't read the words on the screen, all I can see is the image of me sucking Stuart's cock.

'Well, you can report it, I suppose,' says Jonathan, 'but it does seem a shame. I mean, this could be the start of a whole new career for you.'

'I don't want a new career, thank you very much!'

'I'm just trying to be helpful,' he says, putting on his coat to leave, 'because after tomorrow, you might need one.'

I don't sleep, and get into the office absurdly early, as if somehow just by being there I can stop anyone from switching on their computer. I'm sure that Xtube and other such sites are blocked to us mere mortals on the office floor, but what about the managers? I've already been warned once about inappropriate internet postings. This will get me fired for sure.

I know that Stuart did it, and I send him a dozen furious texts, to which he does not reply.

Simon gets in early every day, so for a while we're the only two in the office. He's got his usual cup of takeaway coffee and he's whistling a merry tune, which stops the second he sees me.

'Blimey, you're early,' he says. 'Couldn't wait to see me, I suppose.'

I must be looking as bad as I feel.

'My God, Robert, are you on drugs?'

'No, I'm not on fucking drugs! Christ! What the fuck are you talking about?' I know that it's wrong to take it out on him, but there's nobody else here.

He stiffens. I don't think he likes the swearing. 'Well, if there's anything I can do, you know where to find me.' He sighs, picks up his coffee and turns to go.

'Actually,' I say, 'sorry. I'm really sorry. It's just that something really bad has happened and I don't know …' I'm on the verge of tears, and I have to stop and breathe for a second. 'I don't know …' My voice goes up an octave, like a teenager's. 'I don't know what to do.' I'm really crying now. Simon carefully puts his coffee down, and puts an arm round my shoulders.

'What is it? God, what's the matter?' People will be arriving in a minute, and I've got snot running out of my nose. 'You'd better come into my office. We won't be disturbed in there.'

I tell him the whole sorry story, and he confirms that, should they so wish, anyone with the word 'manager' in their job title can watch me sticking my fingers up my arsehole all day long.

It's up on his screen – the still image of my face, smiling and sleepy-eyed, high as a kite on whatever it was, heedless and crazy with lust. The image judders into life, and Simon hits the pause button.

'What the fuck am I going to do, Simon? What the fuck …'

'Just leave it with me,' he says, patting me awkwardly on the back. People are starting to turn up to work. 'Don't worry about a thing.' He hands me a little plastic pack of tissues from his ridiculously tidy top drawer, and I blow my nose. My eyes must be as red as tomatoes.

I spend the rest of the morning hunched over my computer, not daring to look right or left, not wanting anyone to catch sight of my face in case it reminds them of something that they might just have seen on screen …

Every time the phone rings or an email pings into my inbox, I jump. Is this it? The sack? The end of everything? Shame, disgrace, loss of income, repossession, moving back home, everyone knowing, nobody talking …

Ping! Jump. Heart fluttering, stomach knotting.

It's from Simon.

'Mission accomplished,' it says. 'The bunny is dead. You may now buy me lunch. Simon aka The Hacker.' Then, a little lower down: 'PS You deserve an Oscar.'

My face is flaming, my eyes are watering, but the griping nausea has turned to butterflies and I write 'Lunch? B******s. I'm taking you out for dinner. Tomorrow night. Thank you. Robert xxx.' I hit the send button with a flourish, cackle madly and spin in my chair. My co-workers look up, shrug, look down.

Jonathan calls me in the afternoon.

'I've got to see you tomorrow night. It's an emergency.'

'I can't,' I say, 'I'm busy.' Jonathan has cried wolf so many times that, despite the fact that he almost killed himself, I take his emergencies with a large shovelful of salt.

'Busy? You're never busy. What's up? Something good on the telly?' He starts laughing uproariously, then suddenly stops. 'This is important.'

'I'm afraid it will have to wait.' I'm not going to stand Simon up after what he's done for me.

'Well in that case I'll see you at my funeral.' He puts the phone down. It nags at me for the rest of the day, so I call him back.

'What's the big crisis, then?'

'Oh, it's over. You're too late. Don't worry.'

'Jonathan, what are you talking about?'

'You're interested now, aren't you? Well don't bother. I've decided to face the music alone.'

It turns out that he was arrested back in June for possession with intent to supply class A drugs, and was bailed until tomorrow, when he has to turn himself in at Kennington Police Station. He never mentioned this to anyone because he thought it might 'blow over', and knowing Jonathan he has ignored or recycled a number of letters reminding him of his date with destiny.

I'm angry with him, but I say, 'Of course I'll come with you,' because that's what friends do.

'Oh don't force yourself, dear,' he says. 'I can take care of myself. You've obviously got something much more important on.'

Then, stupidly, I tell him that I've got a date.

'What?' He sounds furious. 'Who with?'

'Simon. From work.'

'Never heard of him.'

'The New Boy.'

Silence.

'You are not serious.'

'Yes. Why not?'

'The one you said was so naff that he buys his clothes at … where was it?'

'Next.'

'You must be desperate.'

'I was wrong.'

'What, you mean he gets his shirts from Asda?'

'No. You wouldn't understand.'

'You're right there,' says Jonathan, 'I wouldn't.'

When I get home it occurs to me that I don't know Simon's number, so I can't call him or text him to cancel our date. It will have to wait till the morning.

There's a ring at the doorbell. What fresh hell is this?

It's Stephen, and it looks as if he's been drinking. His shirt collar is askew, one wing sticking up over his jacket, and – or is this just my imagination? – his wig looks crooked. I've always assumed it's a wig, anyway.

'You're not dead, then.'

'Not quite.'

'Then why the fuck aren't you answering my letters?'

It's true. He's sent me a few terse notes insisting that we need to talk. 'I've been so busy at work, Stephen. I'm sorry. Come in.'

'Hmm.' He walks into the living room. 'Yes, I'll have a G&T, ta very much.'

I haven't offered him anything, and it looks like he's had enough. 'I haven't got any gin. Or tonic, for that matter.'

'My God, what is the world coming to? No gin? Call yourself queer?'

'I can open a bottle of wine.'

'Oh, I fucking hate wine,' he says, then interrupts before I have a chance to offer anything soft, 'but on this occasion I'm willing to make sacrifices. Just make it a large one.'

I hand him the best part of a pint of wine, and we sit opposite each other, the coffee table between us. He's looking around.

'Where is it?'

'What?'

'You know perfectly well what I mean.' I do. 'It was in here.' He points to the corner, where Michael's boxes were stacked up last time Stephen paid a call. 'Tell me … Oh God, tell me you haven't thrown it away. I told him not to trust you with it. I told him. Oh God, Robert, say it hasn't gone.'

He's sitting bolt upright, looking wild.

'It's okay,' I say, 'it's perfectly safe.' But it might not be. I haven't checked the bin store for weeks. For all I know, it's been taken away, or flooded, or eaten by mice.

Stephen jumps to his feet, eyes blazing. 'Then where?' His hands are clenched like claws.

'Calm down! I'll show you.'

'Oh fuck,' he spits when I take him out to the bin store, 'is that what you really think of us? Just rubbish? Just a load of smelly old rubbish that you can chuck out when it suits you? Is it?'

That's pretty much exactly what I'm thinking at the moment, because Stephen does smell – of liquor – and I would love to chuck him out.

'Okay, okay,' I say, lugging the first box off the top of the pile. 'I'll bring them back in, if it means that much to you.'

He watches me with folded arms, hiccupping occasionally, as

I carry all four boxes from the bin store along the landing and into my living room. When he's satisfied that everything is there, he snaps his fingers and points to his empty glass, which I refill. Only then does he sit down, drink and sigh.

'I apologise for the language,' he says. 'A lady should never resort to swearing. It's a very bad habit I picked up in the Air Force.'

I can't picture Stephen in the forces, and he reads my look.

'Oh yes, dear, I was in the RAF, albeit briefly. There's no need to look quite so surprised. Where do you think I met Michael?'

'I don't know … I suppose I thought you just met … at a club, or something.'

He cocks his head to one side, like a bird, and then laughs till there are tears at the corners of his eyes. 'A club? A club? And what sort of club exactly would that be?'

'A gay club.'

'Do you have any idea when we met?'

'I don't know.' I've never thought about it, but I remember Michael saying that he and Mervyn had been together for forty-something years. 'Sometime in the sixties?'

'The fifties, actually. 1957 to be precise. Not exactly a vintage year for gay clubs.'

'I'm sorry. I didn't know.'

'And why should you, dear? They don't teach it at schools.'

'Go on, then.' I fill up my glass. 'Tell me about it.'

'Oh God, no,' he says. 'It's a long mucky story and I'm far too pissed to go into all that now. You don't want me crying on your shoulder all night, which I inevitably would.'

'I don't mind.' I want to tell him that I don't sleep at night, that I'd enjoy the company.

'I tell you what, dear. If you're really interested, you can read all about it.'

'Where?'

He nods towards the boxes. 'There, of course. Were you never curious enough even to take a little peek?'

'No. I thought it was just …'

'What?'

'Old junk.'

The words clunk down on to the coffee table between us. Stephen takes a long drink, and looks out of the window. We both watch the lights of a plane traverse the sky from left to right, bound who knows where.

'I suppose I seem terribly old to you, don't I? No, don't say anything. I remember what it's like to be young. You don't think about the past, and as for the future, it's just the next drink, the next party, the next man. At least, it was for me.'

He sighs, and I try to picture him as a twenty-one-year-old.

'Oh, don't you worry, I had my fair share. More than my fair share, as my proctologist can testify. You keep on running, running, running, and then suddenly one day you wake up and you're sixty years old and you're on your own and you wonder what happened to all that fun and all that hope, all those fabulous nights, the outfits, the camping, all those friends you thought you'd have forever …'

He takes off his glasses and cleans the lenses. Without them, he looks less like a crazy old bird, more like a tired old man.

'When you're young, you look at old people and you wonder why they're still breathing and walking around. You just think they are waiting to die. You think we're the past. But I'm telling you, boy, we're your future.'

He drinks up, and gets to his feet. He's rather wobbly, and holds out a hand, which I grab to steady him.

'I'm sorry, dear. I've been unforgivably rude. Thank you for not throwing me down the stairs. Michael said I did it deliberately, rubbing young men up the wrong way so that they'd treat me rough. And I must say, I did rather like it.'

He straightens himself, adjusts his collar in the hall mirror. 'Oh, child, why didn't you tell me I was looking like a mad old tramp!'

'Now you really must let me go,' he says when I open the flat door, loud enough for anyone to hear. 'I'm sorry, but I simply will not let you have your wicked way with me. I'm old enough to be your mother!'

And he's off down the stairs, cackling away, as he weaves into the night.

I wash up the glasses, rinse out the bottle and open the first of the boxes. It's full of diaries. A glance at the spines: 1967, 1968, 1973, 1977. There must be about twenty of them. Twenty more in another box. More diaries, and letters and papers and certificates, in a third.

And in the fourth, the photographs.

Mervyn alone, Mervyn with friends. In the studio, posed under lights, with props – a sword, a spear, a classical column. In costume – a sailor's hat, a biker's cap, a kilt, a military tunic. In pouches and shorts and slips and briefs. On stage, posing and smiling, showing off his muscles, taking prizes, kissing girls. Outdoors by the sea, in the woods, in gardens and parks, always a pose and a smile, the hair thick and dark, the eyes laughing and sexy, the body … Oh, the body.

There's a large brown envelope at the bottom of the box, once sealed with Sellotape which has long since gone dry and brittle. It crumbles in my fingers.

Inside are prints, maybe twenty in all, taken in the same studio on the same day, Mervyn posing against a black curtain in boxer shorts, in a white pouch and, finally, naked. He's hard.

And I'm hard too, harder than I've been for months, without Viagra, without Tina, without GHB. I push my pants down round my knees and wank like a schoolboy, in such a hurry to come that I can't even get to the bathroom or the bedroom.

Before my eyes close and my orgasm comes, the last thing I see is Mervyn, staring back at me across time. A man I only ever saw as a shape on a stretcher.

I can't remember the last time I came. I can't remember. I try, in that last moment of rationality, to remember, as if it matters, but I can't, and then all thought is washed away.

Ten

The charges against Mervyn keep mounting up. Not only is he suspected of murdering Gerald, and stealing money and expensive photographic equipment from the ransacked studio, and attempted arson – there is now an additional charge of buggery. Certain negatives have been found in the studio – according to what I hear, they were in a safe concealed in the brickwork behind a framed picture – which show just how far Gerald had gone into the realms of hardcore pornography. These were the photographs that he sold to trusted clients only – some of them, it appears, overseas. If it can be proven that the photographs went by Royal Mail, then there will be yet another charge on the table, for sending obscene materials through the post. Mervyn may only have posed for the pictures, but in the absence of anyone else to charge in what's beginning to look like a very juicy vice case, he'll do. The police are gunning for a conviction, so that they can put this down as a successful 'clean-up' and get the Sunday papers off their back.

As to the content of the photographs, reports differ, and Mervyn is reticent. He says it was 'a bit of larking around' in Gerald's studio with a fellow bodybuilder who also happened to be doing the rounds at the same time, both of them broke and hungry and eager for admiration. But they must have been pretty convincing if the police think they can hang a buggery charge on them.

I've been to see him as often as I can over these last dreadful weeks. Incarceration doesn't suit him. He's losing weight, and I fear that he's starting to lose his mind. He alternates between vicious bouts of temper and pitiful wheedling. He vents his frustration on me, and has even suggested that it's somehow my fault that he 'got caught up in the queer world' at all. In fairness, he immediately regretted saying this, and apologised, but I'm beginning to worry that he sees me as part of the problem. If I hadn't taken those photographs, taken him to Blackpool, and everything that followed, he could now be shooting his first starring movie role out at Pinewood opposite the delectable Maxine Trent. When he heard that the long-delayed boxing epic had been announced for an autumn release under the title *The Gloves are Off!*, starring Edward Templeton's latest discovery, he became even more discouraged.

'That little bastard stole my fucking job,' he said, leaning across the table during one of our increasingly painful visits. 'And you know how he got the job, don't you? He's letting that old bastard fuck him. That's why I didn't get the job. I wouldn't put out for that fucking dirty old queer.'

'Keep your voice down, Wright.'

'I'll fucking kill him when I get out of here.'

'What are you saying?'

'I'm only … for Christ's sake, Michael, I'm not … Oh Jesus.'

There was something about his eyes that I didn't like, glancing from side to side, catching mine only for moments. It's at times like this that I realise I hardly know Mervyn Wright at all, and suspicion flickers across my mind. He could have killed Gerald. I can see it all too clearly – an argument, Gerald's dreadful insinuations and veiled threats, Wright losing his temper, whacking the old man, realising what he's done and trying to cover it up to look like a robbery … I hate myself at these times, but not wanting to believe something doesn't make it any less plausible.

'And what the fuck is buggery?' he said, smashing his fists on the table.

'Among other things, it's a crime.'

'Since when?'

'Since about a hundred years ago.'

'I thought your lot had got all that sorted out. Wolfenden and that.'

'I'm afraid not.'

'So you mean what we've been doing all along is … a crime? You should have fucking told me.'

'Would it have stopped you?'

I knew the answer to this – the law never stopped Wright from doing anything he wanted to do – but I wanted to hear it from his mouth. And I knew I wouldn't.

'What the fuck have you got me into? Jesus Christ.'

I couldn't answer this without making a fool of myself in front of the guards and the other prisoners and visitors, who watch us and talk about us enough as it is. I changed the subject.

'How's your lawyer getting on?'

'He's a cunt. I sacked him.'

'You're joking.'

'He wants me to go down. He's one of Templeton's cronies. Pretends to be helping me but every time he sees me there's another charge. He's doing deals with the cops to protect Templeton. I'm the fucking fall guy. They've set me up, Mikey. You've got to get me out of this.'

This is another of Wright's refrains: how his current situation is the result of a massive conspiracy between the cops and the queers. His theories get wilder with every visit. The entire British film industry is apparently to blame. He sees himself as a scapegoat for something – but he's not quite sure what. Locked up, left alone, branded as a queer, he's lashing out at everyone and everything that put him there. The only person who never gets the blame is Mervyn Wright – the man who loves another man, who used his body to get him and who wasn't averse to trading it for fame and fortune either.

How much can I do for Mervyn? And what is the point? If he gets off this time, he's going to turn his back on me and everyone else. I can't alter the facts – Gerald is dead, Mervyn had motive and opportunity galore – and I can't provide an alibi. Even if I could, I'd be putting myself in danger of prosecution as well. No doubt it will all come out at the trial in any case, and I could be the next one in the dock. It's happened to enough people I know, including one man who went to the police to complain about blackmail and ended up being charged with gross indecency himself.

None of us is eager to stand up to the law. The police are getting vicious, seizing address books and letters and paying calls in the middle of the night. Those of us who can are hiding our true nature, keeping our hair short and our clothes drab. The pubs and clubs, those that have escaped the raids, are empty. There aren't the parties any more. Edward Templeton, once the host with the most, the reigning queen of London queenery, has relocated to the south of France, officially to set up a distribution office down there, more probably to avoid unwelcome questions from the police. The house in Pimlico is closed up, Don has mothballed his chauffeur's uniform, the Bentley is in a garage somewhere. Rumour has it that Templeton's extensive collection of military uniforms, and the photographs in which they featured, modelled by those convenient soldiers from the Wellington barracks, have been consigned to the waters of the Thames.

And those who can't hide? What of them – the screaming queens who flocked in the bars and clubs of the West End, who flapped across Leicester Square like brightly-coloured parrots, defying the police and the bashers and the blackmailers, high on bravado, confident that good times were just around the corner? Where have they gone, now that the Wolfenden Report is on the shelf and the vultures of the law and the jackals of the press are circling, eager for reprisals? I've searched for Stephen in all the regular haunts, the Standard, the Captain's Cabin, Lyon's Corner House, the handful of other seats of gaiety, but he's nowhere to be seen. I knew so little about his life, his connections outside our little world. Of Tony – our landlord, his employer, lover and possibly pimp, I knew nothing beyond the name. *Muscle Boy* magazine has closed, the office, above a chemist's shop in Kensington, gutted by fire. I've even tried to contact some of the other photographers who contributed to those titles, on the off-chance that they might know Stephen, or Tony, or something, anything, that might help – but their addresses turn out to be sweet shops or newsagents or dry cleaners, PO Box numbers or 'gone away'. The world in which Stephen lived and worked seems to have evaporated like a feast in a fairy tale, and Stephen with it.

I'm in the pubs so often that I'm mistaken for one of the lonely souls who looks for company in such places, and could have a different bed mate each night if I so chose. I certainly wouldn't be the only young man in the YMCA who entertained in this way. But I'm not interested, and I've turned so many down so often that they now regard me as part of the furniture and ignore me. I ask everyone about Stephen and Gerald, and some of them think I'm a copper's nark. The landlords don't like me.

'You look like charpery, dear,' said Max, still pouring the watered-down gin at the Captain's Cabin, where he presides over a seriously reduced clientele. 'People are very suspicious these days. You should know better than to come round here asking questions.' But he tolerates me because, I think, in the event of a raid I look straight.

'I've not seen hide nor hair of her,' he said, when I asked about Stephen. When I asked about Tony, he clammed up altogether. 'Ask me no questions, I'll tell you no lies.' The next time I visited, he asked to see my membership card – I've never had one – and informed me that he would no longer be able to serve me. 'I don't want trouble,' he said, and there was fear in his eyes.

One night after work, eating egg on toast at Lyon's Corner House, a haggard, middle-aged man sat down at my table. I didn't recognise him, and pointedly read my *Evening News*.

'You're Stevie's friend.' I looked up. A pair of beady eyes, a deeply lined face. 'You don't remember me, do you? And why should you. In happier times I was known as Vera.' He extended a hand, the nails cut short, no longer polished. 'Vauxhall Vera. *A votre service.*'

We shook.

'Where is he?'

'Chez moi, dear. Kipping on the couch. And a right bloody slut she is as well. Coffee cups. Fag ends. Oh!' He waved a hand in the air, quickly aborted the gesture and glanced around. 'Well,' he said, lowering his voice, 'he says he doesn't want to see a soul. It's like the final act of *La Traviata*, it really is. Pitiful. But if you was to pay a call, I think it might not be spurned. Got a vogue, dear?' He took the cigarette packet, wrote an address with a stub of pencil on the back, lit one and put one in his pocket. 'Sorry, dear, but times is 'ard. The Dilly isn't what it used to be.' He touched the back of his hair, and his hand recoiled when it found stubble rather than the heavy fall he once favoured.

'Don't let me down,' he said, digging his fingers into my arm. 'I don't want to be dramatic, but I think she's dying.'

Stephen looked like a waxwork, or an embalmed corpse, the pale, yellowish skin stretched over his skull, his features too large. He lay on the sofa in pyjamas and a dressing gown, surrounded by ashtrays, all of them in need of emptying.

'My God,' he said, propping himself up on one elbow, 'look what the cat dragged in.'

Vera made himself scarce.

'How are you, Stephen? I've been looking everywhere for you.'

'I prefer to remain incognito at the moment.'

There was nowhere to sit, the armchairs covered in clothes and books and records, and so I perched on the arm of the sofa near his feet. 'You don't look well, Stephen.'

'Thank you for caring all of a sudden. What do you want?'

'You should see a doctor.'

He put a hand to his chest. 'Mine is a sickness no doctor can cure …' He feigned a delicate cough, which became a real cough. 'Isn't this nice,' he said, when he'd recovered. 'Just like being at Reville again. Not much has changed, has it?'

'I don't know. Mervyn's in prison.'

'Poor little chicken.'

'Gerald's dead.'

'No great loss.'

'I'm living out of a suitcase at the Y.'

'And I'm expiring rather decoratively in a hovel in Vauxhall. Aren't we a marvellous advert for National Service.' He saluted. 'For Queen and Country! I'm sure Sergeant Kelsey would be proud.'

'What happened, Stephen?'

'The world turned, dear.'

'And not in our favour.'

'No.' He moved his feet, patted the cushion next to him, and I sat. 'It would appear not. Now why are you here?'

'I've been looking for you everywhere.'

'Not, I presume, to propose marriage. Don't answer that question. You want something from me.'

'I was rather hoping …'

'Here we go. Never wants me for myself.'

'That you might know something about Gerald.'

'Yesss … I thought it might be something along those lines.'

'And do you?'

He shifted around, lay on his back and extended his feet across my lap. 'What could a poor girl like me possibly know of such affairs?'

'You told me you were the spider in the middle of the web, Stephen.'

'That's as may be.' He reached to the floor, found a packet of cigarettes and lit up without offering me one. 'But there's knowing and there's knowing, isn't there?'

'If it's a question of money …'

He laughed, and dug me hard in the thigh with the ball of his foot. 'Don't presume too far on our long-standing friendship, Michael. I may be a hardened bitch, but I am still capable of being hurt.'

'Sorry. I just thought I could help you out.'

'Well, darling, let's see. How much have you got? First of all, I'll need a ticket to Istanbul, or perhaps Tokyo, or Moscow. Somewhere very far away indeed, where nobody could ever find me. Then of course I'll need a new identity – I'm sure such things can be bought for a few thou – and a place to live. I'll need an allowance, because I really don't see how I can be expected to work in such a place. So, adding it all up, plus of course some appropriate new wardrobe, I should say about a hundred thousand pounds would do. Give or take a quid.'

'Why the sudden urge to travel?'

'Oh, call it a whim. Call it an interest in foreign trade.' He dragged on his cigarette, brushed ash from his dressing gown. 'And there's also the little matter of not wanting to be murdered, of course.'

'What?'

'Oh Michael, Michael, Michael, you've lived in London for so long but you're still a babe in the woods. If I were to open these ruby lips for any purpose other than the usual, the next time you'd see me would be in the morgue. Fished out of the river, perhaps, or pieced together from little bits they've found scattered around the woods of south-east England.'

'So you do know something.'

'You said it, not me.'

'Who are you frightened of, Stephen?'

He cocked a hand behind his ear, counting footsteps as Vera descended the stairs. The street door slammed.

'Quick, go to the window and see if she's gone.'

'Yes. He's walking down the street.'

'Right. Now listen well. No, stay there. You're on guard.'

'Don't you trust him?'

'I don't trust anyone, dear. Spare me the soulful expression. If I were to trust anyone, it would be you, but it's so much easier to be a suspicious cow.'

'But Mervyn's in prison and ...'

'Yes, I know. Sympathy, and all that. But there is nothing I can do.'

I stepped over to the couch, stood over him. 'But you must.'

'Oh, go on then,' he said, putting one hand behind his head and adopting a Mae West voice, 'persuade me.'

'Stephen, for Christ's sake, an innocent man is in prison ...'

'Innocent? Your Mervyn? Pull the other one, dear, it's got bells on.'

'You don't think he did it.' I sat down.

'Oh dear. That's taken the wind out of your whatsits, hasn't it? Well no, for what it's worth, I don't think Mervyn killed Gerald. But someone's got to go down, and it looks like it's going to be him.'

'Why? He didn't do it.'

'Maybe not, but he did plenty of other things. I hate to be the one to break this to you, Michael, I really do, but Mervyn wasn't exactly Snow White.'

'I know about the pictures he did for Gerald.'

'Oh, them.' He waved a dismissive hand. 'And did he tell you about Lady Templeton and her little circle? And his many friends and shall we say investors in the West End?'

'I don't want to hear this.'

'I don't imagine you do. But I'm sorry to say that Mervyn put himself about a bit and was not very careful about covering his tracks. Gerald wasn't the only one who caught him with his knickers down. Quite the flasher, was our Airman Wright, as you well know.'

I swallowed hard. 'But he did not kill Gerald.'

'Granted.'

'So who did?'

'We may never know. But as far as the police are concerned, he will do very nicely.'

'What about evidence?'

'Darling, I hate to disillusion you, but in a case like this, evidence is the very last thing on anyone's minds. The police have their reasons for wanting a quick, clean conviction. Mervyn suits everyone's purposes very well. He's so … visible.'

'So someone's framing him?'

Stephen held his hand over his mouth and shook his head.

'Look, Stephen, there's no one here. Nobody will hear you. Anything you tell me …'

'Will be treated in the strictest confidence. Yes. I'm sure. But you don't know what they're like.'

'Who? The police?'

'Them as well.'

'For Christ's sake!'

'Don't shout, dear, and stop striding around in that masculine way. You're upsetting me.'

I sat down, and he hooked me with his legs again. My chest heaved, and tears started pouring out of my eyes.

'There there,' said Stephen. 'Crying won't help.'

'That's easy for you to say. The man you love isn't in prison for a crime he didn't commit.'

Stephen slowly withdrew his feet, and sat upright.

'*The man I love.*' He hummed a few bars of Gershwin. '*Someday he'll come along, the man I love, and he'll be big and strong …*'

I stopped crying and lit a cigarette.

'Do you remember that night at Reville, Michael? When I flew the coop?'

'I'm not likely to forget it.'

'Did you ever wonder what was going on in my pretty little head when I lured you into my improvised boudoir?'

'It was pretty obvious, Stephen. You wanted to get out.'

'Mmm …' He stared towards the window. 'Among other things.'

I opened my mouth, and closed it again.

'Was that the sound of a penny dropping, dear?'

'Go on.'

'Do you remember when I showed you that drawing I'd done, and I said that I drew what I saw in here?' He tapped his forehead. 'Well, that was always my trouble, you see, ever since I was little. An overactive imagination. I had it all worked out, you know. You'd sink into my arms and taste my womanly charms, and we'd get busted and sent to the loony bin together but somehow love would triumph over adversity and we'd troll into the sunset, hand in hand.' He blew out a long grey stream of smoke. 'Daft, isn't it? I never was your type. You like 'em butch.'

'I see.'

'You do? Well fuck me. You took your time.'

A lorry rumbled past, rattling the window frame.

'I'm sorry, Stephen.'

'What for?'

'I must have caused you a lot of pain.'

'Don't flatter yourself, Hot Stuff.' He leaned against me. 'Now do me a favour, and leave now.'

'Why?'

'Because I think I'm about to do something very stupid.'

'What?'

'Darling, put your arms around me. Just for once. Hold me. Let me think that this is worthwhile. Just for ten minutes or so. That's all it'll take.'

And so I held Stephen in my arms on that dirty old sofa, the Vauxhall traffic circulating around us, as he gave me the answers to the questions I had never even thought to ask.

'I met Tony the first week I got to London after they let me out of Halton. He picked me up in Leicester Square and took me to a flat on Tottenham Court Road and fucked me so hard that I was bandy. Well, it was just what the doctor ordered, wasn't it, after all the frustrations and the disappointments and the bromide in the tea. He was dark-haired and handsome in a rather cruel sort of way – made me weak at the knees. Well I was on them often enough. I fell in love, and I thought he felt the same way. You know how stupid I am. But he set me up in that flat in Queensway, and he got me a job on *Muscle Boy*, and he was always popping round in the middle of the day or the middle of the night wanting his oats, saying he was going to leave his wife, and mug that I was I believed him.

'It was all hunky dory for the first few months, and I was enjoying working at the mag, going to the parties, meeting all those models, living the life. But then he started to ask more of me – a little favour here, a delivery there, oh, just sign for this, sign for that, meet this client, make that payment. Of course I did as I was told. I thought I was doing rather well for myself, having so much responsibility, like a real career girl. He told me I was his right-hand man, that he couldn't manage without me, blah blah blah, and I soaked it all up. And he was still taking care of me in other ways, as you know. He didn't mind you moving in, did he? And if he slapped me around a bit, got a bit rough, well, that was all part of the fun. I knew which side my bread was buttered on, and I didn't complain, even when he hurt me.

'Then I began to twig, dear. It wasn't just the magazines that he was involved in. He always told me that he was a business-man, something to do with import-export, all terribly butch. Well he was doing business, that's for sure. Flats all over town, each and every one with a couple of girls in them. He used to send me round to pick up the rent, at least that's what he called it. Living off immoral earnings, that's what the courts call it, isn't it? You read about it all the time in the *Pictorial*. And then there was the porn. Dirty pictures. Girls, boys, you name it. He got it from Germany and Scandinavia and he sold it through the

Muscle Boy mailing lists. Got me to write the envelopes, keep the accounts, log in all the money. And some of it was home grown, of course, as your Mervyn knows to his cost. Oh, the money that came flooding into that office! Envelopes with a tenner, twenty, fifty quid. And I wrote it all in the ledger, kept his books straight for him, handed it over like a good little soldier, never a penny short.

'But then Gerald started getting restless. Well, she was a drunk, dear, and they're the worst. Started complaining that he was being ripped off, that Tony was getting the cream, why shouldn't he cut out the middleman and set up for himself? He had his own mailing lists, and he knew all the models, he had something on all of them, so it was in their interests to cooperate. He pissed off everyone. You saw what Teddy Templeton was like! Oooh! If looks could kill, it would be Lady T in that prison cell, not your Mervyn. But Gerald didn't care. She was a reckless queen, and she paid the price. People like Tony don't like competition. He tolerated it for a while, and he tried to warn Gerald often enough. But Gerald didn't listen, did he? And we all know what happened next.'

'So Tony killed Gerald?'

Stephen laughed. 'Don't be ridiculous, dear. Tony's hands are clean. But he has friends in low places, shall we say. It's not difficult to get someone killed, if you have money and influence. Life is really quite inexpensive.'

'But why Mervyn?'

'I told you. The police need a conviction.'

'Why don't they go after the real killer?'

'Oh, that. Didn't I mention? Tony's on very good terms with the Metropolitan Police. I believe he plays golf with the Commissioner. And of course he provides them all with girls.'

'What?'

'Don't look so surprised. Many's the pair of police boots that have been parked under beds in Tony's flats. So of course nobody's going to give Tony trouble. He makes sure the boys in blue are well entertained, he gives generously to police charities, if you know what I mean, and he takes his wife to the dinners and dances. It's a very civilised arrangement.'

'He's bribing them.'

'Oh must you be so direct?'

'And so he makes it look like Mervyn's killed Gerald, and they let him get away with it.'

'Exactly. And they get a nice story in the paper about how they've cleaned up the West End, one less dangerous criminal on the streets of London, we can all sleep safer in our beds.'

'So Mervyn goes to prison, and Tony just carries on as normal.'

'Not exactly, no. He's getting out of the vice game. Too risky, and the margins are too low. I mean, all those flats to keep up, all the photographers and the mailing lists and the printing and so on. Not to mention the girls. Oh! Don't get me started on the girls. So he's moving on. He's cleaning up his act. He's going in for drugs. Much easier, less fuss, huge profits.'

'It's hopeless, then.' I sat forward, my head between my hands, imagining Mervyn after a twenty-year stretch, bitter, middle-aged, hating me.

'That's not like you, Michael.' Stephen put a hand on my shoulder. 'Come on, dear. Never say die.'

'Oh, and you have a plan, I suppose? What were you going to suggest? That you and I set up a florist somewhere in Chelsea and get matching poodles?'

'I shall pretend I didn't hear that, because I know you're upset.' He got up, and rummaged under the sofa. 'There.' He placed an exercise book on my knee, orange cover, stapled at the centre, ruled.

'What's that?'

'You're not the only one who keeps notes, you know, dear.'

I flicked through the pages: dates, times, names, addresses, figures.

'If National Service taught me one thing, Michael, it's that desperate situations require desperate remedies. And under the circumstances, I am willing to do something that goes against the very nature of my being.'

'And what's that?'

'Tell the truth.'

11

I haven't blogged for so long that it feels quite strange to open a new document and start writing about myself all over again after all these months. It's an activity that I associate with the bad times – the drug come-downs, the lonely nights unable to sleep, tapping away in a room lit only by the glow of the screen, pouring it out to an indifferent cyberworld. And these last months have not been bad times. They've been happy, and as Jonathan likes to remind me, I'm so boring when I'm happy.

I see Simon every day at work, but we give each other a wide berth. Neither of us is comfortable with the idea of the 'office romance'. The morning after we spent our first night together, after several weeks of dating, we entered the building separately and communicated only by email. Since then, we've seen each other outside work maybe four times a week, and slept together on half of those occasions, either at his place or mine. Neither of us has said anything about moving in together, or the future, or 'us', but there are plans for a long weekend in Scotland next month. Sometimes we go out to bars and clubs, but he dislikes the noise and I'm not crazy about the ghosts, so it tends to be meals, cinema, he's even dragged me to the theatre. On my bachelor nights, I read or work or watch TV, or I go out with Jonathan, who still officially doesn't like Simon but has at least stopped constantly telling me why.

And I see Stephen. After I read the first few diaries, I find his number and I call him.

'That got your attention, then.'

'Would you like to come over for dinner?'

'Oh, and what would that be then? Brown rice on a bed of lettuce? No thanks.'

'My boyfriend will cook. He's a very good cook.'

'I'm pleased to hear it, dear. Boyfriend indeed.' He sounds pleased. 'Whatever next?'

Stephen arrives at six o'clock on a Saturday evening, dressed in his best, his hair bigger than ever, a crisp white shirt and a burgundy silk cravat. I greet him at the door with a hug and a kiss on both cheeks, which he receives like a potentate receiving homage. Simon is busy in the kitchen, and so we sit in the living room with drinks.

'So what happened?' Michael's diaries are tormentingly silent for a year, after the crisis of the murder. 'Was Mervyn convicted?'

'No.'

'Thank God.'

'I was.'

My mouth hangs open.

'Mmm, hard to imagine, isn't it? Little old me, breaking rocks in the hot sun. I fought Lily Law, dear, and Lily Law won.'

'But you didn't … you hadn't …'

'I didn't kill the old bastard, if that's what you're driving at, no. But as I told Michael, there had to be a scapegoat, and in the end it came down to the lesser of two evils.'

Dinner won't be ready for another hour. Simon nips in and out with drinks and nibbles.

'To put it crudely, I did a deal. I went to the police and I told them that I knew who killed Gerald, and that if they didn't release Mervyn Wright I would go to the papers with my little orange book. There was enough in there to end a few distinguished police careers and quite possibly topple the government as well. In a way, I rather regret not doing it. I could have been the Mandy Rice-Davies of the queer set. But the police were very keen to buy my silence, and so they agreed to drop the murder charge against Mervyn.

'I was about to rush off to tell Michael the good news, but that's when things got complicated. The inspector reminded me of the fact that he was a good friend of Tony's, and that if Tony found out that his little bird had been singing, I might never chirp again. So I sat down. Then they said that there were several other charges against Mervyn, enough to put him away for a number of years, and that if I wanted them to be dropped as well, I'd have to give them something in return. Like what, I said. Like information about the porn and prostitution racket, he said. Well, I said, you can just go and ask your good friend Tony about that next time you see him, and he said, I've already done just that and he's handed over all the books and what do you know, your writing is all over them.

'Well, in the end it turned out that one sacrificial lamb was as good as another, and before the interview went very much further they were reading me my rights. I was charged with everything under the sun, from obscene publications to running a brothel, in the hope that something might stick. And stick it did. I got four years.'

'What for?'

'This'll make you laugh, dear. Conspiracy. Me! Who couldn't conspire her way out of a paper bag! They might have done me for any number of things, really, but this gave them the best chance of sending me down for a good long stretch. So they gathered up all the evidence, all the pictures of all the trade, all the accounts books and the letters and the envelopes and the receipts in my handwriting, and they said well, dear, you've been a busy girl, ain't you? Quite a one-woman crime wave. And rather than getting me on some minor technicality that might have got me a fine or a suspended sentence or a measly six months, they went for conspiracy to commit gross indecency. In other words, I'd lured all these poor little flies into my web and made them flash the gash and do the you-know-what for the cameras. I mean it was ridiculous. If I'd had that kind of power over men,

I wouldn't have ended up as the lonely old spinster I am today.'

'And what happened to Tony?'

'Got off scot-free, dear. Clean as a whistle. Teflon Tony. Nothing stuck to him. Last heard of in the early eighties, when he was busted as one of London's crime barons and buggers off to South America where I imagine he has a nice respectable wife and a great big house and a little flat somewhere so he can bugger the brown arse.'

'But prison … That must have been awful.'

'It wasn't exactly Butlins, dear, but one managed. I served two years. Michael and Mervyn came to see me every week, regular as clockwork, even when I was transferred up to Norwich, never missed, not even to go on holiday. I don't know what I'd have done without them. Killed myself, I suppose. Lots did.'

'You wouldn't. You're tougher than that.'

'I may seem like an old boot to you, but I was once a relatively delicate flower, you know. Even after National Service and the loony bin and all my trials and tribulations in London. But there were two things that kept me going. First of all, I've always been an optimist, and I wanted to see what would happen to the world when I got out. And secondly, I was happy for the boys, and I didn't want them to have my death on their conscience.'

'And did they live happily ever after?'

He sips his drink, nibbles on a piece of bread. 'I wouldn't say that, exactly. I mean there were dramas.' He rolls his eyes. 'Dramas, dear! Oh, I've had him crying on my shoulder more times than I care to mention. Mervyn had what you might call a wandering eye. Men, women, you know – he wasn't fussy. But he always came back. He loved him, you see.'

I think about Stuart, how it never once occurred to me to take him back after what he did to me. So that, I suppose, was not love, never had been, never would be. Simon comes in, tops up our glasses, says dinner will be ready in twenty minutes, takes away the hors d'oeuvres so we won't spoil our appetites.

'So why did you do it, Stephen? Why did you go to the police, knowing that you could easily end up in prison yourself?'

'You make it sound as if it was all carefully planned and thought through, but really it wasn't. I did it on instinct. I never thought about the consequences. I just couldn't stand seeing Michael so unhappy, and I knew that there was something I could do to help him, so off I trolled, very pleased with myself, into the lions' den. I was brave, I suppose. Brave, or stupid.' He got up, went to the window, looked out. 'But I loved him. I never stopped loving him.' He rummages in his jacket pocket for cigarettes. 'I suppose this is one of those bloody no smoking flats, isn't it, and I'll have to go and freeze my fanny out on the balcony.'

'Go ahead.' I find matches, and light his cigarette.

'Bless you, dear. You're not all bad.' He smokes quietly for a while. 'Once you get to know you, that is.'

'I suppose I made a very poor impression.'

'I won't lie, dear. I told Michael you were trash. I didn't see why he bothered with you … Well, apart from the obvious, that is. He always did have an eye. But he seemed to think you were worth the trouble and so I went along with it for his sake. Anything that took his mind off Mervyn's death was a blessed relief, even if it was an infatuation with a boy who could have been his grandson.'

'Infatuation? Oh, I hardly think …'

'No, I don't imagine you do. Well, I won't embarrass you.' He smokes his cigarette down to the stub, and flicks it out of the window. 'Now there's a really common habit for you. I feel quite ashamed. Where was I? Boring you rigid with some sordid tale I've no doubt.'

'What happened to Michael and Mervyn? What did they do?'

'It's all in there, if you can be bothered to read it. Michael carried on in the Civil Service. Never got the promotions. We always said there must be a big black mark against his name on a file somewhere. Mervyn scratched around in the lower depths of the film industry for a while, doing stunts, waiting to be discovered, did a couple of bits of telly, then he got into wrestling. He did well, dear. That's how they afforded the flat. Always on the telly on a Sunday afternoon. Oh, he was camp! Mad Mel Wright, he called himself. Dyed his hair blond, came flouncing on in a satin cape, blowing kisses, flapping his wrists, then he'd beat the shit out of his opponent. The old ladies loved him. Nobody would ever have believed that he was queer.'

'And what about you, Stephen?'

'What about me?'

'When you got out of prison. When the world changed.'

'Well, they were exciting times, weren't they. The sixties. Swinging London, all that caper, and I swung harder than any of them. Bona days, dear, bona days. The summer of love, 1967, the change in the law, gay liberation, my generation saw it all.'

We sit down for dinner, and Stephen asks Simon about his family, his work, his hopes for the future, his plans, specifically his wedding plans. By the time dessert is finished, he's practically booked the marquee and sent out the invitations. We drink a lot, and get quite merry, and I tell Stephen he can stay the night, and he screams and calls me a vile seducer.

The doorbell rings, and it's Jonathan.

I always rather hoped that Jonathan and Stephen would get on, and they're both pissed, so they have something in common, which is a good start.

However they take one look at each other and immediately they're like two cats having a stand-off, hissing and yowling, the fur standing up, any second now there will be spitting and claws and they'll be rolling around in a heap on the floor.

'Oh,' says Jonathan, dumping his bag in a chair, 'I didn't realise you were having one of your help the aged evenings.'

Stephen sits up very straight, his hands resting on his knees, and makes no attempt to introduce himself.

'Jonathan, this is Stephen. Stephen, this is Jonathan, one of my oldest friends.'

'Oldest!' says Jonathan. 'That's a laugh.'

'How do you do, Jonathan,' says Stephen, who has obviously decided to play the grande dame. Jonathan does not take his hand.

'I need a drink.' He heads for the kitchen to help himself as usual. Simon follows him.

'Your friend needs to learn some manners,' says Stephen, getting to his feet, rubbing his tired legs. 'Anyway, thank you for a lovely evening.' He looks at his watch. 'Heavens, is that the time, I must fly.'

'Stay, Stephen.'

'I won't stay where I'm not wanted.'

'You are wanted. I want you to stay. Please. Sit down and have another drink.'

Jonathan is back with a huge glass of what looks like neat vodka. 'I'm fucking exhausted. Got any drugs?'

Simon winces.

'No, Jonathan,' I say, 'I don't do that any more. I told you.'

'Well I hope you don't mind if I do.' He's about to start setting up on the coffee table, as we've done a hundred times in the past. Stephen looks as if someone's just farted, but he's fascinated too.

'Actually, I'd rather you didn't.'

'Oh, I forgot. He doesn't like them.' He jerks a thumb towards the kitchen, where Simon is getting him something to eat. 'You're so wholesome these days.' He gets his phone out and starts texting. Stephen sits and watches him. 'My God!' says Jonathan, suddenly, 'what the fuck are you looking at?'

'Certainly not you, dear.'

A text bings into Jonathan's phone. 'Rob, I need some money.'

'Oh, that's why she's here,' says Stephen. 'I didn't think it had the air of a social call.'

'I haven't got any …'

'Mind your own business, grandma.' Jonathan opens a wrap and dumps a little pile of coke on to the tabletop. 'Well I'm very sorry, Robert, but I need it.' He produces a Marks and Spencer store card from his back pocket – and for a moment he looks embarrassed – then starts chopping. His hands are shaking, and the coke is going all over the place. 'Shit! Fucking stuff!' He's picking up crumbs with his fingertips, rubbing them into his gums. The coke is going under magazines, into cracks on the tabletop.

'Oh for Christ's sake, daughter.' Stephen snatches the card out of Jonathan's hand and stands over him. For a moment I think he's going to sweep the whole lot on to the floor, or strike Jonathan across the face, but instead he kneels slowly on the floor and starts neatly, methodically chopping the powder, first this way, then that, forming little herringbone patterns in the fine white powder, before scooping it into two lines like vapour trails, elegantly tapered at each end.

'That's the way to do it.' He smacks his hands clean. 'Honestly. Don't they teach the children anything these days?'

Jonathan is speechless, which is a first.

'And I don't suppose you even have the necessary tenner, do you?' Jonathan shakes his head while Stephen fishes in his pocket for a neat fold of banknotes, peels off a tenner and rolls it into a tube. 'We used pound notes in my day. They were just the right size. Still, inflation and all that.' He hands the tube to Jonathan. 'After you.'

Jonathan is sulking now. He knows he's beaten, but he's not yet willing to concede defeat.

Stephen sits back, folds his legs, takes a sip of wine. 'I saw the look on your face when you walked in here, my girl. Oh God, look at the old queen, how disgusting, what's she doing here, shouldn't she be in a home or something? You just think of us as the sad old bastards who missed out on the party. Well let me inform you that without us, there wouldn't have been a party. You with your drugs and your clubs and your hair looking like a haystack and your trousers hanging round your arsehole, you think you invented it, don't you? But you didn't. You just bought it. You had it all handed to you on a plate and you never stopped to wonder who put it there. Your generation seems to have lost the ability to love or to care or to fight for change, or to do anything other than fuck each other and shop. You treat Robbie like shit, you're jealous of his boyfriend, you're bitter as hell because you're lonely as hell and you're drinking and snorting your way to an early grave. And don't give me that look, daughter, because I've done it all myself and I can read you like a fucking book.'

He stands for a moment with his arms folded, then flourishes the rolled-up note like a dandy flourishing his fan.

'Now will you stop snivelling and blow your nose and take this fucking line?'

I retreat into the kitchen, almost colliding with Simon, who has been doing the washing-up and is still wearing an apron. I pull him after me, and close the door, turn off the light, and spy on Stephen and Jonathan through a gap in the hatchway.

They sit in facing armchairs, dabbing at their noses, not speaking.

After a while, Stephen gets out his cigarettes, and offers them to Jonathan. There is a little whispered conversation, and – did I hear right? – a certain amount of giggling. A lighter clicks, a flame flares, sucked in once, twice, and smoke begins to fill the room.

Simon and I finish the washing-up, the wiping up, the putting away, we clean the surfaces and empty the bin, and when there is nothing more to do we pour a glass of wine, toast each other, kiss and drink in silence.

The living room is dark, but for the glow of the television. Jonathan and Stephen are sitting on the sofa – not quite together, there's still a foot or two between them – smoking and drinking and sniggering. It's the new series of *Star Search*, and they're busy picking their favourite.

'Oh, I say! He's nice.'

'Him! Oh, come on. Look at his hair!'

'No, but he's got a sweet face.'

'He can't sing a note!'

'Who fucking cares about that?'

And so on.

It's after two when I finally take Stephen down to his cab. He's unsteady on his feet, but his eyes are shining.

'And what about you, Stephen? When you got out of prison, what sort of life did you have? Did you work? Did you have a lover?'

'A lover, dear? I had plenty, don't you worry.' He gets in the car, winds down the window. 'But that, as they say, is another story for another day.'

And the car pulls away, Stephen's hand at the window blowing kisses.

Acknowledgements

This book could not have been written without a number of people who shared their memories, archives and expertise. I would like to thank them all, in particular Harry Woodman, Ronald Wright, Adrian Street, Adan Julian, Brian Robinson, Spencer Churchill, Stuart Waterman, Tony Parker, Alan Edwards, Michael Dee, John McKay, Tony Field, Edward Smith, Tim Wilbur (www.timinvermont.com/vintage), Norman Hibbert, James Gardiner and the late Victor Burdett. Thanks also to my agent Sheila Crowley at Curtis Brown, and to Peter Burton for his support and advocacy.

The research for this book was supported by the Arts Council of England. Many collections and archives were consulted, including the Hall Carpenter Archives, the Imperial War Museum, the RAF Museum and the British Library.